IRON MAIDEN

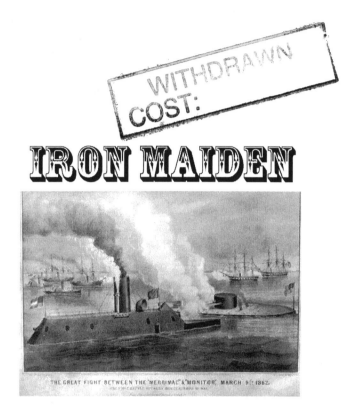

THE GREAT FIGHT BETWEEN THE "MERRIMAC" & "MONITOR", MARCH 9th 1862.

Jim Mu

DEDICATION

Dedicated to my father, Elvis Ray Musgrave (Pearl Harbor Survivor), 1921-2001 and to my mother, Jean Elizabeth Mandeville, 1925-2005.

CONTENTS

ACKNOWLEDGMENTS

This book could not have been written without the research done by many others. I owe a special debt of gratitude to Dr. Jared Diamond of UCLA for his book *Collapse: How Societies Choose to Fail or Succeed* for the basic thematic impetus of this novel, and to all those researchers on the Internet and elsewhere who have put down the facts and details relating to the naval engagements of the American Civil War, especially as concerns the period 1860- 1863.

PROLOGUE: THE RACE

January 28, 1862, Brooklyn

Inside the Continental Shipyard, there was a flurry of activity. In two days, the *U.S.S. Monitor* would be launched for her maiden voyage. Carpenters, ship fitters, metal workers, sailors and officers were climbing all over the dark little craft, which was sitting in the early morning shadows in dry dock near the East River. She resembled a medieval instrument of torture, with sharp pieces of metal sticking out of her hull and the round turret sitting amidships, as if it were the block for a colossal guillotine, waiting for the executioner to appear. In a short while, she was going to be transferred to the Brooklyn Navy Yard for final touches and the launching ceremony.

Inside the Drafting Office, John Ericsson and Captain John Worden were going over the final plans with Lead Draftsman, Charles McCord. McCord was pointing out some questions he had about the weight of the cannons.

"I must go along with the Navy Department on this, Mister Ericsson, sir. If we were to put 12-inch Dahlgrens in that turret, she would surely go under. We must install 11-inchers for the safety of the craft."

Ericsson looked fatigued and unusually disheveled. He had been fighting the Navy's Supply Office to get building supplies delivered, even though the Navy was behind on payments, and now he had to refit cannons on his craft. He knew he had to make it look as though he was doing everything he could to defeat the Southern monster, even if his real plan was to come to a standoff. However, he had heard some good news from Washington. The Senate had refused to pass the bill, which would have allowed an increase in the amount of gunpowder permitted for firing all naval cannons. Ironically, this bill was passed following the disaster of the U.S.S. Princeton, of which Ericsson was well aware. Thus, even if the cannons were 12-inch Dahlgrens,

Ericsson knew they would probably not have the firepower needed to penetrate the metal hull of the *Virginia*.

"All right, we'll convert those guns as best we can. If we don't start working faster, then we won't make the deadline. And if we don't make the deadline . . ." Ericsson was unable to complete the sentence before the two other men broke in.

"We don't get the money!" they said, in unison, and then began to laugh.

The newspapers in the Union States were all talking about the impossible task ahead of these men, and the epithet of "Ericsson's Folly" seemed to make the men work that much harder. They all knew this ship was a first in many more ways than just its outer design. There were 40 unique patents used on the *Monitor*, and some journalists, more sympathetic to the cause, often featured this in their stories, contrasting the originality of her construction with the lack of ingenuity in the construction of the *Virginia*. In fact, most journalists refused to call the Confederate ship by her proper name. They insisted upon calling it the *Merrimack*, in order to insult the Rebels in Norfolk.

"Where is Lieutenant Greene? I haven't seen him all morning," said Ericsson. He knew the young Executive Officer had been acting strangely ever since they returned from Christmas leave in Maryland. The young man was in love, and John knew what that felt like. As you work, there is a gnawing deep inside your heart, which tells you all such martial pursuits are meaningless when placed beside the tender beauty of your loved one. However, he also knew that this young lieutenant was an important ingredient in the plan to get more ships of the *Monitor* class constructed by the Navy Department. Without the big money, Ericsson knew he could not regain his love's interest. Amelia's parents were against her marriage to Ericsson, from the time he had been arrested for patent infringements, and they did not provide a dowry when they were married. Greene, on the other hand, was young and handsome, and he would be able to go back to his Anna Cameron and live out life in tender bliss, supported by their wealthy parents. Ericsson had no such money upon which to rely. He had left home as a young man, and all that he owned had been earned through his genius and hard work. No, this was his only chance to live the good life, and he was not going to allow Greene, a young romantic, stupefied by love's early passion, to spoil his own future.

"I'm going out to look for him. You two men get the workers on the conversion of those cannons. We need to have the ship moved tomorrow," said Ericsson, pulling on his overcoat.

"The men are ready for action, John, and I am proud to be serving with them," said Captain Worden, who had become quite admired by the crew since he had come aboard. He always had a kind word for everyone aboard, and he took time to get to know each of them by name, where they were from, and if they needed anything special. And Chip Jefferson, the young steward, followed Worden around like his shadow, fetching him drinks, running errands, and doing any other odd jobs the Captain required of him.

Ericsson walked out into the morning sunshine, straightening his waistcoat and tie, and thinking about what he was going to do to make the young man finally understand the importance of this mission. He had been reading Emerson and Greene's beloved Whitman, and he had finally come upon an idea he believed could work. As he reached the other side of the yard, he spotted Greene, who was sitting on the end of a short pier near a tugboat, which was moored quietly for minor repairs to her engine. Lieutenant Greene had his shoes and stockings off, and his pale legs were dangling over the edge of the pier in the water. He was reading another of his books, probably more poetry, and his gaze was fixed in concentration, and he did not notice when Ericsson approached.

"Your father is very proud of you, Dana," said Ericsson, and Greene looked up from his reading. The young man's blue eyes were moist from some passage of prose or poem.

"I'm glad you think so, Captain. I do so want them to believe I will be a good husband for Anna. But... I am rather afraid of what is to come in my immediate future."

Ericsson sat down, with some awkwardness, next to his protégé. "I've been meaning to discuss this with you, my boy. Remember how we talked about how we will go to our paradise of Easter Island? Well, we will need to be assured that we have enough capital to get us there and keep us in supplies for some time."

"Yes, I can see how we would need to be supplied," said Greene, nodding slowly. "All we need do is tell my parents, or even Anna's folks certainly have the money."

"No! Now, I told you this was to be our secret. If we are to live with our women in this tropical paradise, then we must not let anyone else know of our whereabouts, or how we got

there. This is extremely important. If others discover where we are, then our secret life away from civilized madness will soon disappear. They will bring their technology and warfare to our island, and we shall have destroyed a beautiful and innocent culture forever!"

Dana's face became wistful with regret. "Oh, I don't want that to happen! I know we will find the innocent paradise, just as you described it to me, and our women would enjoy it as well."

"That's what I want to explain to you. In order for us to get the money we need, my *Monitor* must not defeat the *Virginia* at Hampton Roads." Ericsson watched the young man's face, and he saw a certain surprise, but there was inquisitiveness as well, just as he had hoped there would be.

"Not defeat? What do you mean, Captain? How can we not defeat our enemy?"

"The business of warfare is a strange one, Lieutenant. One would assume that the business was one of victory at any price. However, this is not the case. If one's ship is victorious over the enemy, then the government does not choose to purchase more of these ships to ensure future victories. No, but if there is a confrontation, what we called in the War with Mexico a 'Mexican Standoff,' then the government believes it must build upon this in order to increase the profits of everyone involved."

"I really do not understand. How can the war be won by a draw?" Greene pounded the book of poetry on his legs. "I have never heard of such things!"

"This is the logic of modern war. Certainly no warrior or industrialist wants to lose lives. This is very costly to all concerned. However, if the war can be continued through the

fair development of modern armaments which keep both sides protected . . . well, then, don't you see, both sides continue the chess game, and both sides continue the profit-making industry and no lives are lost! It's rather ingenious, in a modern way, I must admit."

"How do I help to do this? I am only one man, a lowly lieutenant, at that."

"Aye, but you are also an inventor's son, are you not? You will also be in charge of the guns aboard our *Monitor*. I will show you how to cause the turret to spread the shots so they do not hit the *Virginia* in damaging locations. Our craft is much faster and much more maneuverable than her foe. She will be just crafty enough to keep us in the money. We will still stop the South from breaking the blockade, and we will most certainly win the war, but we shall also have a wealthy contract for thousands of *Monitor*-class ships! See the brilliance of the idea? You will have saved many lives, and you will have also given us our passport to tropical paradise!"

Lieutenant Greene looked down at a poem he was reading. His eyes sparkled with impulsive insight. It was as if he had seen his true, heroic calling for the first time.

"Yes, I do see what you mean, Mister Ericsson! It's just like Walt says in his poem about democracy. We will be doing this for future humanity. *Listen, Come, I will make the continent indissoluble, I will make the most splendid race the sun ever shone upon, I will make the divine magnetic lands, With the love of comrades, With the life-long love of comrades.*"

"That's the spirit, Lad! Come; let's get back to work. I'll show you what I mean about the trajectory of the turret." Ericsson put his arm around the lieutenant's shoulder as he put his shoes and stockings back on, and then they both stood up together. The wind was picking up, as if on cue, and the whistle for work began the daily routine. Two conspirators of fortune walked toward the dry dock where the Iron Maiden, a medieval instrument of torture, was miraculously being transformed into an instrument for love.

Or was it? There were still two other men, who were planning a different rendezvous upon the waves, with a different goal in mind. Robert Whitehead and his invention, the torpedo, and Walter Sinclair, the Confederate spy, were at that very moment watching the two men walk toward their craft, envisioning the flaming hell they would create once their instrument of torture was freed from its lair.

PART I: THE LETTERS

April 12, 1859 – September 1, 1861

CHAPTER 1: COMING TO AMERICA

"The Inventor," New York City, April 12, 1859

Dear Cornelius,

When I came to the United States from Great Britain, in November of 1839, my young bride Amelia and I were fortunate to begin lodging at the John Jacob Astor House in New York City. It was fortunate because I, who was an inventor by profession and a Swede by birth, had, just two years earlier, been languishing in British debtor's prison on Fleet Street, due to some surreptitious thefts of patents, which caused me a devastating bankruptcy. As I often told my associates, one can live in ostentatious surroundings, as I have lived in the Astor House, and still be destitute. As the philosopher Kierkegaard would say, engineering was my "existential conditioning" for the first twenty-five years of my life here in America. My work was my salvation, but it was my wife's downfall.

Amelia, God love her, was the only decent event to happen to me during my stay in England. And she had some good humor about her when she told me why they call the United Kingdom the Emerald Isles. "Because we're green with envy, and we want all the riches of the world!" she said, her sparkling blue orbs flashing with coquetry. When I attended the church to marry my Amelia, it was the first time I had been inside a house of worship in ten years. I whispered to my nineteen-year-old bride that I hoped it would be another ten years before I returned. I have no patience with superstition and myths that cannot be observed with careful scientific experiment.

I must agree with my wife, even though her years are a score fewer than my own two. I have noted in my travels that the British are jolly good fellows to visitors, as long as you are doing creative things for them on their home soil. But, alas, once they become colonial masters, as was the case in the

7

United States, for instance, they at once wax into tyrannical overlords who demand total obedience and financial obsequiousness.

However, unlike Kierkegaard's *Fear and Trembling*, I thank my stars that I am not philosophically rooted in angst about my fellow man. I simply put forth that I am misanthropic by nature, and which incarceration I had no control, I knew my time in the "Emerald when I saw that British authorities were locking me up for dishonesty, over Isles" had been spent.

I must say that I am fond of the American philosopher, Ralph Waldo Emerson, and I am especially pleased with his essay, "Self-Reliance." For it was this brand of "self-reliance" upon which I have based my life. For example, at twelve years of age, I was commissioned to produce drawings for the Gota Canal Company in Sweden. At sixteen, I was a cadet in the Mechanical Corps of the Swedish Navy and then an officer in the Army at seventeen. And, at twenty-two, I traveled to London to see what my acquired engineering skills could gain on the free market.

I am a rather stone-faced man, a bit under six feet in height, with a massive forehead that reminds me of a drawing I once viewed, by anthropologist Dr. Raymond Pile, in the *Encyclopedia of Homo Sapiens* in which an ape-man entitled "Cro-Magnon" is stupidly glaring out at the reader with a club slung over his hairy shoulder. People have said, I must admit, that I have "a bludgeoning self-confidence."

My years in England are noteworthy, if only for the excitement I caused with my inventions. First, I devised an air- compressor pump for removing water from the mines. I also perfected coolers for breweries and refrigerators, and applied new tubular condensers for marine boilers. In point of fact, I had a direct hand in developing the means whereby Sir John Ross's Arctic exploration ship, *Victory*, was able to navigate with its entire engine system below the freezing waterline. But Sir Ross, who was impatient with modern machinery because it "kept him up at ungodly hours," had it disconnected and thrown overboard. I, of course, as the impudent young foreigner, was blamed for the failure.

But perhaps my best venture in England came when the 1829 Liverpool Line was being planned, and inventors were asked to develop a "steam-driven coach" to compete for a 500-pound prize. The conditions of the contest were that the engine must be capable of drawing a weight of twenty tons at the rate of ten miles per hour.

I built my *Novelty* in seven weeks. My only competitor was an engine designed by George Stephenson called the *Rocket*. There were thousands of spectators assembled on the grounds of the railway in October 1829. My vehicle started admirably enough, getting up to a speed of thirty miles an hour in minutes. However, the engineer, a usually quiet man, suddenly began pouring on the steam; he was obviously trying to impress all those gathered with his speed. The *Novelty* did impress, gaining a maximum speed of sixty . . .

when the boiler burst . . . hurtling shattered metal and wood thousands of yards in every direction! Thank goodness, the flying debris injured no person.

Although I lost the competition, I did, four years later, build a caloric heat engine that actually worked and could be considered the first internal combustion engine. Rudolph Diesel also built a similar creation that used another fuel. Michael Faraday, a respected senior scientist of the day, called my youthful effort, "A fine contrivance, but I can't for the life of me see how it works at all!"

In general, it is said, Swedes are a rather oafish and stubborn breed of men. Perhaps we are. At least, when I arrived in New York City, I felt as though I had been thrust into a zany, illogical world, where citizens ran wild in the streets, and where it took every ounce of courage I could muster just to walk with my wife around Central Park.

In fact, in all my years in New York, I have never ridden the satanic transportation that rumbles through the skies above the chaos they call "city life." I came upon the monstrosity called the Brooklyn Bridge one day, quite by accident. I have no use for what New Yorkers call their engineering "wonders of the world." Rather than ride the elevator trains or cross that grotesque bridge, I would that they tie me to a steam-driven propeller of one of my frigates and let me spin my way across the seas—underwater!

When I arrived in America in 1839, I entertained notions of building a big frigate for the Navy. The result was the unconventional 600-ton frigate *Princeton* that was built during the period 1841-44. The hulk was constructed in the Philadelphia Navy Yard and the engine in New York. It was with great admiration that the newspapers of the time boasted that my craft was a first in many areas of navigational genius.

The *Princeton* was the first direct-acting, screw-driven metal-hulled steamship of war with all machinery below the waterline, furnaces designed for anthracite, forced draft by blowers, telescopic stack—and the biggest gun ever carried by a fighting vessel, of twelve-inch caliber. I was quite pleased to be producing this craft because it was far superior to any British frigate of the time.

However, there was an accident, which occurred aboard the vessel that was the fault of an early American partner of mine, one Captain Robert F. Stockton. I first became acquainted with the Captain when my wife and I crossed the Atlantic—England to America—in his ship, a little twin-propeller steamer that he financed, the *Great Western*. He was a tall, pipe-smoking gentleman, with willowy black hair and big spectacles, which encircled his great ears like grappling hooks. Captain Stockton, like many Americans I have met, was enamored of "bigness." If it were his choice, it was better to be bigger. "America is for big thinkers like us, Swede," he used to tell me, puffing on his pipe like one of the boilers in the *Princeton*. "If we don't think big, then we won't succeed!"

So, it was the captain's idea to take the ship out for a test firing of weapons; but, unbeknownst to me, he was also sailing out with one of his own cannons added to the *Princeton's* arsenal. It was nicknamed the "Peacemaker," and it was a foot more in diameter at the breech than the ones I had constructed and much heavier. It was "the largest mass of iron to be brought under the forging hammer," Stockton later told me. But it also had an Achilles' heel: unlike my guns, the Peacemaker was not reinforced with hooplike iron rings forged into the breech and extending for a partial length to protect the metal during the concussion of firing.

As a result, on February 28, 1844, a notable party headed by President John Tyler went on board our ship docked on the Potomac River, for a cruise and demonstration of Stockton's wondrous "Frankenstein" naval rifle. It was a bright unusually warm winter's day, an electioneering candidate's delight with some four hundred political and social leaders and their ladies coming on board to see the event.

I was not present, but Stockton reported the news to me shortly afterward. I had to meet him at a pub in downtown New York, near those dreaded cable cars. He was already "three sheets to the wind" when I approached. His eyes glared at me intensely from out of the smoke-filled darkness, and I thought he was going to fall off his stool.

"Swede! It was disastrous! I put the fire to her fuse myself. There was a flash of light—then an explosion like hell itself erupted from that black beast! We felt the vessel lurch under the concussion. When the smoke cleared, there they were. Five persons dead. Secretary of State Upshur and Navy Secretary Gilmer. Three others. President Tyler was on board but below decks at the time—thank God! A score were seriously wounded and were writhing in agony on the decks. Blood was everywhere! The Peacemaker blew-up, Swede! What are we going to do?"

It was something I had expected, given Captain Stockton's proclivity for "bigness." I reassured him and told him I was working on other projects, and that I still needed his financial help. But he was obviously shocked to the marrow. "The United States Government will not pay us the rest of our money, Swede. And I ... I have murdered the Secretary of State!"

This fiasco was to come back to haunt me, but I did continue with my other tasks, leaving Captain Stockton to his despair. I heard rumors that he took to drink and was eventually committed into a sanatorium by his wife, Rachel. This was not the last time I would see rich and noble men come to ruin.

I devoted much of my time on smaller projects. It was in this time period that my wife, Amelia, advised me she was heading back to London to stay with her parents for a while. I must admit, I was quite busy, and I had been neglecting her. Women are quite soulful beings, forever parading about and wanting you to pay them constant attention. I spent most of my time working at my drawing boards or supervising construction at the shipyards, so I am ashamed to say that I was a bit relieved when she told me the news. I could finally get down to some real work at last.

The 260-foot *Ericsson*, powered by my caloric engine, sank in a squall off New Jersey but was raised and refitted for steam. Steam machinery for various light tonnage vessels earned me as high as $84,000 in one year—1845—but I lost my money on the *Iron Witch*, a New York-to-Albany Hudson River steamer equipped with both a propeller and paddles. She vibrated so much that none wanted to embark on her pulsating decks. This craft served as a metaphor for my marriage, it seemed.

I spent most of my time defending my patent rights to the screw or "spiral" propeller in the courts, especially with respect to those U.S. Government steamers found using them. I failed, however, to win a $15,000 claim. In spite of my rebuffs and shabby treatment with regard to funds owed to me for the *Princeton* (I was blamed for Captain Stockton's escapade on the Potomac), I became a naturalized citizen in October 1848.

I remember the day clearly. I walked down to the doorman, Alfred, and I told him I was now an American, at the age of 37. The grizzled old ruffian looked me up and down, shook his head, and exclaimed, "Well, the country was named after an Italian explorer, Vespucci, discovered by an Italian explorer, Columbus, but some have said the first man who founded these United States was from your area, Captain."

"Oh? And who might that be, Alfred?" I asked.

"I don't exactly remember his right name, but I think it was somethin' like Leaf. Yes, that's it! Leaf Ericson! He had the same damned name you have, Captain!"

Thus, I was initiated as an honorary relative of the Scandinavian Viking founder of these United States, Leif Ericson.

Yours truly,

John Ericsson

CHAPTER TWO: LEAVING ANNAPOLIS

"The Officer," Annapolis Maryland, June 10, 1860

Dearest Anna,

Well, I have done it! At long last, the years of study and hardship have given me the diploma and an appointment to Midshipman by the President of these United States. When you come to the graduation ceremonies, you will see how well we have fitted the grounds for feminine splendor. There will be rest rooms where the women can spruce-up before the long-winded speeches by our commanding officers. I wish I could spare you all the pomp and circumstance, but such is the plight of the military service. If you are to wed an officer, you must learn to put up with these formal occasions, I am afraid.

I am apprehensive father is disappointed that I finished seventh in my class. How can I compete with the man who invented the famous "elevator trains" of New York? I did, however, finish second in Mathematics and Astronomy, so perhaps I can impress you with my calculations of the stars? I sat last night at my dormitory window and found "our star." It is in the Spiral Nebulae, and I have named it "Lovers' Retreat." It is here we shall stay when our time on this earth is finished. This will be a planet for our dreams, my Anna. There will be no conflicts to break us apart, no oceans to separate us. Whatever you can imagine in your female dreams, we shall have it on our planet! Alas, the Master-at-Arms, who came poking his long nose into my room and saying, "Lights out", broke my reverie! But, as we both know, the Navy will never extinguish our love light in the heavens!

I will meet you at the station in Annapolis, my love. I want to escort you around the campus during our pre- graduation festivities. We shall have a ball on the evening of our commencement ceremony, and I will be the luckiest midshipman attending with you at my side. I have been practicing my waltz, and I can even do a fair Virginia Reel, although I doubt that with politics as they are we will hear such tunes! All the men are discussing the possibility of war, but I do not think it will come to that. The Southern States may have differences with the Union, but they must realize that we could leave ourselves open to foreign aggression if we were to fight over slavery and King Cotton.

Well, the Master-at-Arms will arrive soon, and I must extinguish the lamp. My love is pulsating out of my heart and into my quill. Please, kiss these words and feel my life's blood rush to your brain! Oh, my love, I miss you so!

Until I can see you step down from the train, I will be the saddest midshipman in the Navy.

Love, Dana

CHAPTER THREE: BLOCKADE!

"The Spy," Liverpool, June 12, 1861

Heavenly Penelope,
I have received word that my schooner, *H.M.S. Caine*, shall be ready in a fortnight. I will meet with the American at the Silver Tide Inn on Shropshire Court, just as the sun goes down. There is a great profit to be made, Penny, and I pray you not be abashed by these bold actions of mine. It is inevitable that this war will take place. The northern business owners are refusing to let the southern farmers run their plantations as they see fit.

The boys up north are trying to say it is because of the negro. But no, on the contrary, I have heard these southern gentlemen speak in great detail about the true cause of this pending conflict. They tell me their "darkies," as they politely refer to them, live extremely comfortable lives; indeed, they have much better lives than the factory workers whose existences are in constant danger because of the unsanitary slum hovels and countless, labouring hours toiling in those horrendous sweat shops. Those northern pigs even put the children to work inside those metal tombs in New York City! It seems they need a good Charlie Dickens to show the people who the true villains are over there in the colonies!

Do not fret over me, Pen. I know you worry about the peril, but the Union Navy is an abysmally sad collection of torpid old frigates and ineffectual sailing vessels. With her steam-driven propeller below the water line, my schooner will glide past these old dowagers like a good pickpocket on the run at Piccadilly Square.

The "Confederates" as they call themselves, plan to wage a long and bitter conflict with their northern brethren. They want to keep the same genteel values we have long esteemed under the Crown. Profit is not as important to these gentlemen as their way of living. They see the demonic tendencies of capitalistic greed and social permissiveness taking over in the north, and they say they will fight to the last man to preserve their "southern dignity."

They plan to buy tons of supplies, and they are opening hundreds of stock lines here and in France. But I, and many other professional captains, will be "running the gauntlets" for them as they have little or no naval force. You know I have always sided with the underdog, Penny, and especially when the dog has a gigantic bone for me as well!

Please, do come out to Liverpool! We can celebrate my contract with the Americans and plan for our wedding vows. I must say if your father rattles his saber one more time when I come to visit, I shall flail the old buzzard like an American turkey! Sincerely, however, I am certain he will agree to our marriage once he sees what the monetary award is for running the blockades in America!

Until we meet again,

Walter

CHAPTER FOUR: THE UNION CRUMBLES

"The Inventor," New York, July 4, 1861

Dear Cornelius,

It has been several months now since my wife, Amelia, left. I have moved to less auspicious surroundings at 36 Beach Street, near Canal Street and City Hall. Amelia's parents, Mr. and Mrs. Ralph Blackstone, are very wealthy Londoners, and I am afraid my constant work for little money drove her back to them. She appears in my dreams, however, and I can't get her out of my mind. It is as if her lovely image can project itself upon any task I have in front of me. I am immediately interrupted, and it takes me quite some time to become focused once more. Quite scandalous, really!

My work habits, however, remain the same. My workroom is now located on the second floor, with drawing boards stretched the full twenty-five feet beneath the five bright windows overlooking the city's traffic. My parlor and dining room, dominated by heavy chandeliers and mantel mirrors, exude grandfatherly, old-fashioned dignity. I am told by Mrs. Hasbro, my house woman, that I should attend the theatre or visit a symphony. She says I am too much of a "busy bee," and that a person of my age should learn to relax. She has even observed that the pins in the cushion on my bedroom bureau are arranged so that they are in mathematical rows, and that I have all my canned goods filed in the cupboards alphabetically. She says I am obsessed with order.

My dress is as meticulous and uniform as my home furnishings. Invariably, I will wear a black frock surtout coat with rolling collar, velvet vest over a fresh shirt front, gold chain hung about my neck, looped at the first buttonhole and attached to a watch in the fob of the vest. My trousers are usually of light shade, and when I walk out of my front door, I top-off my attire with a dressy beaver hat and kid gloves.

Mrs. Hasbro's husband, Neil, often comes in the evenings to play chess and to discuss politics. He is now sitting across from me; we are celebrating Independence Day, and he is going on about the American election campaign. It seems that in June there was a clamor for secession at the Southern Democratic National Convention, which met successively in Charleston, Richmond, and Baltimore and nominated its own candidates, a Mr. John C. Breckinridge of Kentucky, President, and a Mr. Joseph Lane of Oregon, Vice-President. This little southern party has insisted, says Mr. Hasbro, that the federal government protect slavery as a state right.

It is interesting to me that these Americans elect people called "presidents," as though they were appointing the heads of corporations, and not commanders-in-chief of the armed forces. Indeed, one cannot move an inch in this country without the talk of money. As Mr. Hasbro so quaintly phrases it, "If we could charge people for breathin' air, we sure as hell would do it!"

Well, there will most likely be a new President in the American White House. He will defeat a short little man named Douglas, who was supposed to have been a superb orator. I have heard this tall, gawky new president speak. Hasbro says he is from the state of Illinois and that he was raised in a log cabin. I must say, I expected him to speak in the homespun vernacular of many of these fools, but he surprised me. He has some wit about him. When a gentleman——a Wall Street financier, I believe——asked him why he wanted to alienate the South by abolishing slavery, the big, bearded fellow replied, "What if the cotton farmers in the South had decided to pass a law that said they could own white men with black beards and work these men for nothing, and beat them or kill them if they tried to seek other employment? Why, you and I would be hallowing for the abolishment of slavery, would we not?"

The Wall Streeter said, "But that is not the case, dear sir, those slaves are black all over! We merely have black beards."

Whereupon Abe Lincoln replied, "There you have it! We can shave our faces and roam free as rabbits, but these poor devils are trapped in their own skins. What justice is there in that?"

Mr. Hasbro believes this Mr. Lincoln will win the elections in November but that the South will leave the Union. As I look across at him, his eyes sparkle with an absurd twinkle, as he moves his white knight right into my trap. "But that means a civil war," I say, taking his knight and preparing for my usual conquest.

Mr. Hasbro is a sixty-five-year-old cobbler, and his gray beard curls up like a little girl's on the ends. But his green eyes flash as he replies, "Abe says, 'if the Union crumbles, there won't be nothin' civil left!'"

After Mr. Hasbro leaves, I go to the back of my bedroom to an old trunk.

I take out a brown-wrapped drawing of a small, black, iron-plated battery craft I invented for Emperor Napoleon III of France to use in his little conflict in the Crimea in 1855 against those barbarians of Russia. I must say I have no love for those czarist pigs! But my little monitor, as I call it, had only one revolving turret with cannon, and the grandiose emperor believed it did not fit his expectations. I now raise the letter from "his majesty's personal secretary" and hold it near the gas lamp.

"The Emperor himself examined with the greatest care the new system of naval attack, and he has found your ideas very ingenious."

Then he explained that His Majesty was concerned about the expense as well as "the small number of guns which could be brought into use."

As I hold these drawings, I can't help but think that my invention still has value. There is an English inventor named William A. Armstrong, whom I met in a pub on Canal Street not too long ago. He was bragging that he has invented a rifled- cannon of such powerful explosive strength that it could destroy any American vessel on the seas today. He further bragged that he had met with some southern "gentlemen," and they were willing to pay him over eighty thousand pounds for exclusive rights to his gun.

I still hate the British. And, as I gaze upon my little ironclad, my little iron maiden, I can't help but conclude that Mr. Armstrong has erred. His cannon could perhaps penetrate every American vessel . . . excluding one . . . and I was now looking down upon it.

Yours truly,

John Ericsson

CHAPTER FIVE: THE MERRIMACK IS RAISED!

"The Officer," Brooklyn, New York, August 29, 1861

Dearest Anna,

It was so wonderful being with you for those few short days before war began. Our moonlit nights on the lake will be etched in my memory forever! Christmas was such a joy with your parents and mine getting together at long last. My father has seemed to reconcile our marriage, even though he abhors my choice of the military as a career. I am the first Greene to leave the engineering ranks, and now I feel like the Ugly Duckling out on the lake. When Mr. Lincoln won the election, we thought he could avert war, but those rebel bastards were up to no good from the start!

After the Confederate batteries fired from Fort Sumter on the *Star of the West*, I knew we would be in for it. Now I am waiting in Brooklyn for orders, standing outside the Bachelor Officers' Quarters gazing up at the stars, just like Walt Whitman, looking for our "lovers' retreat."

Anna, I hope you'll understand, as I am afraid to tell father. The news in the local papers tells a tale of exigent urgency for our naval forces. It seems the Confederates at the Norfolk Gosport Navy Yard have resurrected one of our own ships, the *Merrimack*, which was inside the yard when the Rebels took it over in their bloody uprising of April 21. When the fires were finally abated, the Confederates had captured over $10 million of scuttled war ships, including the above- mentioned ship, as well as some three thousand pieces of ordnance of all calibers and three hundred of the latest big eleven-inch Dahlgren cannons, thousands of rounds of ammunition, powder barrels, food, clothing, uniforms, an intact stone dry dock and many other buildings. In effect, sweet one, the Rebels have themselves a navy!

But this is not the true worry, I am afraid. Reports have circulated that they are presently working on the former *Merrimack*, so as to cloak her with heavy armored plating and arm her with those giant Dahlgren cannons! It is feared this new *C.S.A. Virginia* (but we shall forever call her the *Merrimack*) will be able to destroy our entire fleet at Hampton Roads. Some have even said she might continue up the Potomac and fire at will upon our installations—even to the White House itself!

This will most certainly not happen, if I can do anything to stop it! This is why I must let you read a letter I have clipped from today's Brooklyn Eagle. It is from an inventor—an engineer like father—who is working on a project he hopes will counter the threat posed by the South at Norfolk's Gosport Yard. Here it is in full:

The writer, having introduced the present system of naval propulsion and constructed the first screw ship of the war, now offers to construct a vessel for the destruction of the rebel fleet at Norfolk and for scouring the Southern rivers and inlets of all craft protected by rebel batteries . . . please look carefully at the enclosed plans and you will see that the means I propose to employ are simple—so simple indeed that within ten weeks after commencing the structure I would engage to be ready to take up position under the rebel guns at Norfolk, and so efficient too, I trust, that within a few hours the stolen ships would be sunk and the harbor purged of traitors. Apart from the fact that the proposed vessel is very simple in construction, due to weight, I respectfully submit, should be given to the circumstance that its projector possesses practical and constructive skill shared by no engineer living. I have planned upward of 100 marine engines and I furnish daily working-plans made with my own hands of mechanical and naval structures of various kinds, and I have done so for thirty years. Besides this, I have received a military education and feel at home in the science of artillery. You will not, sir, attribute these statements to any other cause than my anxiety to prove that you may safely entrust me with the work I propose. If you cannot do so then the country must lose the benefit of my services.

I cannot conclude without respectfully calling your attention to the now well-established fact that steel-clad vessels cannot be arrested in their course by land batteries, and that hence our great city is quite at the mercy of such intruders and may at any moment be laid in ruins unless we possess means which, in defiance of Armstrong guns, can crush the sides of such dangerous visitors.

P. S. It is not for me, sir, to remind you of the immense moral effect that will result from your discomfiting the rebels at Norfolk and showing that batteries can no longer protect vessels robbed from the nation, nor need I allude to the effect in Europe if you demonstrate that you can effectively keep hostile fleets away from our shores. At the moment of putting this communication under envelope, it occurs to me finally that it is unsafe to trust the plans to the mails. I therefore respectfully suggest that you reflect on my proposition. Should you decide to put the work in hand, if my plan meets your own approbation, please telegraph and within forty-eight hours the writer will report himself at the White House.

The editor goes on to say, in jest, that this dispatch was written by one Captain John Ericsson of New York City, who was responsible for the *U.S.S. Princeton* disaster in '44, when five men, including the Secretary of State, were killed by a monstrous cannon which misfired. He finished by saying, "The White House will get many more of these insane inventors who will try to foist their dangerous engines of terror upon our good cause, but this newspaper's diligence will keep our readers appraised!"

You may judge me insane, Anna, but I believe in this inventor. I know of the true culprit in the *Princeton* affair. He was a Captain Robert Stockton, whose company I was with while we were on liberty in the Barbadoes. He was seated at the rear of a local tavern, and he told me the true story of that memorable day in 1844. Mr. Ericsson, it seems, was completely ignorant of the gun, which Captain Stockton constructed and later saw exploded in the Potomac Harbor. He went on to say that John Ericsson was a genius that was in no way responsible for the disaster. Captain Stockton then said that he planned to stay inebriated for the rest of his days, due to the ignominy of his actions. By the looks of him, I would assume he had been in that said "alcoholic condition" for some days, perhaps even weeks, before then.

Remember that father also had a difficult time of it when he attempted to get his patent for the elevator train. Dreams have an absurd way of coming true Anna, and I believe this John Ericsson will see the construction of his little "iron maiden." I plan to keep my eye on the newspapers and keep visiting the shipyards to watch for the imminent construction. We are waging a war against a desperate enemy, and if we don't act quickly, then we may all be suffering the dire consequences!

Love, Dana

CHAPTER SIX: VENTURE CAPITAL

"The Inventor," New York City, September 2, 1861

Dearest Amelia,
I was extremely disappointed to find my letter published in the *Eagle*. It becomes treachery when a citizen cannot trust the United States postal system to deliver a letter to the White House! I am told a young clerk at the president's mansion sold my letter for a profit. I was about ready to leave this thankless country and return to Sweden, but then I remembered my old Auntie's saying about "an ill wind often brings good news."

My Aunt's superstitious musing came true the next day, as I was visited from Washington D.C. by a friend of mine, one Cornelius S. Bushnell, a thirty-one-year-old New Haven, Connecticut shipbuilder and former wholesale grocer. It seems he had recently secured a contract from the government to build his own ironclad, the *Galena*, and someone had informed him that he might consult the wisdom of an "architect," as he was doubtful if his craft could withstand the weight of iron with which he was planning to outfit his vessel. The informant had read my letter to President Lincoln in the newspaper, and I supposed he wanted to play a trick on Bushnell for some reason. So, at the Willard Hotel in Washington, this young Bushnell decided he would make the inconvenient journey out to New York to pay me a visit.

The country at war made travel very difficult. When Bushnell finally arrived, he was quite distraught, and he explained how his discomfiture was caused by the horrendous state of anarchy afoot in the countryside.

"It was quite a slow, jolting ride," he explained, sipping on one of Mrs. Hasbro's famous New England Ice Teas. "I made transfers to four, single-track lines to go between Washington and New York City. I also rode two ferries, with state taxes levied upon all passengers in New Jersey and

Maryland. Can you quite imagine?"

I slowly nodded my head in sad agreement.

"Why, even the gauge of the tracks varies from line to line. It is a virtual impossibility for the same engine to travel between major East Coast cities. I am often thankful that I have thrown my investment money into shipbuilding. Thank goodness, they have yet to come up with a way to lay track on the water! Of course, Mr. Lincoln's blockade has done its share to confuse the Confederate shipping!"

"Indeed he has, sir!" I responded. "And what have you to tell me about my correspondence to the president? I am ashamed to hear you read about my venture in the newspapers. It was supposed to be privy information."

Bushnell set his mug down and stared hard at me. He has quite a penetrating gaze for a man of such early years. "Well, Captain Ericsson, I was informed by a friend staying at the Willard Hotel that you may be able to help me. He read your letter and advised me to make the trip out here to see you."

"Yes?" I again asked.

"I have garnered a contract with the government for my ship the *Galena*. She is an ironclad vessel of 3,296 tons, with six Dahlgren cannons and steam-driven propellers. I was planning on outfitting her with extra plating—about ten thousand pounds worth. I was wondering if you would calculate whether she could withstand the extra weight."

"I suppose she has the plating on an inward slope, so the cannon shells might ricochet off her sides?" I asked.

"Yes, you are quite astute. My friend was correct in his estimation of your architectural genius."

"Architecture? Sir, I am afraid you are mistaken. I am an engineer!"

"Ah, so you are! See, that's why I need you. I am afraid I am nothing but an old grocery man. Cannon balls and watermelons—they are all the same to me!" Bushnell slapped his knees and laughed. He then rose up and handed me the plans of his ship.

"Sir, I will calculate for you, if you could do me one favor?" I took the rolled blueprints. He cocked his head inquisitively. "I have some plans as well. They concern the letter published in the Washington news. You see, it was never delivered to Mr. Lincoln, and I am afraid I have missed the deadline for proposals to him for ironclads to meet the threat of the Confederates' skullduggery at Gosport Yard."

"So! You are attempting to gain some of the fame by meeting the challenge of those rascals? Certainly I will look at your plans."

"It's quite a good floating battery, if I do say so myself. It is absolutely impregnable to the heaviest shot and shell. I am excited about getting it into the proper hands. I recently had conversation with a Brit who is selling strong weaponry to the Rebels for a huge sum of money. We must combat this Mr. Armstrong's guns!" I was gaining momentum, and I could see by the expression on Bushnell's face that he was duly impressed with my bravado.

"Well, you have come to the right man! I happen to have had a personal audience with Secretary of the Navy, Mr. Gideon Welles, and I know that he is anxious to see any reasonable invention. Are you prepared to invest in your craft, sir? You know, the government needs a letter of credit in the bank to ensure you are stable."

I was dumbfounded. How could the government refuse to loan money when I had the only invention around that could withstand the Armstrong shells? This Bushnell craft would last five minutes against an Armstrong rifled cannon, while my *Monitor* would never flinch. "No, you see, I have had some hard times. Perhaps you have heard of the *Princeton* affair? I was mistakenly held responsible for that and in the meantime . . ."

"That's enough! Give me your plans, sir, and I will take them to my hotel room and peruse them carefully. If this craft of yours is what you claim, and you are able to help me, then there will be a letter of credit made out for your venture. Or my name isn't Cornelius S. Bushnell!"

Mr. Bushnell went on to explain that he had two other investors who wanted to back enterprising inventors like myself, and that it was their patriotic duty to see that all feasible ideas come before the president. The nation was in a state of great emergency, he explained, and we could leave no stone left unturned.

That was all I heard from Mr. Bushnell. He wanted to retire to his hotel room and look at my plans. I said I would retire soon myself. Before he left, however, I handed him the dust-covered black box, which contained my model of the *Monitor* prepared for Napoleon III those many years before. He took it from me and shook my hand warmly, wishing me all the best. He said I should expect a visit from him on the morrow, if a trip to Secretary Welles' home was called for. In the meanwhile, he requested that I go over the plans of his *Galena*. If need be, I was to send my estimate to him in Washington, and that I would be liberally compensated——would two hundred dollars be enough, he asked, arching his thick eyebrows.

"Quite proper," I said, and I saw him to the door. "I hope your trip by cab to the hotel proves more favorable than your one to the city," I put in, and he smiled as he turned to leave.

"Mark my words! We will soon be making a journey down to Virginia to knock-off that Rebel *Merrimack* which was pirated from under our noses! We'll show those scalawags who is boss!"

I shall be working hard to earn the money we need so you can move back here with me. Until then, please remember me!

Love always,
John

PART II: THE MONITOR FIGHTS

September 1, 1861 - April 2, 1862

CHAPTER SEVEN: MEN AT WAR

Washington, D. C, September 1, 1861

When Giddeon Welles saw the replica of the little fighting vessel called "the monitor" he laughed out loud. The other uniformed Union Naval Officers and civilian members of congress passed around the model, smiling and poking at it with their index fingers, and as it made its way around the square conference table, Navy Secretary Welles stood up to speak. Its inventor, John Ericsson of New York City, who was in the foyer, was unaware of the conversations being held inside the war room.

"Gentlemen, I am in the custody of a recent cable that was confiscated by our spies to the Confederate Congress." Welles pushed his spectacles up on his nose and held the paper out so he could read it better.

"It is from Confederate Navy Secretary Mallory, and in it he says to regard the possession of an iron-armored fleet as a matter of first necessity. Such a vessel at this time could traverse the entire coast of the United States, prevent all blockades, and encounter, with a fair prospect of success, their entire Navy.' This is what we are fighting, gentlemen. The massive construction of their new ironclad must be matched by a similar craft of our own. This little cheese box, as we have previously determined, does not match the two-inch thick armor being laid upon the huge, converted Merrimack. This *Monitor* would be crushed in minutes!"

"Well said, Mister Secretary!" said Jeffrey Johnstone, one of the members of the board from congress. "That is why we rejected it in the first place. Why have you brought him back?"

Welles peered over his glasses at Johnstone. "I respect a man who has met this engineer, John Ericsson, who is the inventor of the craft you see before you. Cornelius Bushnell is well respected by the War Department, by President Lincoln, and especially by me, and I have told him to bring Mr. Ericsson here to plead his case. I told him that if this Ericsson can convince us that his craft is worthy, then perhaps we should reconsider our rejection of his invention."

One of the Naval officers holding the little model of the *Monitor* stood up. It was obvious that he spoke only when he believed it was important. "I rejected this contraption simply because there is no precedent for this design in the annals of Naval engineering. This craft was made in the image of nothing in the heaven above, or in the earth below, or in the waters under the earth!"

"Well stated, Admiral, but we shall see what Mr. Ericsson has to say. Lieutenant, bring in the inventor," said Welles, sitting back down. The fourteen men seated at the table all fidgeted in their seats, lit up cigars and pipes, and anxiously awaited an important moment in history to run its course. There could be no room for error in this decision, as these men knew the South was, at this very moment, readying its armored ship to wreak havoc against Federal blockades.

Ericsson entered the room with a firm stride, as if he were there on a mission. He placed his notes on the rostrum set up in his behalf, and he looked calmly out upon the faces of sea-worn officers. He had nothing to fear from these men. After all, they were there for the same reason as he was: the country was at war.

"Gentlemen, thank you for giving me this opportunity to defend myself and my invention. Whenever I am asked what makes this country great, I always have the same reply; there is only greatness where there is the freedom to debate, and this country has always provided the means by which common citizens such as myself can have a forum. What concerns me is the fact that sometimes your citizens make judgments based on what they read in the newspapers. In Sweden, we have a saying, 'a fish is never caught until he's in the boat.' I mean, how can you condemn me because of what my partner, Captain Robert F. Stockton, an American, decided to do on his own? Gentlemen, I was not aware that Captain Stockton was going to test his new gun that day on the Potomac when your statesmen were tragically killed. In fact, had I known of his utter foolishness, I would have forbidden it!"

Secretary Welles cleared his throat. "Thanks for your candid thoughts, Captain Ericsson, I am glad to have your side of the story. Our press does indeed make a lot out of such disasters. However, we are here to listen to your proposal for this iron ship of yours."

"Hear, hear!" several of the men called out.

John pointed across at the model of his little *Monitor* being held by a tall naval officer at the corner of the conference table. "Give me this contract, and I swear by my mother's grave, I will give you the only vessel that can defeat the Rebels' ship at Hampton Roads!"

"But, sir, how are we to be guaranteed that your craft will succeed at stopping the *Merrimack*?" said Welles.

"Give me ten weeks. I have been an engineer for over twenty years, and I will devote my entire intellectual genius to making this craft a vessel which can rout the Rebel thieves and keep the waterways and inlets clear for Union ships.

Gentlemen, consider this. When my monitor is floating, she will show very little above the surface of the water as a target. In addition, her steel plating and revolving turret will allow the maximum firing power against this metal monster, the *Virginia*. No other invention will succeed! You have my word. I will produce my monitor in time to save the Union!"

There was a hushed silence in the room. The cynical military men stared hard at this bulldog of a man in front of them who was pleading with them to let him create a war ship that had never before been tested. They knew time was of the essence, and soon the Confederate Navy would move on the Union ships stationed in Norfolk harbor. Stories were being circulated that the Rebels were planning to blast their way up the Potomac with this huge metal ship, raping and pillaging along the way, until, finally, they would invade Washington itself. Unless these Union men moved quickly, the fate of the nation could be at risk.

A young officer opened the door and peeked into the smoke-filled room. "Luncheon is being served in the State Dining Room. The President will be in attendance."

* * *

President Lincoln held the model of the little monitor in his big, rail-splitter's hands, and he slowly began to turn the revolving turret with his index finger by applying pressure on the cannon's barrel. The other men were seated around the large dining table, eating and drinking, but when their Commander-in-Chief picked-up the device, they immediately stopped and began to watch him carefully.

"As the young woman said when she tried on her new stockings, 'I think there might be something in it!'" President Lincoln said, with his usual sense of humor. The men laughed, and the State Dining Room seemed infused with new possibilities.

"Sir, does that mean you believe we should give this Ericsson our approval to begin construction?" said Secretary Welles, nodding seriously over at Assistant Secretary Gustavus Fox, as if to say, "Be ready to move!"

"If he can build this craft within the 100-day period we have demanded, then I say we should give him a chance," said Fox, sitting up straight to emphasize his point. His red, mutton chop sideburns shone under the chandeliers like fiery bands of fur. "I've seen his plans, Mister President, and the man's a genius. In addition to the revolving gun turret and the low profile in the water, he's designed a fan-powered ventilation system and a below-the-waterline flush toilet!"

President Lincoln chuckled. "Well, it seems the ventilation system and the toilet go together quite handily! The Navy beans we've been serving our boys have been known to cause quite a stir below decks."

The men all laughed and rubbed their whiskers with delight.

* * *

The inventor, John Ericsson, had already departed for New York. He seemed so enthused about his presentation that he decided not to wait to see if the committee had given him their approval to go ahead with the development of the new ship. He remarked to his friend, Cornelius Bushnell, as they were riding in the carriage to the train station, "I'm going to begin my plans for the *Monitor* as soon as I get back. I don't believe your government has much choice. I am their only hope."

John Ericsson rode home with his partner, Cornelius Bushnell. The train ride to New York would last several hours, and the inventor was busy working on plans for his new *Monitor*. As the trees and countryside beyond Washington passed by their club car, the sounds of the clacking rails beneath the two men vibrated the papers, which were spread out on the desk, as Ericsson was hard at work, making lines with his compass, and Bushnell was fast asleep, snoring to wake the dead.

I'll call on Charles McCord when I get into New York. He's the best man for this work, Ericsson thought to himself, musing over the designs in front of him and smiling at the sleeping Bushnell. *I knew I could convince Bushnell to let me speak to the committee. He's such an old curmudgeon. I didn't have the heart to tell him his ship would most likely sink to the bottom with all that steel he wanted to drape on her hull.*

The inventor took a creased letter out of his breast pocket and opened it to read under the gas lamp. It was from his young wife, Amelia, who was now in London with her parents. The words he read caused tears to well in his eyes and his jaws to tighten.

"I am still very much in love with you, John, my darling. However, unless you can provide for me in the way my parents are able to do, I am afraid we shall never be together again. Father says it is much too dangerous to live with you in these dramatic times of turmoil. The only way we can be one is for you to get enough money to come and get me! Don't you see, my love, we need to be aristocrats and nouveau riche. This is the American way, is it not? I do long to hold you in my arms again, my dearest. Tell me when, and I shall be packed and ready to fly on Cupid's wings!"

I shall get the money we need my love! If I must, I will kidnap President Lincoln and collect his ransom! I will do anything to get you back. You have been in my dreams each and every night. I fight it, but your face haunts my mind like an avenging angel. This war will bring us the money we need—I just know it will. War creates millionaires overnight—and I will be one of these men—or I shall die trying!

CHAPTER EIGHT: DUTY CALLS

Liverpool, England, September 2, 1861

The Union Navy was setting up blockades at all the Southern ports of call. From the Carolinas to Virginia, all along the coast down to Florida and around to Texas, huge frigates, schooners, and armored batteries were moving into place to stop all shipping activity going in and out of these ports. Walter Sinclair had seen them from his own ship, *H.M.S. Caine*, as he had been running tobacco from Virginia and the Carolinas across the Atlantic Ocean to Scotland and England, before the blockades began.

Walter knew that the new Confederate government was offering sailors 100 pounds a month in gold and a 50-pound bonus at the end of a good trip, which usually took about seven days. More importantly, the captains and pilots earned as much as 5,000 pounds a year. This was good news to Walter, as he was planning to wed his dearest Penelope as soon as he could save enough money.

Walter breathed in the salt sea air of Liverpool as he walked along the cobblestones toward the Silver Tide Inn. Shropshire Court was just around the next bend, and as he walked, Walter speculated about who would be meeting with him to hire his services for the Confederacy.

The *London Times* was covering the outbreak of America's Civil War with some amount of caustic humor and usual British wit. Many of the Southern plantation owners were negotiating with English ship owners to convert passenger steamers into streamlined blockade-runners. They would then hire ship captains and sailors to serve the Confederacy on board these ships, which would serve as a trading lifeline between the South and the rest of the world. The British newspapers showed many cartoons of these "ignorant country gentlemen" dressed in lively, but bombastic squire outfits, sitting down with professional English sea captains and getting bamboozled out of their money. It was all ripping good sport, with the colonies as the butt of the humor.

The Silver Tide Inn was a favorite pub of sailors in Liverpool, and it had a thatched roof with green ivy climbing the walls outside the structure. The sign above the front entrance showed a massive, ocean wave cresting above a giant tankard of ale. As Walter entered, he was enveloped in tobacco smoke and the odor of liquor, and he had to wait a few moments by the door so his eyes could become accustomed to the darkness. A pretty Irish serving wench, with a white-laced hat, greeted him with a big smile and even bigger cleavage, and he followed her to an enclosed booth in the back of the tavern. As she pulled back the maroon drapes covering the booth inside, she said, "Walter, please be seated. And what shall I be getting for you, then?"

Walter was startled by the girl's impertinence, as he had never met her before. "I beg your pardon? I don't believe we've been introduced," he said, sitting down inside the booth.

A tall figure appeared at the waitress's side and handed her a pound note. "Thank you very much, Mollie. You can get my guest a tankard of ale. And bring me one as well."

"Right you are, governor," said the girl, and she turned to leave.

Walter looked over at an extraordinary American. He was a tall man, with piercing green eyes, and he bore the reddest sideburns Walter had ever seen. His dark blue coat was the latest fashion from Europe—probably Italian—and he had a long, gold watch chain curling out of his side vest.

This man is indeed a gentleman, Walter thought, straightening his own tie.

The gentleman took a folded newspaper from his coat pocket and thrust it over to Walter, where he could read the headlines under the flickering overhead gas lantern. "UNION GOVERNMENT WILL BUILD A NEW IRON SHIP TO CONFRONT THE REBEL *VIRGINIA* AT HAMPTON ROADS!"

"I don't understand, sir," said Walter, looking up from the newspaper to gaze quizzically at the American. "What has this to do with what we are here to negotiate? I assumed you needed to hire a captain to serve as a blockade runner."

"Indeed, Captain Sinclair, we do wish to hire you in the service of Jefferson Davis and the Confederate States of America. However, there is an emergency right now that needs to be seen to, and I am here to call you to your duty." The gentleman took out a bulky envelope from his coat pocket and placed it next to Walter's hand. "Go ahead, open it," he said, motioning with a flick of his wrist.

As Walter opened the flap on the envelope, he saw what looked to be currency of some kind. The thickness of the stack inside told him this was no small amount. Walter Sinclair's eyes grew wider, as did those of the young serving girl, as she sat the two tankards down on the table for the two men, staring down in disbelief at the dozens of 500-pound notes being rustled between Walter's fingertips.

"Thank you, Mollie," said the American, and the serving girl smiled at him, licking her red lips at the money.

"Yessir! Anything you gents want, now, you just yell out! I can get you both anything you need!" she said, and before leaving, she tugged at Walter's sleeve and whispered, "The angels sure be shinin' down on your head, Captain Walter Sinclair!"

"There are over 50,000 pounds in that envelope, sir," said the American. "And it's all yours when you complete your assignment."

"Assignment?" said Walter, looking up from the money. His throat felt raw and dry, so he picked up the tankard of ale and gulped down a large portion, and then he wiped his foamy lips with the back of his hand. "You want me to assassinate your President Lincoln?" Walter said, and he laughed out loud at his own joke.

However, there was not the slightest hint of a smile on the American's lips, as he whispered, "No, that shall not be necessary. At the present moment, we have things well in hand. But our plans to use our new ironclad to break the Union's stranglehold on our ports and to protect our shore batteries in the South could be halted. Halted by one man. This man is an inventor named John Ericsson."

"Ericsson? An inventor? I don't quite understand, sir. What has this to do with me?" Walter felt the ale warming and gurgling in his stomach, and he belched into his fist.

"Yes, John Ericsson once served prison time in your country. He is a most unscrupulous fellow. But he is also quite an inspired engineer. This is why we want him done away with. The dictatorship of the North has given this little Swede 100 days to build a ship that they say is the only vessel which can stand up to our *Virginia's* armored firepower."

Walter felt dizzy, and the room was imploding in on him. He stood up quickly, hitting his head on the crossbeam, which drove him back down into his seat again. "Are you insane, sir? You want me to murder this man for you?"

"No, not quite, Captain. We don't request that you do this for us. You will do this for us!" the American spat the last words.

Walter became enraged. "Look here, I don't know what you Yanks have up your sleeves, but I am not becoming a conspirator to murder! This Ericsson could be Judas Iscariot, and I would not kill him!"

The American chose to laugh at that moment, and the sound of his deep, guttural bass voice made Walter sick to his stomach. "Do you love Penelope Andrews?" he asked suddenly, taking a swig from his tankard.

"My Penelope? What has she to do with this plot of yours?" Walter asked, terrified of what was to come next.

"If you do not become our Judas, as you so prophetically call yourself, then you will lose your dear Penelope. This mission will be carried out, one way or another. We know you can find a way to sneak into the shipyard and annihilate John Ericsson and his invention. We shall provide you with the location and the false identification you will need to live in the city without being suspect. How you do it will be up to you. The money will be yours when you carry out the death sentence of this Union savior, John Ericsson. Until then, here is a thousand pounds." The American folded two bills into Walter's palm. "Only after you have completed your duty will you get the rest of the payment. Then, and only then, will you and your lovely Penelope be able to live out your days in peace."

Standing up, the tall stranger took a final swallow of his ale and placed the tankard down on the table. "We shall be in frequent contact with you, Captain Sinclair. You are, after all, the best hope for an early Confederate victory. Good day to you, sir." The American pushed back the curtain and stepped out into the commotion of the noisy tavern.

Watching him leave, Walter saw the dense smoke envelop his large figure like a phantom, until he was no more. Walter looked down at the two notes in his hand. The Irish serving girl stuck her head inside the booth and said, "My, my Walter! Were you a naughty boy? Why don't you have the rest?"

"Piss off, damn you!" shouted Walter, finally realizing the deadly serious nature of his predicament. Inside the tavern, the local quartet of piano, horn and two voices—the Liverpool Landsmen—began to play their first song of the evening, a tune of the 65th Yorkshire Regiment, "The Mermaid's Song." Walter listened intently, as the words seemed to portend his future.

> It was Friday morn when we set sail,
> And we were not so far from the land,
> When the captain he spied a mermaid so fair,
> With a comb and a glass in her hand.
> And the ocean waves do roll,
> And the stormy winds do blow,
> And we poor tars go skipping through the tops,
> While the landlubbers lie down
> Below, below, below.
> While the landlubbers lie down.
> Up spoke the captain of our gallant ship,
> And a fine spoken sailor was he.
> 'This fishy mermaid has warned us of our doom.
> We shall sink to the bottom of the sea.'

Walter pulled open the drapes to his booth and shouted into the din, "Mollie! Bring me a pint of ale!"

CHAPTER NINE: TRANSIENT

Brooklyn, New York, September 4, 1861

Lieutenant Samuel Dana Greene, 21 years old, was still infused with youthful optimism and patriotic fervor following his graduation from Annapolis two years before. His fiancée Miss Anna Cameron, of the Shipbuilding Cameron's of New Jersey, was in attendance, as well his parents, engineer and inventor Army General George S. Greene and his wife Elizabeth. After graduation, he was stationed on the steam sloop Hartford, which was sent to China and cruised the seas of the Far East for two years. He was ordered back to Brooklyn when the Civil War broke out in 1861. His family was all proud of him, and they were writing him every day as he served his country in the Bachelor Officers' Transient Quarters in the Brooklyn Navy Yard, awaiting his next orders to duty.

As a transient sailor, Lieutenant Greene served only one duty night at the BOTQ as the Officer of the Deck (OOD), and the rest of the nights he was free to wander the streets of Brooklyn, staring up at the starry sky, walking over the green hills, still believing he could pick out the one special star owned by him and his lover.

On rainy nights, Greene would sit inside the Brooklyn Public Library and read the works of the Transcendentalists such as Henry Thoreau, Ralph Waldo Emerson and the new poet, Walt Whitman, who was making a literary statement with his poems of the war, *Drum Taps*, which were being published in many of the best New York magazines. However, it was Whitman's internal message that got to Dana Greene the most.

Something about the poet's link with nature and the common man gave the young lieutenant deep understanding as he read passages inside the drafty library confines. Shadows danced on the walls, and the stunning visions

Whitman weaved played themselves inside Greene's consciousness like Greek nymphs cavorting in a pasture at the bottom of Olympus.

The words from poems such as "Crossing Brooklyn Ferry" reverberated inside Dana and gave him distinctive feelings of anguish and elation at the same time. It was similar to the emotions of dread and excited anticipation, which he would feel whenever he thought about his wartime future. This man, Walt Whitman, was saying a lot about what was going on inside young Lieutenant Samuel Dana Greene:

> *Whatever it is, it avails not — distance avails not, and place avails not,*
> *I too lived, Brooklyn of ample hills was mine, I too walk'd the streets of Manhattan island, and bathed in the waters around it,*
> *I too felt the curious abrupt questionings stir within me, In the day among crowds of people sometimes they came upon me,*
> *In my walks home late at night or as I lay in my bed they came upon me,*
> *I too had been struck from the float forever held in solution,*
> *I too had receiv'd identity by my body, That I was I knew was of my body, and what I should be I knew I should be of my body.*

Dana looked up from his reading. Across from him, inside an enclosed reading booth, an older gentleman was attentively
reading from some large books. He wore a beaver hat and dark coat, and as Lieutenant Greene looked carefully over at what the man was reading, he noticed that they were books containing pages of ship designs.

Could it be? Dana thought. I wonder. Dare I ask him? By Jove, this may be my chosen fate! The young lieutenant got up from his seat and walked over to where the older man was still busily perusing the texts. "Excuse me, sir. I'm sorry to bother you, but aren't you the inventor, John Ericsson? I saw your letter in the *Brooklyn Eagle* the other day. And, I must say, I was quite impressed by your brilliant new design!"

John Ericsson slowly looked up from his reading. He was trying to find a new way to keep the weight of his Monitor displaced evenly when afloat. This young man in civilian clothes had a certain military bearing, and the confident gaze in his blue eyes made Ericsson pay attention to his flattery. "Yes, I am he. I'm happy to know you approve," said the inventor, pulling out a chair next to his for the young man to sit down. Since they were inside a private reading cubicle, they were free to converse without bothering the other library patrons.

"I'm waiting for my orders at the Brooklyn Transient Barracks. I am an officer graduated from the Naval Academy, and I've been following your effort to build your new invention. What a fantastic idea for a ship!" Dana pulled his chair up close to Ericsson and shut the door behind them.

John liked the boy's enthusiasm. He knew that the glow in this young man's demeanor meant something special, as he had that same glow when he was a young man in Stockholm trying to find his way in the world. As he listened to the boy go on about his family and his girl back home, John was suddenly struck with an idea. In order to proceed with his plan, he first needed to enlist this young man's cooperation.

". . and when father got his patent on the elevator trains, our lives took a dramatic turn," Greene was saying, when John Ericsson interrupted. "I am going to see to it that you get duty on my new ship. Would you like that, Mister Greene?"

The young lieutenant's face lit up with delight. "Me? You want me on your new ship? Why, I just knew that my meeting you today would prove to be my destiny! I can't wait to tell my family and my Anna. They'll be so proud!"

"Yes, well, I'm going to talk to people in the Navy Department about you, son. I'm certain they'll help me get you put on the manifest. I would also like you to watch the building of my Monitor from the ground up. That way, you can better appreciate the way she'll perform for you when you're at sea. As your father was an engineer and inventor, I expect there's some of that blood of the creator in you!"

The two men talked on about the details of shipbuilding and how the new *Monitor* would be able to defeat the Rebel's giant, the *Virginia*. Lieutenant Greene, as he listened to the confident words of his new benefactor, was becoming infused with an inner confidence and resourcefulness he never realized he owned. It was the same confidence that Ralph Waldo Emerson wrote about in his essays. "Great men working together can build great inventions," and Greene now believed he could be part of the effort.

Lieutenant Samuel Dana Greene understood he was part of an anointed few when he left the Brooklyn Public Library that day, with two books of Whitman's poetry under his arm. He couldn't wait to get back to his wardroom to tell all the other young men that he would no longer be a transient looking for orders. Destiny had shined on him, and he was now going to become one of the first crewmembers of a ship that was ordained to make history. Life or death was not an issue because it was the participation that made one heroic. He had been summoned to answer his calling, and Greene believed the days to come would gradually unveil his hero's journey.

As John Ericsson left the library that evening, he was thinking only about his new plan. His calculating, engineer's mind was fixed upon a goal, and when this occurred, there was nothing he would permit to get in his way. It would be quite risky, indeed, but the possible rewards could be astronomical. He would need this young man on the inside in order to pull off the plan, and it seemed quite fortuitous that he had met him. That optimistic face of youthful Lieutenant Greene had immediately set John to thinking about his own early life and how much he now needed his darling young wife, Amelia. His plan, if worked to perfection, would give him the money and influence he would need to become one of the richest Americans of the war. John Ericsson believed he understood the "dirty little secret" behind all wars. Profiteering was the impetus behind the escalation of warfare—not patriotic duty. *We leaders*, thought John, looking out over the waters as he stood on the Brooklyn Bridge, *create patriots by our cunning propaganda. As I shall create my craft for their battle against the South, so shall I also create my unique young patriot, Mister Greene, for my war against all those who would keep me from my bride. My victory will see my precious Amelia returned to me, where she belongs. And America and its uncivil war can go straight to the bottom of the sea!*

Back in the transient barracks, Lieutenant Greene sat upon his rack and read from the 1855 edition of Whitman's Leaves of Grass. From the first words, "I celebrate myself, and what I assume you shall assume, for every atom belonging to me as good belongs to you," Dana was pulled into the author's world. He became fused with the natural splendor of Nature and the God within the man. It was almost three in the morning when Greene read these last few lines and fell asleep dreaming of patriotic oneness with his country, with the genius inventor, John Ericsson, and with his internal God:

This is the breath of laws and songs and behaviour, This is the tasteless water of souls . . . this is the true sustenance, It is for the illiterate . . . it is for the judges of the supreme court... it is for the federal capitol and the state capitols, It is for the admirable communes of literary men and composers and singers and lecturers and engineers and savants, It is for the endless races of working people and farmers and seamen. This is the trill of a thousand clear cornets and scream of the octave flute and strike of triangles. I play not a march for victors only ... I play great marches for conquered and slain persons. Have you heard that it was good to gain the day? I also say it is good to fall. . . battles are lost in the same spirit in which they are won.

* * *

As John entered his house on Beach Street, he had his plan well formulated. He at once went into the study and began laying out two charts. One chart was for the construction of the U.S.S. Monitor and the other one was for the construction of the

patriot: Lieutenant Samuel Dana Greene. Both of these enterprises would take all of his genius, but John believed he would succeed. The United States Government would be his salvation. No more lonely nights inside this cold tenement. No more cold sheets and drafty winter chills. John Ericsson had hit upon a plan that would bring him the money to build an empire in New York, and he would then be able to afford to bring back his empress.

Reaching into a trunk at the end of his worktable, John pulled out a worn letter from his Amelia. He sat back in his chair and reverently unfolded the letter in front of the gas lamp on the desk beside him.

John,

I hope you can afford to soon bring me back to America. I have faith in you, darling.

The days, and especially the long nights, make me yearn for your touch. We can at last be together once you are able to become independently wealthy. I believe you shall be able to do it! America is the place where dreams can come true. And, right now, you are in my dreams, my love! Soon, we shall be one forever!

Love, Amelia

John fell asleep with the letter on his lap and the two charts completed. It was almost daybreak. In addition to a number of paragraphs filled with engineering plans, two words were capitalized in the Greene chart beneath the young officer's name: "MIND" and "MONITOR". Between the words was: =

CHAPTER TEN: RECRUITMENT

Brooklyn, New York, September 5, 1861

Charles W. McCord was a lanky Irish draftsman who lived down the road from John Ericsson, off 42nd Street and Canal. The inventor knew that McCord would be his lead draftsman, as there was a need for hundreds of additional drawings for the workmen to use on the new ideas to be implemented on the *Monitor*.

As John approached the Dutch-style building, he was thinking about how to begin his development of the young Lieutenant Greene. John believed that Greene would best respond to a fantastic scenario rather than a monetary appeal. Young men usually are taken in by propaganda that includes vivid descriptions of a new world to come and other romantic notions that can pique their fancy. After hours of research in the library, Ericsson now had such a notion, and it would be quite stimulating to see if the young man would respond. If Greene did not react, then nothing was lost. The engineer's son would certainly never call his mentor a traitor.

Charles was working on his latest invention at the rear of his one-room apartment. The sun was shining upon his workbench through a small window in the back wall. There were a variety of blueprints hung up on the walls on either side of his bench, and when McCord looked up from his drawings as Ericsson entered, the Irishman gave John the appearance of some insane warden of mysterious secrets of the soul.

Charles McCord always left his door open when working, a habit that John Ericsson found quite irritating, but McCord always insisted, "Thieves who are able to read my chicken scratches would not be of our civilization, so they would be welcome to them!"

"I see you have another nebulous concoction brewing, my dear Charles,"

39

said Ericsson, moving over to stand near the tall and lean Irishman and look over his plans. "What might this contrivance be, pray tell?"

McCord wore brown corduroy trousers and a white shirt with fasteners on the rolled sleeves, and his black jackboots were in memory of his days in the Irish Army in Dublin. He had them ship him a new pair every six months. He had a sweeping black mustache, as Charles was one of the Irish they call "Black," and his thick, wavy hair extended down into broad, midnight sideburns. His face was expansive and good-humored, and his complexion dark, yet his murky eyes contained the sparkle of wit that endeared him to Ericsson.

"You would not care for what I'm doing, John. I am not the inventor of important devices that you are. I have devised a simple way to hold paper on a roll for uses in privies. Outhouses, as you call them, can be quite dark at times, and I thought that having a roller containing paper would make the completion task much easier."

Ericsson slapped McCord on the back until dust rose into the air around them. "Charles, my dear lad, great minds do think alike! You have just invented something that will go quite handily inside my new *Monitor*. We shall build the first below-decks flush toilet system any world navy has ever seen!"

McCord moved into the kitchen and stood by a table covered with a variety of liquors and smoking paraphernalia. He poured a shot of Irish whiskey from a long black bottle into a water-stained cup and thrust it forward toward John. "Here's to you, Mister Ericsson. We had some grand times working together, to be sure. But the last one—when the gentlemen got blown-up on the *Princeton*—that was just too much for me. You'll be needing to find yourself another draftsman."

"Now Charles, we've been over this many times. I was not responsible for the disaster on board the *Princeton*. Captain Stockton was. Indeed, I have come to enlist your service because I know you are the only man who can illustrate what I have in my head. We have almost a psychic affinity for each other. Your country is at war, Charles, and those Rebels down in Virginia have a ship that can destroy any naval vessel you have in the North. However, you can help me build the ship that can surely save the union!"

Charles looked perplexed. He poured another finger of liquor. "You mean, you have a way to combat that iron monster they're building in Gosport? Why, those damned Rebels deserve to go straight to hell!"

Ericsson smiled. "That's the spirit! Yes, you and I can build a craft to sail down to Hampton Roads and stop that giant. I invented her to sell to Emperor Napoleon to use against the Russians, but he refused. Now we can put our novelty together and see what she can do against those mutineers."

"I don't know, Mister Ericsson. You're a hard man to work for, you are. I spent fifteen hour days working on your plans for the *Princeton*." Charles downed the whiskey and wiped his mustaches with the back of his hand.

"This will be even more work, my lad, because we have only 100 days to finish her. President Lincoln himself wants it done! But there's more money to be had, that's for certain. Are you up for it?" John walked over to Charles and held out his hand. "Let's seal our agreement before the sun sets. It will be an omen of our patriotic intentions."

Charles McCord stood for several moments, gazing into the convincing eyes of Captain John Ericsson, and then he inflated his cheeks and blew out a rush of air. Finally, he reached out and shook the older man's hand. "All right, sir, you've got yourself a draftsman. But I get all the whiskey I can drink at the end of the week!"

"Yes, Charles, that shall be written into your contract, I'll see to it myself. My boy, today is a superior day. A fine day for both of us, and an excellent day for the United States of America!" John said, as he vigorously pumped the draftsman's hand and beamed like a Swedish sunrise.

* * *

Mrs. Beulah Scott-Townsend was the widow who owned the Brooklyn Seaward Rooming House on Bedford Avenue at North 10th Street, across from Mug's Ale House, in Green Point, Brooklyn. About five blocks away, as the seagulls flew, was the Continental Ship Yard. When the stranger came into her place of business, Mrs. Townsend greeted him with the same warm welcome she gave all prospective boarders. However, when she heard the young man's British accent, she was especially impressed, as she was a bit of an Anglophile. Inside her rooming house she had collected a variety of Victorian furnishings to decorate all the rooms. Stained glass windows, billowy and tasseled red drapes, and thick mahogany chairs and tables with carved feet and legs were all about, as well as tall fern stands. Bric-a-brac, silver and china collectables covered all the windowsills and smoking room stands. The atmosphere was quite charming and darkly ravishing, or so Mrs. Townsend believed, and when this gentleman began speaking in the King's proper English, she became immediately attentive and formal.

"I would like a room for the month," said the tall young man. He handed Mrs. Townsend cash for the month, and the old widow smiled warmly as he signed the registry.

"Thank you, Mister Ellwood. I am certain you will be quite happy here in my little home. We serve breakfast at seven, and dinner at eight. Also, I would be delighted to offer you a special tea time!" Beulah was beside herself with good humor, and when the gentleman took her hand into his and kissed it, she indeed felt a bit woozy with passion! Nobody had done that since her late husband, Gaspar Townsend, originally of the London Townsends, used to do it before they would enter the dining room for the evening meal.

"I thank you for your kindness, Mrs. Townsend, but I shall be out and about most of the day. I am doing work at the shipyard, and I shall not have need for teatime. I should now like a nice bath, however, if that could be arranged? I have been traveling aboard ship for several days now, and I could use a good sloshing about the gunnels, if I may be so blunt."

"Why, certainly sir! I will have one of my porters heat the water for your bath immediately," said Mrs. Townsend, and she hit the brass bell at her desk. A short black boy came running out from the back of the house. "Chip, please take this gentleman's cases, and then heat him a bath."

"Yes, Mrs. Townsend," said the boy, in a refined voice, and he immediately picked up the two suitcases and began dragging them toward the dumb waiter near the circular stairs in the center of the room.

Mrs. Townsend whispered conspiratorially to the gentleman, "I taught him proper manners. I belong to the Abolitionist Union, and we do our patriotic duty!"

"Indeed," said the gentleman, as he followed the young lad up the stairs. The boy led him to his room on the top floor facing the tavern, and he could hear the clatter of glasses and the occasional shouts of drunken revelry coming from the dark tavern just outside his window. He knew he could use a good pint before turning in for the night.

He gave the boy five cents, and the little urchin's face lit up with a pearly smile, as he dipped low with a grand bow and left the room. "Bloody trained monkeys!" Walter cursed under his breath, as he lifted his biggest suitcase onto the four-poster bed. The bed had a large blue canopy above it that reminded him of some kind of funeral home.

Captain Walter Sinclair spread out three sets of strategies on the bedspread. One was a long black box containing a British Enfield rifle, or "musketoon," as the Confederates who were using them against the Yankees were calling them. This was a superb model, used by snipers, and it had a long telescopic sight designed by a Northern inventor, one Cornelius Bushnell. The second device was a collection of poisons guaranteed to kill any human alive, preferably a certain Swedish inventor. Hemlock, arsenic, and cyanide were mixed in a concoction the Confederate contact had called "Yankee Love Potion." The last device was the most impressive. Although it was in the form of a secret plan in writing by a British engineer, Robert Whitehead, Walter believed it to be the most ingenious way to destroy the *Monitor* when it sailed out for its maiden voyage. Walter also thought it quite ironic that this mission would be the first use of a propeller-driven bomb, which would be launched from his own schooner, the *H.M.S. Caine*. After all, it was John Ericsson who had first invented the propeller-driven ship, and it seemed quite proper that Ericsson's own invention was to be sunk by a British torpedo bomb finding its way through the water to explode inside this scourge of an ironclad!

Walter heard a knock on the door, and he quickly threw the large coverlet over the top of his assassin's gear. "One moment," he called, and walked briskly over to the door. He leaned against the entrance and said loudly, "Yes, who is it?"

A high-pitched, very proper voice of young Chip came through the transom above his door. "Mister Ellwood, sir! I got your hot bath ready in the room down the hall. And it ain't even Saturday!" Walter could hear the little black bastard laugh and then run away down the hallway. Breathing a sigh of relief, Walter began to undress, walking slowly over to the other suitcase to get out his long silk dressing gown imported directly from the Japanese islands. He had one hundred days to do his duty, and tomorrow he would see where this demonic ship was going to be built.

CHAPTER ELEVEN: CONSTRUCTION BEGINS

September 6, 1861, Green Point, Brooklyn

A visit from John Ericsson's military courier came into the Navy Department in Washington D. C. at 0800, and by 1000, the new orders for Lieutenant Samuel Dana Greene were cut and on their way by courier to the Brooklyn Officers' Transient Barracks. Although the officer was only 21 years of age, Ericsson successfully argued to get the young Greene listed as the Executive Officer aboard his new ship, the *U.S.S. Monitor.* Ericsson pointed out the fact that he had personally interviewed the young lieutenant and found him quite bright and eager to learn, and he also mentioned that Greene was from an engineering family and also an Academy graduate. This last point went over very well with the career officers on the Union's Naval Personnel Board. In addition, Greene was to be assigned temporary duty at Ericsson's residence in order to work with the inventor during the construction of the lieutenant's new ship.

The shipyard at Green Point on Palyers Street was a busy place when John Ericsson and Lieutenant Dana Greene entered the main gate in their one-horse surrey. A platoon of Marines was drilling inside the wide compound area, and their shouts of "On your left, two, three, four!" split the early morning air with militant precision.

As Greene drove the surrey up to the main administration building, Ericsson spotted his lead draftsman, Charles McCord, who was sitting on the front steps of the building whittling on a branch from a nearby oak tree. Charles was always doing something with his hands, and Ericsson appreciated his hard work. This task would test all of their willpower, as the pressure to build this ship within the government's deadline of 100 days would create a tension amongst these workers that one could slice with a knife.

"Hello, Charles! Where are the workers we were supposed to get? I don't see much commotion around here except those Marines." John stepped down from the surrey cabin, and shook his friend's hand.

"Hell, John, you know the Civil Service. We'll be lucky to get them out here this week. Don't worry; we need to do some rigorous planning before we put those ship fitters and laborers to work. Remember how long it took us to prepare for that *Princeton* job." Charles glanced over at the young lieutenant. "Who did you bring along? Is the Navy recruiting out of the secondary schools already?"

Greene smiled, but he did not shake the older man's hand until it was extended in good humor. "Name's Greene. Lieutenant Samuel Dana Greene. Captain Ericsson has chosen me to be second in command of his new ship."

"That so?" Charles cocked his head at Ericsson. "I suppose if John here checked you out, then you must be wise beyond your years. Nevertheless, I can still see the wetness behind those big ears. Hey, why don't I write that down? It's a rhyme! It can be our first song for the workers to sing."

"Charles, let the boy be. He'll get enough hazing from the old salts we'll get to crew the Monitor. We've got a lot of work to do before they show up, so let's get going!"

* * *

At the top of a green hill overlooking the Continental Ship Yard, with the wide expanse of the East River as a backdrop, Walter stood with his spyglass looking down into the compound. He was watching the men inside the shipyard with a great deal of interest. He was also memorizing every object and daily routine going on inside this complex, as it would be his hunting grounds during the coming weeks. He knew he had to wait for the ship to be built, as those were his orders. Then, he was to kill Captain John Ericsson and capture the architectural plans for the *U.S.S. Monitor*. The Confederacy was paying a big fee for those plans, but the inventor must be dead as part of the bargain. And, with the aid of his British compatriot, Robert Whitehead, he would also be sinking this infernal craft before it could be put to sea on its maiden voyage.

Wind was causing whitecaps to form on the ocean waves, and Walter pulled up his collar. Off in the distance, he could hear a foghorn. At sea, Walter felt more comfortable, as the people on land always seemed to him to be caught up in a game of personal attack and one-upmanship. Life at sea was a competition with Nature, yes, but men soon learned to cooperate rather than to attack each other. These colonies had insisted upon their fanatical idea of individual rights for all men, and now they were paying the price. The Negroid race was expecting the same rights as free white men, and brother was now turning against brother. What did they expect?

45

There could be no freedom aboard a ship. A captain was the ruler aboard his vessel, and all who obeyed orders learned they would survive. These bloody Americans had not learned that lesson. In a strange way, he felt sorry for them. They seemed to be invigorated from this civil war. He imagined they would all be arguing and fighting it again down through the years. Americans were such contentious brutes.

Walter took the glass down from his eye and closed the fuselage. Would they talk about him in their history books? Probably not. As the magnifying glass of the public media came closer, it would turn away, because the candid face of Walter Sinclair would be too much to bear. I am the face of their past had they learned to follow orders. I am the civilized order they forsook for their bloody revolution. Let them choke on their own destiny!

CHAPTER TWELVE: INDOCTRINATION BEGINS

September 7, 1861, Green Point, Brooklyn

John Ericsson and his new executive officer were inside the Continental Ship Yard's Drafting Office. The workers were reporting in one hour to begin construction, and the blueprints for the ship's keel were laid out neatly on the top of the large table in the center of the room. John knew it was time to begin his indoctrination of the young Greene, and so he decided to start with a story. Young men, throughout history, had been fascinated by stories of scientific discovery, and the elder Ericsson believed it would also be true in his experiment with the mind of the young lieutenant.

"Mister Greene, are you familiar with the text of the British scientist, Charles Darwin? It was published in 1859, and he has called it *The Origin of the Species.*" John watched the young man carefully. He wanted to be certain the responses he received were positive before he continued with his story. When he noted that the young man vigorously nodded his head, John became immediately invigorated.

"Why, yes. In fact, I read it while I was home on leave. Father and I had a rousing good discussion about its implications. Do you believe his hypothesis about mankind's evolution from lower mammal forms such as apes? It seems his ideas about natural selection seem to hold up under closer scrutiny." Greene moved his chair closer to Ericsson's, and both men momentarily ignored the ship's building plans. Charles McCord, lead draftsman, was out setting-up the labor routine for the newly arriving workers from the city.

"Quite right you are! In fact, I am convinced that his theories explain the entire evolution of life on this planet. His ideas have directly contradicted the creation myths of the Bible and other mystical texts of superstition." John was warming to his subject, and he could tell by the gleam in the young man's eyes that Greene was becoming charged with a common emotion. Mister Greene was, indeed, a fellow scientist.

John would extend his argument to one more level. "In point of fact, I am in daily correspondence with geologists and biologists from Britain who are exploring lands in India, Africa, South America and Australia. They have been telling me about their findings, and one gentleman, Doctor Ernest Heinrich Haekel, has come up with a theory of his own. Philip Scalter, a biologist, has agreed with Haekel's findings, and they are to publish a text of their own."

Lieutenant Greene was clearly anxious to learn more. "What did they discover, Captain?" he asked, positively beaming with curiosity.

"Haekel discovered the existence of a unique form of prosimian, or pre-monkey, which has existed long before the ape and monkey species. The strange discovery he made was that these Lemur creatures were found in Africa, India, Madagascar, and on the Malaya Peninsula. In addition, Scalter has discovered the identical fossilized remains of plants, prehistoric animals and other life forms on the continents of India, Africa, South America and Australia. The question these men asked was, how did these same species appear on these land forms separated by thousands of miles of open sea?"

"How fascinating! What did they conclude?" Greene was leaning toward his mentor in eager anticipation.

"Well, I suppose a biblical scholar might say they were part of the original creation, when God placed all creatures on earth at the same moment. However, as we know through scientific dating processes and evolutionary theory brought out in Darwin's book, the earth has gone through many stages, with innumerable creatures evolving and disappearing in the course of a variety of natural phenomena such as floods, ice ages and earth quakes. These men concluded that there was once a landmass, which connected the separate continents. This would explain the Lemur problem. This landmass, they say, sank beneath the sea at some point in time, probably over 250 million years past, and left the same species on each of these four continents. In fact, Scalter has named this ancient between-land Lemuria, in honor of the species of prosimian."

"This must be quite a breakthrough! Tell me more," said Greene.

"Not only did they name this land, but they have discovered a small part of the original land mass that they have called 'Easter Island,' in honor of the day the Lord rose from the dead. This island was the minuscule piece that rose from the sea to give us a connection with a lost civilization!"

"Has anybody ever visited this land?" asked Greene, noticeably interested.

"This is where it gets really interesting! The men who have visited Easter Island have brought back incredible tales. They say the inhabitants worship gigantic beings, and they have created huge, carved stone statues to memorialize them. In addition, they are said to be the happiest humans these visitors have ever set eyes upon. They have no prurient tastes, as the females wear no clothes over their top parts, and the men have the slightest palm fronts covering their privates below. They are kind and considerate souls who have never been observed to argue or fight, and this makes me believe they are most likely descendants of the tribes of the connecting land of Lemuria back when it joined the great continents many thousands of years before."

"They do indeed sound like remarkable humans!" Greene exclaimed, his eyes large with wonder. "They sound like the beings that Walt Whitman writes about in his poetry. Wait! I have a book of his writings in my coat. Let me get it to read to you what I mean." The young lieutenant, giddy with exuberance, darted over to his coat hanging on the rack in the corner and brought back a small book. He opened it and turned reverently to a page that had been marked with a slip of paper. "Listen to this. He tells us about the human forms we all share:"

The man's body is sacred and the woman's body is sacred.
No matter who it is, it is sacred—is it the meanest one in the laborers⁹ gang?
Is it one of the dull-faced immigrants just landed on the wharf?
Each belongs here or anywhere just as much as the
well-off, just as much as you,
Each has his or her place in the procession.
(All is a procession; the universe is a procession
with measured and perfect motion.)
Do you know so much yourself that you call the
meanest ignorant?
Do you suppose you have a right to a good sight,
and he or she has no right to a sight?
Do you think matter has cohered together from its
diffuse float, and the soil is on the surface, and
water runs and vegetation sprouts,
For you only, and not for him and her?

Ericsson was pleased. He knew the young lad was ripe for his conditioning. It would take only a few days to prepare him for the plan. "That's certainly a wonderful philosophy you have there, son," he said, patting the young man's knee. "I only wish we could escape this turmoil and join those untainted natives on Easter Island. It would be the ideal territory to live out one's existence in harmonious peace with the woman you love."

"Ah, yes! It does sound magnificent, sir. I am to be wed as soon as this conflict is over. Are you also looking to marry?" Greene asked, making his first inquiry into the older man's personal life.

Ericsson's demeanor became gloomy. "I'm afraid my wife is living in England with her parents. The war has divided us, as it has you and your future bride. We also have the added problem of sparse finances. My Amelia comes from a rather wealthy family, and my coffers have become quite used up these last few years, and this in turn led to her retreat. However, when we finish our construction of the Monitor, we shall be a bit closer to approaching as one. Although, I am afraid it will take much more money to at last bring us together."

The young man looked visibly moved by what Ericsson was telling him. "Don't you fret, sir! I, for one, will work tirelessly to help you build the best craft the United States Navy has ever owned."

"Thanks, Mister Greene. You are quite kind. Now let's go see if Charles has prepared the shop for the workers, shall we?"

The two men walked with a purposeful stride out of the drafting office and into the morning's sunshine. Greene had thoughts of running with his dearest Anna down the warm sands of Easter Island, and they were wearing what Walt Whitman would have called their "natural splendor." John Ericsson was devising another story to lead this military lamb to his fold.

CHAPTER THIRTEEN: TORPEDO MAN

September 8, 1861, Green Point, Brooklyn

Walter Sinclair was sitting inside a booth in the back of Mug's Ale House, waiting for his visitor, and he was thinking about how long it would take to set things in motion. The workers were now organized inside the Continental Ship Yard, and he knew it would be just a matter of days before the construction began on the *Monitor*. All his plans had to be in place before the launch, and it was his new visitor from Austria who was the vital cog in his machinations.

"Could I fetch you another pint, Mister Ellwood?" the serving wench, Grace, was addressing him. At first, Sinclair failed to respond. He was thinking about what to buy his Penelope as a souvenir of the colonies.

"Why, yes. That would be nice. Grace, what would you suggest a young woman of your age should want in the way of a remembrance to this country? I have been through most of the shops, but I can't for the life of me come up with a good idea." Sinclair thought the girl had striking good looks. Her raven hair hung below her shoulder blades, the way Penelope's did when she let it down, and her sparkling brown eyes measured his with a directness that explained she was a woman of the world.

"How thoughtful of you, Mister Ellwood! Let me think about this for a bit. I'm certain we can come up with the best gift!" The young woman giggled and turned to get another pint. She almost ran into a tall young man in a dark blue suit with a flaming red vest. "Oh! Excuse me, sir," she said. The aristocratic-looking gentleman was about five feet ten inches tall and was smoking a briar pipe; something Sinclair had not seen done since he was in England. He had a bushy head of blond hair, and his confident manner convinced Sinclair that this was indeed his guest.

51

"Mister Whitehead?" Sinclair stood up.

"Yes, and you're Mister Ellwood, I presume?" said the young man, seating himself on the hard wood chair inside the booth.

Sinclair had been corresponding with the young inventor for over a year. Robert Whitehead was working in Trieste, on the Adriatic coast, and Walter knew all about him and his new inventions, particularly the new device that was the object of their meeting. Whitehead was originally from Lancaster, near Bolton, and he had left England in 1840 to seek his fortune abroad. His was a family of engineers, and the genius of this young man seemed to coalesce on foreign shores, as he managed to make a good living, working initially in a shipyard in Toulon and setting up as a consultant engineer in Milan. He was, however, forever trying to avoid the numerous European wars and, as a result of boundary changes, lost many of his important patents. He moved on to Trieste on the Adriatic coast, again working for a shipyard where he was credited with producing the first screw propeller and cylindrical marine boiler to be built in Austria. However, it was Whitehead's latest invention that had led Sinclair to seek him out.

"Would you mind closing the long curtains, Mister Whitehead? I would like to keep our conversation secure." Walter said, smiling. "I trust your trip was smooth?"

"We had a bit of a storm off your Cape Hatteras, but other than that it was quite smooth sailing indeed. I am anxious to get started. The Austrian Navy has refused my latest invention, even though Captain de Luppis and I spent many months perfecting the explosion mechanism."

"Yes, I read about that. How is dear Giovanni? It's a shame we Brits get snubbed by our own country and must turn to other countries in order to use our true genius." Walter gave his fellow countryman a conciliatory smirk.

"Actually, as you know, I would not be here to do business with you if it had not been for the Austrian Navy's refusal. Der Kustenbrander's problems with the clockwork engine and tiller controlled steering mechanism have led to my present invention, something I like to call the MK-1. The failure with the clockwork caused me to derive a far better device that uses compressed air." Whitehead's eyes began to light up with enthusiasm as he spoke of his new invention.

"Fantastic! Bravo! You wrote about the problems with the weapon spinning in the water and throwing off the direction. Have you solved that dilemma as well?"

"Yes, I have installed large, vertical fins to compensate for the roll-over of the cylindrical body. It now runs at six to eight knots for over 400 yards. I believe that is satisfactory for your needs, is it not?"

Walter grinned. "Quite! However, have you thought about how I can camouflage this device and lessen the noise? It must run straight and true for

200 yards, because if it is detected, then the mission will have failed miserably."

"Yes, I have. I will take a plate of metal and some sample pigments down to the East River. There, I shall mix and match until I find the color which completely blends with the waters until the metal is invisible beneath the surface. The MK will be propelled about six feet beneath the surface, and there will be only a slightly visible ripple effect on the surface. We cannot prevent this due to the speed of the torpedo needed to intersect with your enemy's craft. By the way, did you find out how many knots this target will be doing? This is crucial to your distance and engine speed preparation."

The serving maid returned with the drinks. "Thank you, Grace," said Sinclair, pulling the large brass ale mug to him and taking a swig. Foam tickled his upper lip, and he wiped it clean.

"You are welcome, Mister Ellwood. I now know of the perfect gift for your lady, sir! We was talkin' about it in the back." The young woman reached over to a box on a table nearby and pulled out what looked to be an intricate quilt with colorful, square designs, which resembled a ladder or tracks of some kind.

"My, how lovely! You are correct, Grace. My Penelope adores quilts."

"Yes, these here are made by women in New York. We call them 'Union Quilts.' This is one we named the 'Jacob's Ladder or the Underground Railroad' print. It's in memory of those poor black souls who are being held in miserable slavery down South. The only way they can find their freedom is to die and go up God's Ladder, or find their way onto the Abolitionists' Railroad up to us in the North!" Grace spread the quilt over the top of the table, and the two men stared down at it.

Walter was about to ask the ignorant wench how she knew these black creatures would be better off in the hands of government profiteers, but he thought better of it. It was best to maintain his neutral decorum. "Quite charming, my dear. Yes, I do believe you have something there. Wrap it up, and I'll purchase it."

CHAPTER FOURTEEN: THE VIRGINIA

Richmond, September 11, 1861

Chief designer and naval ordnance officer of the Confederate Navy, John M. Brooke, was in the office of naval construction supervisor, John L. Porter. The two men were jawing at each other, toe-to-toe, beard-to-beard, and Porter seemed to be losing the shouting match.

"Look here, John, I've got men tearing up the railroad tracks all over Virginia, down the Carolinas and over into Mississippi. Why is that? Because your iron works can't produce anything thicker than 1-inch armor plate! How is that going to stand up to those big Union guns? I need to enclose and protect my rifles and cannons with a gun deck that has over three inches of armor. What can you do for me?"

Porter grabbed a red bandana he had stuffed into his porkpie hat and wiped it across his perspiring brow. "We're short on iron all over the South. I know you think yours is the most important project going, but there are a lot of men dying because we don't have railway transportation to hospitals in Richmond. Why? Because your men are tearing up all of the tracks for that infernal beast of yours!"

"I have men working day and night paring down those charred timbers on this ship, and I need that iron to lay a good cover over her. This government can't get me iron, so I have to get it somewhere! Besides, the Merrimack's engines were so waterlogged they had to be condemned. I'm working to get them ready as well."

"I understand your dilemma, John. No place in the South can produce the iron you need. I'm trying to get some blockade-runners to deliver the goods from France, England and Austria, but I don't know if they'll get here on time." Porter felt sorry for poor Brooke. He had plunged himself totally into the effort to convert this old steamer into an ironclad, and he did want to help in some way. It was just that Brooke was such a difficult man to work with. He would go off into tirades against the entire Confederate government, and Porter often thought he bordered upon treason, if it had not been for the designer's unrelenting drive toward his goal of creating a true battle ship for the cause of Southern states' rights.

Brooke sat down on a stool near the window and pulled open his shirt collar stays. "I don't know if we'll make it. Sometimes I think it's a useless attempt."

Porter walked slowly over to the taller and much grayer man and put a tentative hand on his shoulder. "We're all in this together. You keep forgetting that. In fact, I talked to an officer on Mallory's staff, and he says we have a secret weapon in the works." Porter leaned over to whisper conspiratorially, "He told me there's a spy in New York right now who has orders to destroy any armored ship that the Yankees can build! You just may have clear sailing up the Potomac, my friend. One of your famous Brooke rifles may give old Abe Lincoln a new part in his beard!"

Brooke stood up. "That's all I hear around here, John. Big talk about spies and secret weapons. Well, I didn't join this fight to build a rumor. My Virginia will be ready for Hampton Roads, or I'll die trying! But you have to get me more iron, do you hear?" John Brooke poked a long finger into the shorter man's chest. "And don't you put your hopes on secret assassins. Wars are won with blood, sweat and tears. But you're right about my feeling all alone. You have to show me I am not!"

CHAPTER FIFTEEN: ROMANTIC INTERLUDE

September 12, 1861, New York City

Dana Greene was spending his first three-day leave of the war with his beloved Anna, who had come down from Maryland to spend time with him in New York. Greene was beside himself with passionate joy, as he believed he was truly on a hero's journey, right out of the pages of Walt Whitman. As he waited for his love under the street lamp in front of the New-York Times building on Printing House Square, he felt for the small book of poetry in his uniform's coat pocket.

There was a special poem he wanted to read to Anna before he explained how, after the war, they were going with Captain Ericsson and his wife to Easter Island where they would live out their lives in native splendor under the palm trees. The poem was "A Woman Waits for Me," and Greene knew it would thrill Anna.

He knew a lot of the poem by heart, and it began, "A woman waits for me, she contains all, nothing is lacking, yet all were lacking if sex were lacking, or if the moisture of the right man were lacking. Sex contains all, bodies, souls, meanings, proofs, purities, delicacies, results, promulgations, songs, commands, health, pride, the maternal mystery, the seminal milk, all hopes, benefactions, bestowals, all the passions, loves, beauties, delights of the earth, all the governments, judges, gods, follow'd persons of the earth, these are contain'd in sex, as parts of itself, and justifications of itself."

The poem told of women like the ones on Easter Island, who freely gave of themselves to men, and who were independent and strong, unlike the weak, emotionally clinging women of Europe and the United States. Captain Ericsson had explained to him that the women on Easter Island were equal to the men, as women's suffrage had been part of the early practices of Lemuria.

56

The natives owned nothing in Nature, so all was freely communal, and women were given the same rights as men.

Greene opened the book and read a few more lines from Whitman's poem, "They are not one jot less than I am, they are tann'd in the face by shining suns and blowing winds, their flesh has the old divine suppleness and strength, they know how to swim, row, ride, wrestle, shoot, run, strike, retreat, advance, resist, defend themselves, they are ultimate in their own right— they are calm, clear, well-possess'd of themselves." Anna would be one of these independent women——as they would all be autonomous from war and from the government's tawdry civilization.

When he first saw Anna on foot, walking toward him down 42nd Street, he could see she was proudly wearing her new Coiffure Josephine, the newest chic from France about which she had written in her letters to him. This new hairstyle featured a "birds nest," a small bow formed in the center of the nest (*noeudpapillion*), on which the puffed hair was supported. The chignon, or nape of the neck, was formed of the natural hair arranged over Topseys, or tight curls. Surmounted with a comb, the whole was covered with an invisible net.

As she came even closer, Greene's visions of her running topless in a grass skirt on Easter Island began to fade, and he could make out the expensive bonnet she had purchased that day from the showroom of Miss Mathers on Broadway. It was of white chip, trimmed with a rushing of white blonde lace across the top and down over the crown. White silk curtain, trimmed with white crape was decorated with half-open, large blush roses on the stem so as to form the outside trimming; the roses were set in tulle and intermixed with green grasses. A broad white ribbon extended across the bonnet and terminated in strings that hung down on either side of her beautiful face. She also wore a white, four whale-boned, ruffled hoop dress, with a matching Battenberg Lace Parasol, which she was twirling in nervous expectation as she, smiling broadly, strolled up to him.

"Good afternoon, sir! Is this where I can get an escort for the big city?" Anna's voice held its usual hint of mischievousness. This, above all, was what had attracted her to him. Most of the other girls he had known were always so full of themselves and how their appearance affected others. Anna, in contrast, had always placed her wit and charm before her good looks, even though she dressed impeccably well.

"Yes, Madam, I shall be your escort. We have reservations at the Officers' Club on Broadway. Shall we?" Greene put his hand on his hip, and gave his elbow to Anna. She draped her delicate arm inside the circle, and they began the walk toward Broadway. There was no need for talk, as they were the most dashing couple that day. Men and women turned to stare as they passed, and even a few horse-drawn cabs and surreys slowed down to notice the sharp-dressed young naval officer and his lovely paramour.

A strong breeze came down the avenue and rustled Anna's dress and bonnet, until she turned her head to look full into Lieutenant Greene's face. "I have the most dreadful nightmares about you at sea, my darling. I do hope you will be careful!"

"Don't you fret, dearest. At Annapolis, we were trained to withstand the worst sea conditions. Last year, I was also in a typhoon on the China Sea with a very small vessel. Besides, Captain Ericsson says our new *Monitor* will be a strong, seaworthy craft." Greene squeezed her hand as if to ensure his engaged of his future safety, about which no person could foretell.

"Actually, father was reading an article about the construction of your ship. He said the author had called it 'Ericsson's Folly.' He also said many critics believe your captain to be a charlatan who was responsible for the deaths of Washington political leaders with his other craft, the *Princeton*, I believe it was called?"

Greene raised his eyebrows in exasperation, "Honestly, don't you read my letters, Anna? Captain Ericsson explained all of that to me before. I told you. His partner was to blame for that horrible accident. He had constructed a cannon much too powerful for use aboard a war ship. Mister Ericsson would never risk the safety of his crew, and he certainly would not endanger civilian lives!"

* * *

The Officers' Club on Broadway was a special association where Union officers were welcomed to enjoy billiards, eat a hearty meal, and find a brief "home away from home." Greene had reserved a back room where they could eat alone. A tall, red-haired woman by the name of Mrs. Cross met them at the front desk when they entered and was quite jocular as she led them to the private drawing room. She pointed to the various photos by the war photographer, Matthew Brady, which hung on all the walls. "See, Matt Brady's done all these famous people. There's President Lincoln, General Grant, and over there's Walt Whitman and Edgar Allan Poe."

Greene stopped to gaze at the photo of Whitman. "Quite impressive!" he said.

"Yes, Mister Brady has a gallery off of Fulton Street. Perhaps you can take your lady there after dinner. He has some startling photos in his P. T. Barnum collection. He took pictures of General Tom Thumb, the midget, and his new fiancée, Lavinia Warren, and the Siamese twins—Chang and Eng—can you imagine? Living your life attached to each other like that?" said Mrs. Cross, glancing down at the young lieutenant's arm, which had affixed itself around Anna's waist.

Greene, embarrassed, withdrew his arm and chuckled. "Yes, perhaps I shall take Anna across the street to the American Museum of Oddities. Mister Barnum has a new collection of strange animals. A wooly horse and a white whale. And Jenny Lind—the Swedish Nightingale—once sang there. Captain Ericsson says he has heard her many times—she is quite excellent!"

"Oh yes! We must hear her sing," said Anna, her brown eyes beginning to glow with happiness.

For dinner, they had the "Bubble and Squeak," a beef dish being served to conserve the more prime cuts for the men at the Front. It was boiled beef and carrots but was quite delicious after their "Hour Before the Battle" drinks, consisting of Madeira wine and a dash of bitters. After dinner, Greene walked with his woman over to the P. T. Barnum museum on Fulton. As they strolled in the dark, they gazed up at their star and Dana read from his beloved Whitman. Anna, to his surprise, showed a great deal of enthusiasm for the idea of moving to Easter Island after the war. She told him he deserved anything after having risked his life for others. Greene was filled with a deep joy that knew no bounds. He could barely contain himself, as they walked into the Museum of Oddities.

They stood looking at the prehistoric man frozen in granite when Greene told Anna about the native women on Easter Island and read her the final stanza from Whitman's poem. She squeezed his arm and looked soulfully into his eyes, vowing an eternal dedication to him.

"If you want me to dance naked on the sand under the moon, I swear, I will do it!" she exclaimed, and a tall sailor in dress blues looked over at them. They both laughed, and hugged each other, as they were also becoming American oddities. They made plans to go on a picnic in Central Park the following day, and Greene was to return to work the morning after.

"Would you like me to wear a grass skirt on the picnic?" said Anna, the dimples in her cheeks rising.

Greene put his fingers to her lips. "No, my dearest. If you did that you would surely cause a riot!"

As they left the museum, the tall sailor with blond hair wrote down something in a pad he was carrying inside his blouse pocket. Lieutenant Greene and fiancé discussed the island. The project seems to be going well.

CHAPTER SIXTEEN: CHIP'S NEW JOB

September 13, 1861, Green Point, Brooklyn

Chip Jefferson, whose slave name was Reginald Sims, was a free Negro who had moved two years before with his parents, Emil and Sarah, from a plantation in Virginia. They had traveled the newly constructed Underground Railway to the North, conducted by a white man, James Fairfield, who posed as a slave trader, and purchased the entire family from John and Wendy Sims for two thousand dollars.

It was a wonderful day in May 1861 when they first set sight on the "promised land," as his mother called it, although Chip, at fourteen years of age, did not think New York City was quite as hopeful as Virginia. Brooklyn was a rather crowded, noisy borough, and people did not say, "How y'all doin'?" the way they did back in Tidewater. Chip's family was known as "house niggers," so the Jeffersons had never experienced the degradation that the "field niggers" were subjected to back at the Sims Plantation outside Richmond. In addition, Chip's father, Emil, had learned to read and was constantly devouring the books in the rather substantial Sims' library. Emil often engaged in some rather pointed and heated "discussions" with Master Sims, but Emil was ultimately respected for his intelligence and for his memory of history and geography.

Chip had also been taught to read and write by his parents and by Mrs. Sims, a pale and sickly, yet kind woman, who seriously believed Negroes could become civilized beings. Of course, she did not think they could ever become American citizens, with the legal rights of white people, but she did trust in the Lord that they could "learn to run their own shantytowns with some amount of industry and education."

It was a topic that often escalated into a dinner argument at the Sims table, and Chip and his parents first learned about the "emancipation" for Negroes being "cooked-up" by radical Northern industrialists. Mister Sims said these Yankees were "subjecting their darkies to worse working conditions than the Southern plantations could ever hope to do."

Chip would flit in and out of the white folks' dinner places at the table, like a black ghost, yet he was taking in all that they said with some amount of interest. When his parents told him about Mister Fairfield and the plan to get them to freedom in the North, Chip thought it was all a great adventure. Once, he almost told Mrs. Sims about the plan, but he caught himself at the last moment. "We're going to ride the Underground Railroad, Missus," he began, but then he stopped short, as he watched the eyebrows furrow on the white woman's usually kind face.

"What did you say?" she asked, turning Chip's chin to face her own, as he was reading from the *Holy Bible* seated on her lap.

"Oh, I was saying how my Mamma told us we could one day ride the railroad cars to Richmond. They lets us darkies ride in the cattle car for free."

Nevertheless, Mrs. Sims looked suspiciously at Chip for many days after this near disastrous slip of the tongue.

The New York Abolitionists got jobs for his parents at the new Hotel Belvedere, in downtown New York, and they rode the overhead elevator trains to work every day, and it was a miracle to see them sail off into the sky from his vantage point at the Brooklyn station on Bedford Avenue. Chip liked the feel of the wind as it rushed back at him when the cars took off. He called it the "angels' flight," and the grownups standing around him smiled down at him whenever he said this.

It was Mrs. Townsend who came one day to employ him at her Brooklyn Seaward Rooming House. Chip remembered her wearing a gigantic peacock feather sticking out of her red hat, and it kept tickling his nose whenever she turned her head to talk to his parents. "I shall put your son under my immediate stewardship, Mr. And Mrs. Jefferson," she said, swishing her tail at him. "As a member of the Women's Abolitionist League, it is my sworn duty to advance the cause of Negro sovereignty in this great country of ours!"

The job at the rooming house was hardly showing Chip how to be "sovereign," as he saw it, because he had to do all of the dirty jobs that none of the white boys wanted to do, such as cleaning the toilets, carrying the luggage, and mopping all the wood floors on every level of the hotel. However, his parents also did such menial tasks, so he soon learned to take his predicament into stride, as he received something he had never experienced before in his life: he was paid forty cents a week for his work!

His life changed when Mister Ellwood checked into the hotel. Chip was fascinated with the foreigner's speech, his dress, and his secretive ways. He knew this man was up to something, and he made it his duty to find out what.

From that first day when the gentleman came to the door of his suite in that silk dressing gown with the colored flowers all over it, Chip began to follow his every move. It was not difficult to do, as Chip was short and black, and the shadows were excellent hiding places. He knew this man was in America to watch the shipyard down the street, as he observed him during the first few days, looking down into the grounds with a long spyglass. Was he a spy from England? Chip's father said the English war profiteers were running blockades for the South, as they wanted the cotton and other foodstuffs they needed. But Mister Ellwood did not seem like a sea captain. He seemed as if he were interested in the construction going on inside the Continental Ship Yard.

Chip Jefferson made it his secret duty to follow the mysterious Mister Ellwood whenever he could, and he was bound and determined to discover what this stranger was really up to. Chip expected there would be something important happening inside that ship yard, and the new adventure gave him a purpose beyond the boring drudgery he had to experience each day at his job in the hotel. This new employment made him feel as if he were doing something for the war effort. What if this Mister Ellwood were a spy? What if he were stealing secrets from the Navy? It was all very exciting to Chip's young imagination, and it became his personal, underground obsession.

CHAPTER SEVENTEEN: MEASURE OF MANHOOD

September 14, 1861, Green Point, Brooklyn

Walter Sinclair stood with Robert Whitehead on the banks of the East River. The winds were brisk as the two men gazed out at the passing ships and steamers. The ships were a mixture of military and civilian craft, and Sinclair was thinking about the day he would have to be here with his boat to do his "duty." The Confederates were getting him a fishing sloop just large enough to go unnoticed yet big enough to transport the single torpedo.

Whitehead bent down and opened a satchel he had brought with him. It contained the various colors of paint to be used to smear onto the square of metal he also pulled out of the bag. He wanted to get the perfect camouflage shade to hide the torpedo as it sped underwater toward its target, the newly launched *U.S.S. Monitor*.

Walter hoped his little craft would be able to slip out of the harbor during all the commotion, and then he could concentrate on taking care of the inventor and stealing his plans. Everything had to go perfectly for his plan to work, and with each passing day, Walter was becoming less certain that his plan would go off smoothly. He needed some insurance in case something went wrong, but he had yet to figure out what that assurance could be.

After several attempts at different shades of color, Whitehead finally pulled the metal out of the water and smiled. "There! I think that is a perfect camouflage color. The MK will not be visible to anyone on the surface."

"And are you certain my fishing boat will be able to handle this weapon without suspicion?" said Walter, fingering the metal.

"It should not be difficult to place her in the bow. The lift I will install will get the torpedo into the water, and then the propeller will do the rest. The

63

problem will be the moment of lift. It must be exactly timed with the speed of this Union craft."

"Yes, we need to get that information before the launch date. I believe I'll be able to get into the Ericsson home and find this out. He is employing a lead draftsman who is prone to imbibe a bit too much on the weekends. I will enter on one such evening when I can move around without notice."

Whitehead grinned. "These Americans do love their liquor, eh what?"

"Let's go back to the pub. I'll buy you a pint!" said Sinclair, putting an arm around his compatriot and guiding him away from the banks of the river and away from the future site of their destructive mission.

About fifty yards distance, standing in the shadows of an Elm tree near the Continental Ship Yard fence, Chip Jefferson was watching the two men as they bent over into the waters of the East River. He was wondering what they were doing. He made a silent vow to himself to find out. Chip now knew when Mister Ellwood would be away from his room in the hotel, and this would be a good time to investigate. The prospect of solving this mystery sent a satisfying tremor through his body.

"Excuse me? Do you know this property is off limits to civilians?" Chip jumped at the hand that grasped onto his shoulder. He turned to look up into the face of a young Union naval officer.

"Ah, yes sir! I was just trying to see the ships on the river down there. I aim to join the Navy when they'll have me!" said Chip, not knowing what else to say.

The handsome young man's stern face finally broke into a smile. "Well, that's quite noble of you. I suppose we're all fighting for you folks in this war. I don't suppose it's wrong for you to want to become a part of it. But, aren't you a bit young?"

"I'm sixteen! I've seen a colored man beat to death with a horsewhip whilst in Virginia. We escaped to New York with the Underground Railroad. I reckon I've seen enough for any one man." Chip puffed out his chest and frowned.

"My! I suppose you have seen quite a lot, haven't you?" said the young officer, putting his arm around Chip's shoulders. "I want you to come with me and meet someone who may be able to get you into the service. My name is Greene. Lieutenant Samuel Dana Greene. I am executive officer of the future iron ship of war, the *U.S.S. Monitor.*" Greene held his hand out and Chip took it. They smiled at each other warmly.

"Hey! I read about that ship. She's supposed to go down to Hampton Roads to protect the blockade, ain't she?" Chip's dark eyes flashed with excitement.

"Yep, that's the one. I'm going to introduce you to the inventor of this ship, Captain John Ericsson. If anybody can get you enlisted aboard our vessel, he's the man." Greene stopped for a moment to look seriously into the young lad's mysterious face. He had never been this close to a Negro before, and he wondered at his flat nose and flaring nostrils, and his pink, puffy lips. He did not think it unseemly to be so different. In fact, the youth's strong arms and broad shoulders demonstrated a certain nobility of form that Dana had never before seen on any white man. Dana assumed the natives of Easter Island were much like this young man. In fact, this youthful figure of patriotic zeal reminded him of his beloved Whitman's description of the soldiers of 1861, this year that saw many Union men being killed or wounded in the early Confederate victory at Bull Run. The verse came back to him, as he watched the young man walking, self-assured, childish and yet spirited; like Greene, he was anxious to become part of something bigger than himself:

Saw I your gait and saw I your sinewy limbs clothed in blue, bearing weapons, robust year, heard your determin'd voice launch' d forth again and again, year that suddenly sang by the mouths of the round-lipp'd cannon, I repeat you, hurrying, crashing, sad, distracted year.

Chip wanted to tell this kind young officer all about Mister Ellwood, but he thought better of it and decided he would wait until he could get more information about what the foreigner was up to. It would be a good way to show his patriotism to these Union Navy men. However, Chip was now troubled about what his parents would say about his possible enlistment—especially his mother. She was often telling him how dreadful it was to have brother killing brother in a war that seemed to have no visible end in sight. She said she and his father had been stolen from Africa when they were teenagers, and shipped inside a suffocating British slave trader, where hundreds of them were starved to death or were thrown overboard to lighten the weight during a storm, until they landed in Virginia and were auctioned off to the Sims family in a horrible and inhuman ceremony wherein his mother was stripped to the waist to expose her nakedness to the world. Twelve years later, they were free Negroes living and working in New York. Despite his mother's concern for his personal safety, Chip knew it was high time that he did something to make certain his family remained free forever.

CHAPTER EIGHTEEN: COUNTER-ESPIONAGE

October 15, 1861, Green Point, Brooklyn

Walter Sinclair was ready to put his new plan into operation. By spending several weeks observing the habits of the lead draftsman, Charles McCord, Walter had determined that the best night to break into Ericsson's house would be on a Friday. This was the night. Charles would get drunk inside the house, as usual, and Ericsson would work late at the shipyard. Ericsson and his young officer, Greene, would go to Mug's Ale House before they came home, and this would give Walter about two hours to get the information he needed to put his plan into action.

Walter decided to wear a black fisherman's outfit and a watch cap over his face. He had cut three holes in the cap so he could pull it down over his face when he entered the residence. As he walked over to Ericsson's house on Beach Street, he thought about his insurance plan. Actually, his employer gave him the idea. If the Confederate Government could threaten him by putting his beloved Penelope in mortal danger, then he could return the favor for Mister John Ericsson.

Robert Whitehead had recently informed Walter that Whitehead's relatives knew the Blackstone family of London, and that their daughter, Amelia, was home from America, having left her husband of twenty-five years because of dwindling finances, and what some of the London wives were calling "a deficiency of romantic attention."

"Amelia wishes to return to her husband, the inventor John Ericsson, but the Civil War has given him new employment, yet the pay from the Union Government has not been regular and on time. Thus, the poor couple must wait until they can save enough money so that Mrs. Ericsson can live in the proper surroundings with which she is accustomed," said Whitehead, smiling

66

and rolling his eyes at Walter.

Thus, the plan was hatched in Walter's brain to leave a note for Captain Ericsson describing the details of the "insurance policy." If the assassination and destruction of the *Monitor* were to fail, then this new arrangement would surely keep Walter's beloved Penelope safe.

The twilight lamps were being lit along the streets as Walter rounded the corner of Beech off Canal Street. He enjoyed the fall weather in America, as the odor of leaves and the dampness of the hills filled one's being with a satisfying gift. It was the nearest climate Walter could find to compare with life on the open sea. The swirling tornadoes of foliage all along the boulevard reminded him of the water spouts on the ocean, and the winds that hit one full in the face with their forceful reality were just like those he had felt on the bridge of his *Caine* after the evening's mess with the crew.

No light was visible inside the house as Walter walked up to the window. He knew Ericsson kept this back window open, for some reason, and it was the perfect entryway. Away from the traffic of the street, this porthole was near an alley on the backside of the house. Walter pulled down the front of his watch cap and climbed up on the window ledge. He grunted as his big hands pressed down and pulled the rest of his body up and over the ridge. He sat on the opening for a moment, to catch his breath, and then he stepped down into what proved to be the library.

Walter could see the shadows of the rows of books along the wall, and as he crept inside the room, he couldn't help feeling intimidated. With only a boarding school education, Walter Sinclair had always felt rather inadequate next to educated men. He believed these "Dickens' types" were always showing off their knowledge of history, literature and the like and were constantly looking down on him. Secretly, however, Walter knew his seafaring experience was worth far more than anything one could learn from a book. The sea was the best teacher, and he had spent most of his adult life learning the harsh rules of life on the bounding main.

Walter knew that Ericsson's drafting room was next to the library, so he tiptoed through the doorway into the hall of the adjoining rooms. The drafting room was a large space with a long table that was raised on four wooden legs. There were several desks and cabinets, and Whitehead told Walter that the information they needed would most likely be locked-up inside one of them. With that in mind, Sinclair had brought several lock picks and other tools that were inside pockets of a bandoleer which was wrapped around his chest. Walter walked up to the first cabinet and began to pick inside the iron lock with one of his long instruments. It made a scratching sound but was not very loud. Nonetheless, Walter kept glancing back at the doorway for any sign of Charles McCord.

* * *

Across town, inside the Brooklyn Seaward Rooming House, Chip Jefferson was entering the private room of Mister Simon Ellwood, the strange foreigner the young man had been following for several weeks. Chip believed he could find out what this man was doing in New York, and if he were indeed up to no good. Whatever he could find, Chip believed, would be handed directly over to his new employers, Captain John Ericsson and Lieutenant Samuel Greene.

Even though Ericsson and Greene had no knowledge of what Chip was doing, the new recruit believed they would approve of his actions once he discovered the truth about this Ellwood's activities around the shipyard. Captain Ericsson was like no other white man Chip had ever met. The closest in stature and intelligence was the master of the plantation in Virginia, John Sims. They both had the stern and confident gaze that seemed to go right through you. However, Chip noticed that Ericsson listened to people more, as Master Sims was constantly speaking over you, as if he never heard a word you were saying. Chip liked Captain Ericsson and Lieutenant Greene. They told him he could be their personal steward, and he would be allowed to live in a small space inside the lieutenant's room aboard the newly constructed *Monitor*. Ericsson had shown Chip the blueprint of the design and exactly where the officers would be sleeping when not on duty. Mister Ericsson pointed out that they were to be berthed exactly the opposite of the usual ship's structure in the United State Navy. Inside the *Monitor*, the captain's rooms would be at the farthest point in the bow of the ship, rather than in the stern, as was the usual social architecture. Just behind the captain's rooms was the wardroom, where Chip and three other cooks and stewards would serve the nine commissioned officers their daily meals. Directly aft of the captain's stateroom and cabin, on either side of the wardroom, was Executive Officer Dana Greene's quarters, and this was where Chip would stay.

A big trunk was under the foreigner's bed, and Chip grunted as he pulled it out. Alas, there was a huge lock on the front of it, and he had no tools with which to pry it open. How was he going to impress the two older men? Why hadn't he thought about this possibility? Darn it all! Chip pushed the trunk back under the bed.

This was probably an omen. He needed to confide in Ericsson and Greene about this foreigner. They would then be able to help him find out who he really was and what he was after each day that he watched the Continental Ship Yard. They were all going to Washington to interview the new captain of their ship, Lieutenant John L. Worden. This would be a good time to tell them.

Captain Ericsson said that Captain Worden was forty-three years old, and he had twenty-seven years' experience in the Navy. But, the most exciting aspect of this trip was that Lieutenant Worden had recently served seven

months as a prisoner of war, and the Navy Department had appointed him
captain of the *Monitor* to show the South that Union men did
not succumb to their terrorism.

* * *

"What in blazes are you doing in here?" the dark figure weaving in the
doorway was shouting at him, and Walter knew who it was. There was no
time to discuss the peculiarities of his dilemma. Walter lowered his head and
rushed with all his might at Charles McCord. Bringing his head up into the tall
man's stomach, Walter could feel the air leave McCord's diaphragm with a
whoosh. The lead draftsman went sprawling against the wall, as he was still
quite drunk, and Sinclair was able to rush past him into the next room.
However, the window had been shut, and Walter knew he had to get out, so
he wrapped his arms over his head and flung his entire body against the
window. The shards of glass shattered, and he felt stabs of pain, as the sharp
points dug deeply into his face and shoulders. Nevertheless, he continued to
roll over the windowsill, and he finally fell heavily to the ground. Walter got
up slowly, but he was soon able to regain his energy, and he took off in a
sprint down the alley and out onto Canal Street.

You fool! I got what I came for, thought Sinclair, slowing down his pace so as
not to attract attention. *I'll get the letter to Ericsson in due time.* He pulled the black
watch cap from his face and noticed his cheek had a half-inch gash on the
right side. Blood was streaming into his open palm. He took a handkerchief
from his back pocket and applied it to his wounded face. *The speed of the
Monitor is no longer a secret. Now they suspect me, and I'll have to move. Yes, they'll be
looking for me. But the seed has been planted. Soon, the plan will come together as a
hurricane that gathers inevitable supremacy from its opposing temperatures and gales to
create the Coriolis Force. We shall all be spinning together, toward the unavoidable chasm of
our common fates!*

CHAPTER NINETEEN: THE CAPTAIN

October 21, 1861, Washington D. C.

John Ericsson and his entourage arrived in the nation's capital at sundown. Accompanying him on the three- day journey by steamer, to interview the future captain of the Monitor, were Lieutenant Greene and the newly appointed young steward, Chip Jefferson. Ericsson enjoyed giving them the lay of the land, as they sailed up the Potomac River toward their eventual destination at the United States Navy Yard near 11th Street.

As they crossed the river near the lockkeeper's house on 17th Street and Constitution, Ericsson pointed toward the Washington Memorial. "They have finished only 155 feet up on that monstrosity. The war came, and the engineers decided to leave it unfinished. It seems to me this whole city has been left unfinished. Do you know how many were in the Union Army before the war began?"

"Yes, there were about 16,000 troops. Washington was a southern town, and it was not a very nice one, at that. Only one street is in part paved, I believe, and it is Pennsylvania Avenue." Dana Greene was proud to show Ericsson that he had been paying attention in school at Annapolis.

"Quite right. The biggest employer in Washington is the Navy Yard. They are still constructing the Capital Building. We shall be staying at the Metropolitan Hotel on the north side of Pennsylvania Avenue. One does not venture onto the south side. The brothels and saloons are there, and the crime rate is said to be quite outrageous." Ericsson brought a cigar to his mouth, bit the tip off, and spat it out into the river. At once, Chip was there with his Flintstone, and he lit the inventor's cigar with a flourish. "Thank you, my boy," said John, puffing rapidly and pointing to an atoll of land off the starboard bow. "See that island over there? That's Mason's Island. I've been

70

told that newly recruited Negro men are kept there without pay or pension. They expect to see military service in the war, but right now, the city wants no part of them in the general populace. Your country never ceases to amaze me, Lieutenant."

"I think that is one reason why we will be better off on Easter Island, Captain. I don't believe most of these humans have any love for their fellow man," said Greene, rubbing Chip's head with his hand. The young steward smiled up at him, but he was thinking about something entirely different and quite a bit more somber.

Ericsson looked perturbed. He pulled Dana by the arm and led him to the Navy steamship's opposite railing on the port side. "Mister Greene," he whispered through clenched teeth, "I told you I wanted to keep our adventure a secret. If anybody discovers the location of our island, then we shall soon lose our exclusivity. Please, do keep all of this information to yourself!"

"I'm so sorry! I completely forgot about Chip being there, sir. I shall remember in the future."

"All right. Please go down below with Chip and get ready to disembark. We should be coming up to the Navy Yard in a few minutes." Ericsson patted the lieutenant on the shoulder. "I don't think you did any real harm. The lad most likely has little knowledge of geography or science."

Chip stood by the railing and looked over at Mason's Island. He was thinking about how his father, an educated man who read hundreds of books about islands and lands around the globe, had once told him that Easter Island was, a long time ago, an advanced civilization, and early settlers had called the island Te Pito O Te Henua," which meant "Navel of The World." The landmark statues of gigantic gods called moai were said to weigh over ten tons each and were often over fifteen feet high.

Chip had done research on his own and discovered that Easter Island was located in the South Pacific, some 2,000 miles from both Tahiti and Chile. Recent times had not been so good for the island. After a civil war in the 1500s, the natives had turned to cannibalism, and most recently, according to Chip's father, there were slave ships that descended onto its shores. When Captain Cook arrived in 1722, there were only 600 people left on the island. In 1808, after a bloody battle, an American ship, Nancy, kidnapped twelve men and ten women with the intent of taking them to the Juan Fernandez Islands to work as slaves in seal-hunting efforts there. Three days' sail from Rapa Nui, which was the natives' name for the island, the captain allowed the captives to come out of the hold; they promptly leaped overboard and began swimming away. Attempts to recapture them failed. The ship sailed onward, leaving the islanders to drown at sea. Chip wondered why the lieutenant had mentioned this island as a place to visit? Were these men slave traders as well? Chip decided he was not going to tell Captain Ericsson and Lieutenant

Greene about the English foreigner, Simon Ellwood. At least, not until he found out if they were slave traders!

John Ericsson had not wanted to appoint John Worden captain of his new ship, but Secretary Gideon Welles, who believed in the Union, had a responsibility to show the rebels they could not break an officer who had spent seven months at a swampy prison camp in Pensacola, Florida. President Lincoln had sent the experienced officer to Pensacola to order reinforcements at Fort Pickens, but on his way back to Washington, Worden was captured by five Confederate soldiers and placed in the prison camp.

Ericsson would have preferred a less experienced sailor to captain his new craft, as he was planning to lose the coming battle with the Virginia, but now he knew he had to design a way to put his man Greene in command before there could be a reversal of fortunes and the Monitor sank the rebel monster. If that happened, then Ericsson knew the Department of the Navy would never spend the money for more *Monitor*-class ships. This was the way of the American government. When you were completely successful, you became a hero, but no more money came your way. Thus, the war profiteers who made the big money were the ones who could design ways to arrive at what men called a "Mexican Standoff," a term used following the expensively lucrative war with Mexico in the 1840s that saw many industrial men make millions of dollars from the United States Government in what was basically one big camp- out. In fact, when General Winfield Scott captured Mexico City in September of 1847, he wrote back to President Polk, "I suggest we do not keep this country, as the inhabitants are unclean, lazy and completely uncivilized."

Lincoln, who was a freshman Whig Party congressman from Illinois, was against war with Mexico, and Ericsson believed Lincoln was against spending money for armaments in this war as well. The Mexican War saw the first major use of steamboats in battle. Steamboats were used to transport men and supplies down the Ohio and Mississippi Rivers to New Orleans for subsequent overseas movement. Steamboats also were used to establish a line of communication for Commanding General Zachary Taylor's army along the Rio Grande when, after Resaca de la Palma, Taylor moved his army up the river in the first stage of an offensive against Monterrey.

The Mexican War proved to be a training ground for American officers, such as John Worden, who would later fight on both sides in the Civil War. Grant, Lee, Meade, Bragg, Davis, McClellan, and many others gained experience and learned lessons at Buena Vista and Cerro Gordo that would later serve them well. It was also a politically divisive war in which antislavery Whigs criticized the Democratic administration of James K. Polk for expansionism. However, Ericsson knew, many men became very wealthy— especially the men who invented the steamships that powered the Marines to victory. John Ericsson had plans to do the same with his little Monitor. He believed he could make the *Monitor* the most utilized gunboat in the Civil War. In order to accomplish this, he had to have control of the battle at Hampton Roads, Virginia. This new captain, John Worden, was an obstruction to his plans.

* * *

Chip liked the new captain as soon as he set eyes on him. Unlike many white men, this tall, bearded scarecrow of a man looked easily at him and smiled as if they were long-lost brothers. In fact, Captain Worden totally ignored the other two men, as he marched directly over to Chip and took his hand.

His thinning black hair was pasted down on top of his high forehead like a schoolteacher, and his voice was soothing and calm.

"I am proud to meet you, young man," said Worden, motioning for Chip to sit in the chair in front of his desk. "Come, sit here. You are the guest of honor. The fate of our country's basic human principles is at stake in this war, and you are going to become the beneficiary of our struggle. You deserve to be listened to, and nobody should ever forget this."

Chip felt vaguely uncomfortable as he sat down in the large, leather-covered fixture. Captain Ericsson and Lieutenant Greene nodded for him to do so, hence he sat, but he kept his hands folded on his lap and his feet straightened under his chair.

"When I was inside that bug-infested rat hole in Florida, my best friend was a young black man about your age. He was a slave from one of the mansions nearby, and he was appointed to serve us prisoners our daily bread. That young man told me he was going to run away and join the Union Army because he knew we were fighting for his freedom. Mind you, he had never experienced being a free man, yet he was willing to risk his life just by talking to me about his dream. One day, when he did not bring me my bread and gravy, I asked my captors where he was. They told me someone had overheard this fourteen-year-old lad talking about joining the Union, and the boy was taken out and shot. Do you know the reason they gave for killing him?"

Chip swallowed hard. "No sir," he muttered.

"They told me he was executed for treason against the new Confederate States of America. Can you imagine? A young man, your age, is killed simply because he had a dream to be free. It was at that moment I knew this Civil War was a holy war. Just as the Hebrew slaves in the Bible needed a leader and an army to reach their land of freedom, we too needed Abraham Lincoln and his army to free your people from their bondage."

"Well put, Captain," said Greene, lightly clapping his hands together in applause. "I am certain this is the reason why Chip Jefferson joined us aboard the *Monitor*. Isn't that correct, son?"

"Yes, I guess that's part of it," said Chip, furrowing his brow in concentration. "Actually, my Daddy thinks no group or army will ever be able to defeat Thomas Jefferson's idea of men being endowed by God with life, liberty and the pursuit of happiness. He likes to quote the French writer, Victor Hugo, who said, 'Nothing else in the world...not all the armies...is so powerful as an idea whose time has come.' Daddy says we will win the war because our time has come. We have been down into the Valley of the Shadow of Death, and we shall overcome!"

John Ericsson cleared his throat. "Ahem. I think that is all well and good. However, the French did happen to behead thousands of innocent people in the name of those same ideals. Also, as we were steaming into Washington, we observed Mason's Island. This is where the Union government is housing hundreds of Negro men who have escaped their slave owners, simply wanting to join in this celebrated fight for freedom, only to be once more enslaved inside gloomy dungeons until they are deemed 'fit to fight.' Does this strike you Americans as liberty?"

"Indeed, sir, I have heard of Mason's Island. In fact, I am on the Board of Governors of this installation. I also know that Negro men were refused entry when they attempted to enlist by the thousands in New York City in 1861. When these same black men hired a warehouse and began to drill by themselves, the police chief ordered they be shut down, and they were all arrested. Now we have Mason's Island because many men, myself included, want to train these Negroes to be a special brigade of fighters. Men who know they fight for freedom become infused with a unique power, gentlemen. I have seen it happen! These men may be segregated now, but when they finally do get to fight, they will be more effective than any ten brigades of white men, mark my words."

"Very well, Captain, I appreciate your patriotic fervor. You will do well as our commander. I believe we should now get over to the hotel and prepare for the journey back to New York. I have a contract that says I must finish building your ship in less than four months' time. Are you ready to serve on what the newspapers are calling 'Ericsson's Folly'?"

Captain John Worden kept his mature gaze fixed on Chip's face. "We are soldiers in a holy war, Mister Ericsson. I know you are a capable inventor. I shall serve to the best of my ability, as will my men. Just remember this, Chip Jefferson. This is my favorite quotation from one of our early leaders in this country's revolution for freedom. He said, 'Guard with jealous attention the public liberty. Suspect everyone who approaches that jewel Unfortunately, nothing will preserve it but downright force. Whenever you give up that force, you are inevitably ruined.' It is our task, my lad, to guard the jewel of our liberty with force."

Chip stood up and crisply saluted this tall white man, his new Captain. "Yes sir!" he said, and he brought his hand down to his side so hard that it stung his leg.

CHAPTER TWENTY: RICHMOND REALITY

November 21, 1861, Richmond, Virginia

John Brooke was home on leave during a rainy week, when storms had walloped the Tidewater, and he could barely make-out the courier through the foggy downpour, as the horseman came galloping up to his mansion. The lad was out of breath, and as he stomped his boots on the porch to get the mud off, the plumes of billowy exhales made him look like a human steam engine.

"Lieutenant John M. Brooke?" asked the lad, pulling a waterlogged envelope out of his gray uniform's inside pocket.

"You've met your man," said John, "now why don't you come inside where it's warm, Corporal?"

"No sir, I was told to deliver this to you and get your reply immediately."

John took the envelope from the young man and opened it carefully with his long fingers. The weather was so bad that no work had been done on the *Virginia* for a week, and Brooke assumed this would be some kind of orders from the Confederate Naval Command. He was still having a horrible time getting skilled metal workers and other craftsmen to do the backbreaking labor necessary to get the ship ready for launch. He and Porter, the construction supervisor, had continued to battle over the scarcity of supplies and tools needed to finish the job, and Brooke was just about at his wit's end.

John read the communique out loud. "Reports from a spy in New York say that the production of the *U.S.S. Monitor* is well under way. You are hereby ordered to report back to Gosport to complete the construction the *C.S.S. Virginia*. The commissioning of our ship will take place in February. We have appointed Lieutenant Catesby ap Roger Jones as Executive Officer, and the Flag Officer shall be Admiral Franklin Buchanan." John slapped the letter on his thigh and whistled. "Whoopee! Here they go again. We can't even get enough steel to lay the superstructure, and they've already appointed an Admiral to take her out to fight! Now isn't that just like the Confederate Navy?"

The young enlisted man stared questioningly up at his superior. "Sir, will you write them a reply? I was told to wait for your answer."

"Yes, my reply. I shall give them my reply in a moment.

Do you know what I found out today, son?"

"No sir. I've been riding for five hours straight."

"I received word that the slaves I sold to a trader were, in fact, given their freedom in the North. In New York, to be exact. We treated those slaves as part of our own family. Do you suppose they will get the same treatment by the Yankees?"

The young man shuffled his feet and gave Brooke a sidelong glance. "No sir. I hear tell them Yanks work niggers to death in their factories, and they barely give them darkies enough to live on up there. Why, my cousin Billy says they are even forcing niggers into the war to fight us. But sir, Captain Forrester says we are also gettin' our own slaves into the regiment, and at least we shall keep our niggers fed!"

"I'm glad you said that, son. After my slave family was stolen, I decided to start training slaves to fight for the South. We'll show them Yankees which system is best, won't we? Our niggers know their place is with the land and with their free white masters. We are all indebted to our coloreds, for without them, we would lose our Southern dignity. Without dignity, we are nothing!"

"Yes sir! Long live Jefferson Davis!"

"Good lad. Now you wait here, and I'll go write a reply for you."

CHAPTER TWENTY-ONE: CIVIL WAR CHRISTMAS

December 25, 1861, Annapolis, Maryland

John Ericsson had promised to spend Christmas with his Executive Officer, Lieutenant Greene. The construction of the Monitor was going well, and Ericsson was anxious to get away for a bit of rest and relaxation. Also, it would give him a chance to meet the parents of Dana Greene and his betrothed, Anna Cameron. Ericsson needed to link Greene's mind to the *Monitor* more effectively, and this would give him the chance to see what kind of family he had.

Greene had invited the young steward, Chip Jefferson, but the lad had instead gone home with the new captain, John Worden. Worden promised to take Chip to see the training of the black soldiers on Mason's Island, and the boy became immediately enthralled with the prospect.

The Greene estate was just outside Annapolis, and as Ericsson and his Lieutenant drove up in their surrey from the train station, the youngsters of the neighborhood and their animals greeted them. Two black dogs yelped at the wheels, and a young boy of about twelve tried to climb aboard the back of the buggy, but Ericsson gave him such a scowl of disproval that he yelled loudly and jumped off, quickly becoming an anonymous face in the crowd of fifteen kids running alongside. Many of these children wore miniature versions of the blue and the gray uniforms of the Union and Confederate forces, as Maryland was still deeply divided on the war, even though it was "officially" a non-slave, Union state. The adult forces were building up around them, and the nervous energy expelled in their games of war was a precursor to the raging violence that would soon be part of their daily existence.

The Greene mansion was a three-story colonial, with two huge, white, Greek columns holding up the frontal portico leading up into the estate. The family butler, a Negro with gray hair named Jeremiah, who smiled warmly when he spotted Dana, greeted the surrey.

"Mistah Greene! Lawd in heaven, you made it home." Jeremiah said, motioning for the other two servants to get the luggage of the two guests.

Greene and Ericsson climbed out of the surrey and Greene embraced Jeremiah warmly. The old servant had been with the family for twenty-eight years, and age had turned his head into close-cropped cotton. "Jeremiah, I want you to meet Captain John Ericsson. He's the inventor of the ship, which will soon defeat the Southern monster that's being constructed as we speak. And I will be its first executive officer!"

A tall man, in a wide-brimmed fedora and bristling gray whiskers, came bounding down the stairs toward the two men. "Dana! My son!" cried Army General George S. Greene, clasping his large hands around his son's shoulders and beaming into his face. A graduate of West Point, General Greene was serving in the Union Army, and was himself home on leave.

"How are you, Father? We've come to celebrate the season of joy with you. This, Father, is my superior, the famous inventor, Captain John Ericsson."

"Yes, well now, I have been reading quite a lot about you, sir! Mister Ericsson's Folly, indeed!" he laughed, and Ericsson joined him in the laughter.

"I dare say, when you were constructing those demonic elevator trains in New York, the press was calling you a few splendiferous names as well, am I correct?" said Ericsson, who wanted to quickly endear himself to his fellow inventor.

Just then, the Camerons came out of the house. Anna ran up to Dana, holding a sprig of mistletoe above her head. "Kiss me! I am the messenger of peace and good will. Dana, darling, did you know the ancient Druids worshipped this plant? It's true. And enemies who walked under it on the battlefield were obliged to toss down their weapons and observe a truce until the next day."

Anna's father, Daniel, laughed. "Take care, Lieutenant, if those Johnny Rebs get hold of this plant, and put sprigs up all over their ships and such, we may have to stop the war!"

"Let's all go into the parlor and watch the children decorate the tree," said George Greene, motioning for Jerimiah to go ahead and prepare for guests.

Captain Ericsson put his arm around his young lieutenant's shoulders as they climbed the stairs leading into the mansion. "We shall keep the little secret about Easter Island to ourselves, all right, my boy? I dare say, we will need to release ourselves from this world of greed and subterfuge, if we are to survive following this war."

* * *

Captain John Worden pointed to the long lines of black men waiting for their dinner. Behind the rows of steaming iron kettles and sizzling grills, stood dozens of colored cooks, who were ladling out big gobs of grits, grilled pork chops, baked beans and potatoes into the outstretched and eager tin trays of the Union Army trainees. "See there, Chip? These men are getting the best victuals our government can provide. They eat the same as white men do, and they will receive the same training."

Chip Jefferson smiled, and inside he felt a growing pride welling up. If these men could be accepted into the Army, then it wouldn't be long before they would be accepted into general society. "You reckon one day I can learn to shoot and fire me a cannon?" Chip asked, looking up at the tall captain.

"We're doing all this so you can be free to do anything you need to do, son. And that's a fact!"

"I'm glad I signed on with you, Captain. I'll do my best to win the war, just like my brothers here," said Chip, and he pushed out his chest with pride.

"I'm certain you will, boy, but first, I hear there's going to be a certain gentleman with a red hat and white whiskers, who is waiting over at the Post Exchange for all the children to come and visit him. I don't suppose you're too old to want to see Santa Claus, are you?"

Chip's eyes grew large with excitement. "I hope you can stand beside me when I talk to him, Captain. I got something special in mind to ask for, and you need to hear it."

The captain put his large hand on the boy's shoulder. "Certainly I will stand next to you, Chip. This war's bringing a lot of different folks together, and we're going to be close friends after all this is over, so everything you do, I want to know about!"

Even though Chip had seen the Negro men training with all the latest government weapons, he was more amazed at the dining area, where hundreds of his kind were being treated just like normal soldiers. They did not bow and smile to get their food, they did not call their leaders "Master," and they could eat as much as they needed to live. Chip recalled the days in the South when slaves would come up to the mansion's back door begging for food. They said their master had refused to feed them, and they would have been left to die if it had not been for the kindness of Chip's mother, who gave them leftovers meant for the pigs.

Chip followed Captain Worden down into the mess hall. They stood in line with the soldiers, listening to them talk about the war, about their families back home, and especially about their new president, Abraham Lincoln. "Mistah Lincoln say he will abolish slavery before this war is over," said a tall sergeant, nodding at the large man behind the counter to fill his plate with fried potatoes. "Anybody got the name of the great Bible's Abraham, sure enough got my attention! The Lord told old Abe to worship only Him, and he did it, even though his own Daddy worshipped many gods. The Lord told

Abe to kill his son, Isaac, and he would've done that too, but it was not pleasing to God. You see, the Big Guy was just testing Abe. Well, our Abe Lincoln is sure enough getting tested on slavery, and I do believe God will save all our Isaac asses when the show is finally over! Give me some more of them spuds, Cookie!" The big sergeant's voice boomed out inside the mess hall, and the entire room seemed to fill with expectant courage.

* * *

"Captain Ericsson, I hear the turret on your *Monitor* can turn one-hundred-eighty degrees while firing, is this correct?" Daniel Cameron asked, biting into the leg of turkey at the Christmas Dinner table. The assembled families of Camerons and Greenes were boisterously enjoying the festivities, knowing in their hearts they would soon be bidding these military visitors "God speed" into the jaws of war. Anna Cameron was fastened to the arm of her Dana like a barnacle on the hull of a frigate, and Mrs. Cameron kept smiling over at Captain Ericsson, her glowing face flushed from three glasses of sherry.

"Yes, that's correct. We hope to have her completed by the end of next month, and we shall launch my ship, and the history of naval warfare will be changed forever. I don't know if we will stop the South from doing damage in Virginia, but we will certainly do our best to keep them from the banks of the Potomac!" said Ericsson, puffing on his pipe. He found the rich American food to be too much for his digestion, and he had eaten only the soup and salads.

Anna raised her glass, as Dana, with adoring eyes, watched her carefully. "I want to propose a Christmas toast! To the brave inventor and his men, among them our Samuel Dana Greene, my future husband, and to their success in this war that divides us all. May we all be made whole one day, and may you all stay healthy and become victorious for the coming new year of 1862!"

"Hear, hear!" the rest of the party cried, and the tears flowed solemnly down cheeks while snowflakes blew in the wind outside.

Awhile later, as Jeremiah was bringing in the brandy for the gentlemen to enjoy as an after-dinner cordial, and the women were adjourning to the sitting room, the dining room window was shattered apart, and a large red brick crashed on the table, toppling several wine decanters, and sending silver pieces flying in every direction. There was a note tied around the brick, and Dana, who was closest, untied the knot and read the inscription.

"It says, 'Yankee traitors go home. Maryland is a sister to the Southern rebellion. Long may she be free!'" Dana passed it along to his father. "Who could have done this?"

"I'm terribly sorry, Captain Ericsson. I'm afraid my statesmen have not completely made up their minds about to whose flag they wish to swear allegiance. We've been having these kinds of incidents for over a month now. I didn't want to disappoint Dana's homecoming, but this is the kind of thing with which we must contend here on the home front." George Greene straightened his collar as if he could collect the lost decorum by a gesture.

John Ericsson stood up and gravely smiled at the assemblage. "It is quite clear that these Southern rebels are nothing more than mere anarchists, at heart, and it is you and your kind family who will symbolize the civilized union needed to bring us true peace once more. If your son and I can assist in this endeavor, then God will indeed be with us, and you will be proud, sir, to call yourself a member of the Union!"

"Well said, Captain," said the elder Greene, and all the rest in the room began to applaud.

John Ericsson, who was used to making speeches, was also thinking that he had now made a good impression on these relatives, and that their son would become even more closely aligned to him and his private war to get his darling Amelia back from England.

CHAPTER TWENTY-TWO: MISTER BROOKE, MEET LIEUTENANT JONES

January 4, 1862, Gosport Navy Yard, Norfolk, Virginia

John Brooke knew that the officer in charge of the battery, one Catesby ap Roger Jones, had been at Gosport since November, and it was he John wanted to meet. If there were going to be any work completed, then this was the man with whom he must confer. He also knew when Navy Secretary Mallory finally sent this Admiral Buchanan over to take the flag, there would be little or no work accomplished afterward. They would expect everything to be ready before the Admiral got there.

It was complete chaos inside the small shipyard. Confederate officers were ordering men around who were obviously farmers or country types of one kind or another, and the tools they were wielding were rusted and ill-suited for the intricate work to be done aboard the hull of the *Merrimack*. The conquered ship stood alongside the pier like a gigantic, burnt-out cigar, and the wooden dry-dock on the other side of the pier, which would soon house her during the conversion process, had not yet been half completed. There were groups of marching soldiers all around the perimeter of the ship yard, and the variety of artillery batteries on the walls served as a protective shield against any invasion from without.

John showed his identification papers to the sentry at the gate and walked briskly toward a tall man with a salt-and-pepper, full beard, who was wearing the gray uniform of a Confederate Officer. He was shouting at two workers, who seemed to be imitating carpenters, although they were having a difficult time getting a stack of 4 x 12 feet oak planks into a long cart near the dry-dock.

"Easy there, men! Those aren't bales of hay. We're going to convert a ship, not build a barn! Swing them gently, now. That's it."

"Lieutenant Jones?" said John, raising his voice to be heard above all the noise around the yard.

The officer turned around and frowned at Brooke. "What? And who are you, sir? If you have those punched iron plates from Tredegar Works, bring them around to the supply depot."

"No, I am Lieutenant John Brooke from Richmond. I am in charge of the design of your new ship. Is it possible that we might talk about the problems you're having in a more private location?"

Jones's demeanor changed instantly from mistrust to adoration. "Why, what an astounding pleasure! Your reputation as an inventor and designer are legendary in the Navy. We studied and practiced firing your rifles while I was working for General Robert E. Lee at the fortifications of Jamestown Island. We protected the men who were taking over this very ship yard. Your rifle is the most accurate weapon I have ever had the pleasure of utilizing against an enemy."

Brooke followed Jones into a slant-roofed shack near the dry-dock. There was a gas lantern sitting on a large workbench, and a tall, slender Negro orderly greeted them. "Mistah Jones, sah!" he said, coming to attention.

"Bring us two pints of grog, Sebastian," said Lt. Jones, pulling out one of the wooden stools for his guest to be seated.

John sat down and smoothed his trousers to get the wrinkles out.

"I see you've not completed very much since November, Mister Jones, and I'm sorry to see things in such confusion. What I'm about to tell you won't make the job any easier, I'm afraid. The Secretary of the Navy wants the *Virginia* converted and launched for action by the beginning of March."

Jones took the pint from Sebastian, and blew off the heady froth.

John let his drink sit, as he watched the younger man take a long swig from the mug.

"March? Let me tell you something, Mister Brooke. I respect you and your design, and I don't doubt the patriotism you have in your heart. However, I do suspect those aristocrats in Richmond are unaware that I have been working for two months with country farmers, Army rejects, and slaves. And my workmen have been learning their skills as they labor, with a collection of tools that are damaged, inadequate and mostly unsuited for the task at hand. In addition, the Army has taxed the railroad, and thus I have not been able to get my shipments of iron plating, as I have not had the Confederate currency to pay the taxes to get these goods delivered!"

John made large circles with his mug on the wooden table. "Yes, I'm aware of your predicament, Mister Jones. And I am here to assist you in training your men and in meeting your deadline. But I am also here to make you realize that the *Virginia* will be commissioned in February, and she will be launched in March. And she will not only be armed with four of my single-banded Brooke rifles, but she will also be the first ship in Naval history to utilize six, nine-inch Dahlgren shell guns."

Jones slammed his mug to the table and stood up. "The hell you say! There is no ship on earth, which can withstand that kind of firepower from her decks. Are they crazy? How can we fit this vessel with those guns? This is a navy ship, sir, not a castle on Jamestown Island!"

"Please, be seated, Lieutenant. I have been thinking this over, and there is a way we can fortify our ship enough to withstand the size of these guns. In addition, we are going to add a wedge-shaped battering ram to her prow which will weigh 1,500 pounds."

Jones slumped down on the stool and held his head in his hands. "Oh, dear Lord above! Has the Confederacy has lost its collective sanity? We shall sink like a lead duck!"

Brooke smiled. "Not necessarily. I have a plan, you see, which will utilize the central 160 feet of the 175 total feet of her hull. We shall construct a thirty-six degree inclined roof, of both wood and iron, alternating planks, if you will. The wood planks will be two feet thick and the iron two inches thick, so the complete weight will not be as much as one would believe was necessary. The final covering of a four-inch thickness of armor will be fasted to its wooden backing with one and three- eighths inch bolts, countersunk and secured by iron nuts and washers. Thus, she will not be as heavy as you and others seem to expect. She should be seaworthy and yet still have the protection we will need to fire those big Dahlgrens."

Lieutenant Catesby ap Roger Jones, who had been chosen to lead the first battery of Dahlgren cannons ever to be used on an American ship of war, was now feeling more comfortable with his assignment. The confidence of this man John Brooke gave him a renewed vigor. The South had been victorious in early battles, and now the Navy was going to show the Yankees what the ingenuity and hard work of leaders committed to a cause could do.

"It's good to have you aboard, Mister Brooke. Now let's get to work!"

"Where can I change my clothes?" asked John, pointing down at his dress pants and shoes. "I realize we are Southern gentlemen, but my wife would kill me if I should get this new suit soiled," he added, and they both began to laugh.

CHAPTER TWENTY-THREE: COMMON PURPOSE

January 10, 1862, Brooklyn, New York

Walter Sinclair knew that the *Virginia* was behind schedule due to labor and delivery problems, and yet he was determined to have his end of the bargain completed when the Union's *Monitor* launched. Robert Whitehead was staying at a hotel in New York City, and he was visiting Walter on weekends to discuss the arrangements for the torpedo delivery on January 28, two days before the *Monitor* was supposed to be put to sea for the first time. Walter had discovered this secret information during his sleuthing inside McCord's house.

Having spent Christmas and New Year's at Mug's Ale House, Walter was beginning to detest his assignment in America. Although he had struck a close friendship with the bar maid, Grace Witherspoon, he had no use for most of these citizens of Brooklyn, who were the most uncouth and dull lot he had ever seen. Even the uneducated seamen aboard his ship proved better companions than most of these Americans. They were incessantly discussing the war and how their "sacred Union" was going to win. These citizens had little time for theater or other cultural pursuits that would be the high point of life in England, and Walter found very little to do except to visit the taverns and restaurants with Miss Grace and Mister Whitehead where, to pass the hours, they would make fun of the local community.

His life was becoming an obsession. The days were melding into the true purpose of his existence, and Walter often discussed this point with Whitehead, although they were frequently in their cups and the result often became blurred by drink and romantic musings about their women. It was clear, however, that Walter's mission was taking on an important aspect

86

beyond the money he needed to establish himself in England and perhaps get away from the sea and its transitory nature.

"I have been reading about Captain Ericsson and his life, and he is indeed a worthy opponent," said Walter one evening, as the pub was about to close, and Grace had promised to return with him to the hotel after she closed the bar.

"How so?" said Whitehead, who was rather an objectivist sort, inclined to see people as simply "doers of actions" and not as "thinkers of ideas."

"It seems he has always been creating for himself and for his own aspirations. This, to me, is the mark of an original genius. Whereas many inventors are purchased by governments and become slaves to the state, I can see that this Ericsson is a man for himself, and I applaud him for that," Walter said, taking a healthy swig from his pint.

"Aren't you both doing the bidding of your superiors? How can what you do be seen as individualistic or unique, when the master is watching your every move from above?" Whitehead responded, motioning to Grace to come fill his tankard.

"This Ericsson is a man working for himself only. I have an intuition about these things, and I almost feel sorry for him. Even though I must destroy his invention, I still believe he is not working for the Union as a patriot." Walter stroked his beard and smiled.

"Well then, it seems you are two pigs from the same sty. What makes you believe you can win against him? He may be your doppelganger," said Whitehead, and they both began to laugh uproariously.

"Yes! He even has a lady in jolly old England, same as myself, and we are both laboring for love, it seems."

As he said the word "love," Grace came by and frowned down at the two men. "I do believe we'll have to cut-off the tap for you boys. You seem to be losing your gentlemanly ways."

When Grace was out of earshot, Walter continued, "That's how my insurance comes into play. If something were to go wrong with your torpedo, then I shall be following Captain Ericsson—to the ends of the earth, if need be—and I will smash his independent spirit once and for all!"

CHAPTER TWENTY-FOUR: ERICSSON'S FOLLY

January 30, 1862, Brooklyn

The wind had blown mightily for most of the night, but by the time the two tugs were moving the *Monitor* from her berth in the Continental Shipyard to the launching site inside the Brooklyn Navy Yard, it was calm and clear, albeit the temperature hovered in the low 30s. John Ericsson and Lieutenant Greene journeyed together by carriage, and Captain Worden stayed with his craft, together with the new crew and his young steward, Chip Jefferson.

Chip loved the thrill of this new experience aboard ship, and he had a difficult time sleeping that whole week. He had spent a week from Christmas to New Year's Day with his family, and they had a hard time controlling the young boy's enthusiasm. He told them about the new Captain Worden, about Easter Island, and all about the new training camp for Negro men on Mason's Island. Chip's father warned him about the two white men, as he believed they were scheming about something "nefarious if he ever heard such things." However, he agreed with his son that Captain Worden was probably a good man, especially after Chip told him the story about when he was a prisoner to the Rebs in Florida.

"Son, decent white men are fighting this war to help us, and you must stay next to them to be safe," his father told him, opening one of his many history books as way of illustration. "See here, this is Mister John Brown. Isn't he a pugnacious and noble looking white man? Well, he attempted to capture an ammunitions arsenal at Harper's Ferry, Virginia, and then arm the slaves so they could raid plantations and free others. Sadly, they were stopped because too many slaves failed to rally behind him, as they were house slaves, just like we were, and they didn't wish to risk their position. So, this white man, John

Brown, died, along with some of his own sons, and only five Negroes were there with them. But now, son, you have a chance to show them we can fight too!"

"He looks a lot like Captain Worden," Chip exclaimed, staring at the photo. "I know he's a good man, Papa, and I will stand by him."

As Chip stood on the bow in front of the captain, he watched the hundreds of people who were standing on the banks of the East River, pointing and waving at their craft. Many were laughing, and Chip felt a bit strange. Was it his fault the ship looked like a "cheese box on a raft"? Even the seagulls seemed to want to come down low and take a look at what these humans had created. They swooped down and called out in their screeching, mournful way, a sound Chip Jefferson had never heard, but one that Captain Worden said was something every sailor longed to hear, as he knew he was not far from land. The captain had also told the young steward about the bad luck of the Albatross landing on your deck when you're at sea, and he even read to him a poem by Samuel Taylor Coleridge, "The Rhyme of the Ancient Mariner," and Chip was enthralled as the Captain read: "God save thee, ancient Mariner! From the fiends, that plague thee thus! - Why look'st thou so?" — With my cross-bow I shot the Albatross."

Chip could picture himself as the cabin boy in the poem, his imagination increasing with each moment on the ship. The other men were kind to him; at least, they said nothing to his face, and he seemed to be a favorite of many of them, especially the surgeon steward, a young man of 20 named Jesse Jones and the Acting Assistant Paymaster, Lieutenant William F. Keeler. When the dead Albatross was put around the mariner's neck, Chip felt the weight of the sea, and the possible dangers all around. He couldn't wait to see what adventures lay ahead for him and his fellow crewmembers.

* * *

Sinclair and Whitehead were up early that morning. They had to get down to the river and load the torpedo in the darkness before the Continental Ship Yard workers came in. They also knew there would be hundreds of people watching from the banks of the East River as the new ship, the *U.S.S. Monitor*, was pulled down to the Brooklyn Navy Yard for launching and a shake-down cruise. Time was of the essence, as they say, and Walter knew if he did not get his fishing boat out into the channel, he would not be ready to launch his little Christening gift. He now knew the speed the ship could do, and where she was going to be going for her short cruise. It was only a matter of getting his small vessel in place so when he put his torpedo into the water, it would have clear running to its target.

Sinclair knew that even if he were able to sink this bloody monstrosity, he would still have won only half the battle. Ericsson needed to be done away with, or the Confederates would be after him or his fiancée, Penelope. They had been in touch with him twice since he had been in New York, and each time they reinforced the deadly serious nature of his task.

Walter pushed open the cabin door to the small fishing craft. His hands were almost frostbitten from the walk down to the river, and when he opened the door, he was overjoyed to see that Whitehead had a fire going for tea and biscuits. "I say, all the comforts of home, eh what?" said the torpedo man, pushing out a dilapidated chair for Walter to be seated.

"Yes, it is excruciatingly cold out there! Do you have the missile loaded?" Walter sat down and drew the cup of steaming tea close to him. He waved its warmth toward him and breathed in deeply.

Whitehead passed him a tray of almond and peppermint pastries. "Indeed, it took me from four in the A. M. until now, but I got her packed into the bow. I cut a good hole out of the starboard side, and put in my ramp. I even greased it up for the slide down into the water when the time comes. Jolly good biscuits. Grace made them last night and gave them to me to bring out here."

"She's a dear. I have the map that will get us out into the river right where the ship will be testing her maneuvers. We shouldn't attract too much attention in this bloody cod boat!"

Sinclair was beginning to like Whitehead. He was a rebel, just like he was, and he hoped they could keep their friendship after this was over. "If this proves successful, I suppose you will be able to name your price with just about any country in the world. They will want to buy the weapon that destroyed the famous *Monitor*, eh what?"

Whitehead brushed some crumbs from his lapel and picked up his teacup. "Yes, and I suppose England and France will be posting their observation ships to see how the South fares at the blockade in Norfolk. I read today that Lincoln is moving his soldiers into position to attack the entire peninsula."

"Indeed," said Sinclair, pushing himself away from the table. "The actions we take here can determine the outcome of this war, and if we can stop the Union, then England and France will certainly lend their support to the Southern cause."

"Let's get this ugly fish trawler out into the bay. We have a rendezvous with destiny!" said Whitehead, and he stomped out of the door leading to the pilot house.

* * *

John Ericsson waited at the dock of the Brooklyn Navy Yard. He could see his ship coming down the river, and his being was filled with anticipation. He was going to meet the government's deadline for construction, and soon the craft would be fit to enter the conflict down in Virginia. However, he had to get Lieutenant Greene sufficiently prepared for the battle, as the resultant confrontation could mean the difference between his loneliness and being together with his precious Amelia once more. Ericsson was planning to take the young man out for dinner following the shakedown cruise. This would give him the opportunity to explain just how the ship could be prevented from winning at Hampton Roads. Greene was now getting the crew ready for the cruise. Ericsson could see him talking with the crew near the dry-dock. His hands were gesticulating fervently, and it seemed absurd to Ericsson that such a young man would determine their fates.

The *Monitor* pulled into the docking port at 0900 hours. Little Chip Jefferson threw one of the main lines onto the pier and several sailors took up the small rope and led the larger docking rope onto the planks, where it was gathered and wrapped securely around the cleat. Other men followed Chip's example until all four ropes were secured and Captain Worden guided the ship into its place against the pier.

Dana had interviewed the new crew, and only six men would come with them out on the maiden voyage. Peter Williams, Quartermaster Seaman; George Burrows, Landsman; John Corwey, Fireman; Thomas Feeny, Coalheaver; Moses Stearns, Quartermaster; and Captain's Orderly, Chip Jefferson. The rest of the men were going to stay onshore and get the supplies ready for the voyage to meet their nemesis, the *C. S. S. Virginia*.

"What we gonna do 'bout all these people, Lieutenant?" asked Stearns, a tall, willowy farmer from Maine, who pointed to the hundreds of New York citizens who were lined-up against the fence. They were there to see "Ericsson's Folly" sink into the river, and many of the sailors in the crew were almost as suspicious of this strange craft as the public was.

"These people, Quartermaster, do not understand genius. These same citizens were making disparaging remarks about my father when he constructed the Elevator trains. Today, they all ride them, high above the city, without a care in the world. So, what does this tell us about the public?" Dana was quizzing them like schoolboys.

"Yes sir, you are correct," said little Chip, who was anxious to get on board with Captain Worden, as he had promised Chip he could watch from the bridge. "My family rides them all the time, and they're wonderful!" All the sea stories Chip had read as a child were coming back to him. Melville's *Moby Dick* kept him up for three nights straight, reading under the lamp in their rooms on the plantation. Mrs. Sims had recommended it to him, and Chip was immediately drawn into the tale about the obsessed Captain Ahab and the narrator, Ishmael. There was even a Cabin boy named Pip, and this fact electrified him, as he read over the passage about the young Negro lad as he was knocked overboard during a chase for the whales. After falling, little Pip became transfigured by the sea and its miraculous depths. Chip wondered if he, too, fell overboard, would the same hold true? Chip could quote that passage word for word to this very day, as he kept it inside his wallet, neatly folded, and he would bring it out to read whenever he felt closer to God and Nature, and as he read it that day, just before their first voyage, it seemed to symbolize what lay ahead for him:

By the merest chance the ship itself at last rescued him; but from that hour the little negro went about the deck an idiot; such, at least, they said he was. The sea had jeeringly kept his finite body up, but drowned the infinite of his soul Not drowned entirely, though. Rather carried down alive to wondrous depths, where strange shapes of the unwarped primal world glided to and fro before his passive eyes; and the miser-merman, Wisdom, revealed his hoarded heaps; and among the joyous, heartless, ever-juvenile eternities, Pip saw the multitudinous, God-omnipresent, coral insects, that out of the firmament of waters heaved the colossal orbs. He saw God's foot upon the treadle of the loom, and spoke it; and therefore his shipmates called him mad. So man's insanity is heaven's sense; and wandering from all mortal reason, man comes at last to that celestial thought, which, to reason, is absurd and frantic; and weal or woe, feels then uncompromised, indifferent as his God.

Chip believed slavery had been his ocean bottom, and that he, too, had gone mad. But now Captain Worden had saved him for the war and he could go on to fight injustice. Just as Captain Ahab's quest for the White Whale led little Pip to a great adventure, so Captain Worden's obsession to prove himself a worthy foe of his former captors, a great gray whale of Rebellion, had led Chip on the most exciting adventure of his life.

CHAPTER TWENTY-FIVE: RENDEZVOUS

January 30, 1862, Brooklyn Navy Yard

Walter Sinclair and Robert Whitehead were able to navigate smoothly into the channel before the *U.S.S. Monitor* launched to the hoopla of a military brass band, a 21-gun salute, and the roaring cheers and jeers of thousands of New York citizens, who were lined-up along the shore of the East River waiting for the ship to sink like a Confederate war bond in Manhattan.

Chip Jefferson stood next to Captain Worden in the Pilot house. He could see the inventor, John Ericsson, standing in the stern of the ship, as it was about to launch. Just a few minutes before, Chip had delivered a letter from the captain to the office in the Navy Yard where the mail was processed. Chip had read it before putting it into the envelope, and he felt proud to be a part of this ship's crew as Worden described it to the Secretary of the Navy:

Report of Lieutenant Worden, U. S. Navy, regarding the complement of officers and crew for the U. S. S. Monitor.

NAVY YARD, NEW YORK, January 30, 1862.

Hon. GIDEON WELLES, Secretary of the Navy.

SIR: I have the honor to acknowledge the receipt of your communication of the 24th instant, in relation to the complement of officers and crew for Ericsson's ironclad battery.

In estimating the number of her crew, I allowed 15 men and a quarter gunner for the two guns, 11 men for the powder division, and 1 for the wheel, which I deem ample for the efficient working of her guns in action. That would leave 12 men (including those available in the engineer's department) to supply deficiencies at the guns, caused by sickness or casualties. I propose to use a portion of the petty officers at the guns, and in naming the number of that class I thought I would be enabled to obtain a better class of men for that purpose. It is believed that 17 men and 2 officers in the turret would be as many as could work there with advantage; a greater number would be in each other's way and cause embarrassment.

The limited accommodations of the battery and the insufficiency of ventilation renders it important that as few as is consistent with her efficiency in action should be put in her. In relation to masters' mates, one might be ordered; more would overcrowd her accommodations and seems to be unnecessary.

Very respectfully, your obedient servant, JOHN L. WORDEN, Lieutenant, Commanding

Chip had been taken inside the turret, and the darkly ominous nature of the two guns mounted on the revolving platform sent a shiver down his back. As he waited alone, while the captain went to fetch his pipe, Chip could imagine the explosions coming from those caverns of heavy metal, as they spun around inside the turret, pointing at the enemy through the battery's seaward exposure. Chip pictured the giant *Merrimack* as she took the full brunt of the guns' onslaught. *Ka-boom*!

Rebels would fly into the air like gray rag dolls, and Captain Worden would let him fire the cannon. "Take that you dirty scoundrels!" he shouted, his face beaming with indignation, "this is for all the slaves you have imprisoned, and all the pain you have caused us for a hundred years!"

John Ericsson was still standing at the stern of his ship, as if he were a monument of defiance to all those on shore who would disbelieve that his craft could accomplish what he said it could do. Lieutenant Greene stood beside him, smiling proudly, as the ship was ready for its maiden launch. Matthew Brady, the famous New York photographer and war correspondent, was set-up on the shore right next to the launching dock, ready to capture the success or failure of this strange vessel called *Monitor*. The photo would, no doubt, after being distributed to all the major newspapers of the world, hang in his personal gallery downtown on Broadway. In addition, several rescue vessels were out in the river, ready to collect survivors when and if the ship sank.

"Mister Greene, prepare to get underway!" Captain Worden shouted, and the band picked up its cadence with "Battle Hymn of the Republic," and the crowd along the banks cheered, as the shadowy craft eased down the wooden launching sled, causing the planks to moan and creak, as the heavy iron hull hit the river with a gigantic splash, and water gushed up and over the sides, drenching Captain Ericsson and two sailors. Greene rushed over to the older man to see if he were injured. "Captain, are you all right?"

Ericsson sputtered a bit, but he was smiling. The ship, although it had dipped under the waves, and had taken a full-sized drench over her bow, immediately became seaworthy and was ready for her first adventure. "See? What did I tell you, Mister Greene? This ship was made for the open sea!"

Greene grabbed Ericsson's hand and shook it vigorously. "Indeed, Sir! It certainly was. And now they shall see us in a different light, won't they? Ericsson's Folly is no more!"

* * *

Captain Worden put the new vessel into a rigorous test of her abilities. First, he ran through the engine functions to see the maximum speed that could be reached. Although Ericsson had said she could reach a speed of 14 knots, the most Worden could get her to do was seven. As most of the craft was under the water line, Worden believed she would prove to be a poor target for anything but a ramming maneuver by the enemy. This was a good thing because the armor on the craft had to be reduced to one-inch plating, and the Pilot house, where he was now standing was most vulnerable to a direct hit. She displaced 987 tons, and was 41.5 feet long and 10.5 feet wide. Although he privately had grave misgivings about the ultimate seaworthiness of his ship, Captain Worden decided to keep his reservations to himself. When Captain Ericsson and Lieutenant Greene came in, Worden was giving orders to Quartermaster Stearnes. "We shall take her out near the breakwater, Quartermaster. I want to see how she rides in conditions similar to what we'll be experiencing on our journey down the coast to Virginia."

"Yes, Captain. But remember, you'll be having an escort on your journey to do battle with the *Merrimack*. I can understand your misgivings about her maneuverability in high seas. But our Monitor will not have to do much until she reaches Hampton Roads Harbor." John Ericsson spoke as he inspected the various instruments on the Quartermaster's wheel.

It was gloomy inside the Pilot house, and the only light came from two horizontal slits in the fore and aft bulkheads. It was like being inside a coffin, Greene thought, and he shivered involuntarily. "Can't we open these panels somehow? It's like living inside a dungeon."

Ericsson walked over to the foremost bulkhead and pushed. "See? I have built an eight-inch, hinged metal panel that can swing down." The panel flapped down, and sunlight streamed into the compartment. The four men had to squint to look out at the scene in the East River. People were lined up on the banks waving and cheering the ship as it moved onward to the mouth of the river.

Chip Jefferson entered the Pilot house, his face alive with the excitement of being at sea. His youthful exuberance seemed to fill the older men with renewed purpose whenever he was near them. "Captain Worden, sir, lunch will be served in the wardroom in ten minutes."

"Thank you, Chip. Lieutenant? Want to take over until I get some victuals? She's been running pretty smoothly, although I've been concerned about some sluggishness in the steering."

Greene walked over to take the Captain's position next to the

Quartermaster and his wheel. "You go ahead, Captain. I'll take her. Mister Ericsson and I had lunch earlier."

"The beef steaks are quite tasty, I might add," said Ericsson, smiling. "I saw one of your new men eat three of them as I consumed my one. Our new Lincoln greenback money will be going into the human furnaces also!" Ericsson added, referring to the recent printing of Union money to finance the war effort.

"Yes, it seems we'll all be living on borrowed time and money for the duration of this war," said Worden, as he exited the compartment. Greene looked over at Ericsson and smiled.

They both knew how true those words really were.

* * *

Walter Sinclair was lying on the deck of the fishing boat, which was anchored near the shore, his long body covered by a sealskin tarp. Robert Whitehead was at the bow, near his beloved torpedo, also covered, but he was sitting up, looking out into the mouth of the East River. They were both waiting for the arrival of their prey, the *U.S.S. Monitor*, which would soon be coming their way on its journey out into the breakwater of the Atlantic.

Sinclair and Whitehead agreed that they needed to be close to shore in case something went wrong with their plan. They could then quickly escape to an awaiting one-horse surrey, which was tied to a big elm tree nearby on a country road.

Whitehead had earlier set the compressed air container to maximum pressure, as he realized the torpedo's propeller would need extra speed in the harsh currents near the breakwater. If the explosive tip were to hit any part the armor less, exposed underbelly of the *Monitor*, she would sink like a cannon ball in a birdbath. Sinclair could then retrieve Ericsson from the water and bring him to the Confederates as a trophy.

A brisk wind rustled the sail overhead, and seagulls swooped down to warily inspect the vessel, as if they knew this was a poor imitation of a fishing boat. Walter stretched his legs, and he could feel the numbness beginning to set in. He had to be ready to spring up from his supine position when the moment came. The long months of subterfuge and spying had finally come to this. The black beast was approaching, as he knew it would. He never believed these stupid Americans when they talked in the pubs about the crazy Swedish inventor, John Ericsson. Even though they were a nation of castaways, Americans had a difficult time accepting foreigners. It was quite ironic, indeed. Ericsson, the Swede, had proved to be a most noble and creative adversary. He was much more creative and resilient than any one of these Americans. Walter saw Whitehead's body stiffen, and then he watched as Robert got up, peeked over the railing, and said, "She's coming!" in a low, harsh whisper. "Get ready to move!"

CHAPTER TWENTY-SIX: THE FISH

January 30, 1862, East River Breakwater

Chip was cleaning up the dishes in the Captain's wardroom, trying to finish in time to get back to his reading of *Moby Dick*. Ahab was just about to set out to find the white whale, and Chip was entranced. He kept visualizing himself in the role of the little Negro Cabin Boy, Pip, and his reading made him believe he was aboard the *Pequod*. As he journeyed aboard the *Monitor*, his imagination often made him glimpse scenes from the book. The strange Captain Ericsson became Ahab, Captain Worden was Ishmael, and Lieutenant Greene was Starbuck. It made his routine life much more exciting to have this inner fantasy going on.

Lieutenant Greene poked his head inside the wardroom. "Hello, Chip. Captain Worden wants his pipe. Could you fetch it for him? There's a good lad."

"Yes sir!" said Chip, snapping off a sharp salute. This gave him a chance to visit the Captain's Quarters and keep his little fiction going! He cleaned up the rest of the silver from the table and took it into the pantry for washing later. He then walked down the passageway to the Captain's Room. "Captain J. L. Worden, U.S.N." the door said, in military stencil. He opened the door and stepped inside.

The teacher, Ishmael, has many books, Chip thought, as he looked around for the briar pipe. *Navigation by the Stars*, *The Seagoing Phoenicians*, and, look at this! *The Mysterious Easter Island*. I wonder how teacher became interested in this island? Could he be working together with Ahab and Starbuck?

Chip picked up the book and riffled through the pages. No! He can't be a slave trader! Chip slammed the book down and opened the small drawer on

97

the Captain's nightstand. He spotted the pipe, snatched it up, and ran out of compartment, securing the hatch after him.

On deck, Chip made his way out to the Pilot house. There are Ahab and Starbuck, standing together near the starboard railing. Are they conspiring, as they whisper, nodding their heads knowingly? Are they preparing for the battle with the giant whale? Must we all go out to die with them? As he walked along the edge of the port railing, he looked out at the sea. What he saw became a recurring nightmare for weeks to follow. About one hundred yards out, directly in front of a small fishing boat, Chip saw what looked like a giant gray fish, swimming just beneath the waves directly toward them! Moby Dick! It is the white whale that has come to destroy us!

Chip stood, frozen in place, as the giant fish came rushing at them. He did what his mind told him. He screamed at the top of his voice, "We're being attacked! The giant whale is swimming right at us!"

* * *

Inside the Pilot house, Captain John Worden was watching his Quartermaster, Stearns. The tall blonde fellow was having a difficult time with the wheel.

"Captain, sir, I can't control her. She keeps pulling hard right rudder!" The two men felt the craft as she moved sharply right. "I can't keep on course!"

Worden realized the rudder needed work, and he decided not to risk the lives of the men on board. "All stop!" he yelled into the pneumatic microphone to the fore and aft engine rooms. The ship slowed until she was dead in the water.

* * *

When he and Whitehead watched the torpedo slide easily down the sled and into the water, they smiled at each other. When they heard the steady whir of the propeller as it churned up the water beneath the surface, they allowed themselves another nod of hope. The destruction of the *U.S.S. Monitor* was at hand! Soon, they would put the dinghy into the water to retrieve Ericsson, if he survived the explosion. Whitehead said the concussion would simply tear a hole into the vulnerable hull, and the ship would sink, leaving the sailors to fend for themselves.

However, when the torpedo looked like it was right on target, they suddenly saw that the ship was turning away from the oncoming missile! "What in blazes?" Walter whispered, not believing what he was seeing with his own eyes. Now the ship was stopping in the water! Sinclair panicked. Did they know they were being attacked? Who told them? Should he and Whitehead run away now? The fear fed into his being like gangrene. All these months of careful planning preparations and subterfuge—were they to be lost because of some traitor onboard this Union freak ship?

* * *

Chip was the only one on the port side of the ship when the fish sped past. It was long and cylindrical. It had no fins. He knew it was no whale. When Ericsson and Greene came up to him, they asked what he had seen. Chip looked out at the water one last time. He then turned to face these two men he did not trust. Somehow, he believed they were responsible for that mechanical fish.

"What was it, boy? Did you see something out there?" asked Ericsson.

"No, sir, I guess I was just a bit frightened. I've been reading *Moby Dick*, and I guess I thought I saw me a whale out there," said Chip, pointing backward at the water in the East River and smiling.

Greene laughed. "Well, now, that's quite an imagination you have there! You better stop reading so many of those adventure books. You'll soon be seeing pirates!"

Ericsson thought it ironic that the lieutenant was chastising the little Negro about his imagination, as it was Greene's own Romantic notions that allowed him to be controlled by the inventor. "Go below and have the cook give you some dessert. I think you've been on deck too long," Ericsson told the boy. "I must go see Captain Worden to see what has caused the engines to stop."

Worden exited the Pilot house and walked up to them, followed by Quartermaster Stearns. The captain took his pipe from Chip and frowned. "It looks like we'll need to be towed back, Mister Ericsson. It seems your little *Monitor* has a steering problem."

* * *

Walter Sinclair and Robert Whitehead were able to leave in their fishing boat once the *Monitor* was towed back to the shipyard. They would come back in the morning to retrieve the torpedo.

Sinclair knew he had ruined his one and only chance to sink the ship with this novel weapon. The Union monster's steering malfunction had saved it. Now it would be repaired, and the next time she passed this way she would have a heavily armed escort. There would be no more chances with Whitehead's invention. Walter knew it was now a race against time to kill Ericsson and steal the plans to the *Monitor* before the Confederates found out he had failed. The noose was tightening around his neck, and Walter also knew his darling Penelope would be in danger if he failed again. Sinclair set his jaw and glanced over at his friend. "I'm sorry you didn't get to see your torpedo succeed, Robert. Perhaps there will be time before this war is over."

Whitehead shrugged. "I don't suppose so, Simon, as I hear the French are planning to invade Mexico while the colonies are busy fighting each other to the death up here. I may go down there to see if they want to see what my torpedo can do."

Alone again. Walter knew it would probably come to this. He trimmed the sail on the little fishing boat hard into the wind.

CHAPTER TWENTY-SEVEN: ANOTHER PLAN

February 10, 1862, Greenpoint, Brooklyn

After the Monitor was towed back to the Brooklyn Navy Yard, Lieutenant Greene dismissed the men and walked alone back to the Bachelor's Officer Barracks. Captains Worden and Ericsson were supervising the repair schedule for the steering malfunction, and they supposed it would be completed in a few weeks. Until then, Greene would be in charge of getting the men ready for combat. But it was the secret mission that was making him uncomfortable. As he was going to be in charge of the turret guns, he had to learn how to aim the Dahlgrens so that they would not inflict heavy damage on the *Virginia*. This went against his military training and his will to win, and it also seemed to be a traitorous act.

However, later that evening, as they dined at Wheelers' Steak House on Broadway, Ericsson began describing Easter Island again and what lay ahead for them and their wives, and Greene went into a reverie that placed him far away from the chaos of guns and war, and he was able to see the "Over Soul," as Ericsson told him the Transcendentalists were calling Man's communal harmony with Nature. Their goal was to live on the island peacefully, for the rest of their lives, and the idyllic image was now firmly implanted in Greene's subconscious.

All Greene had to do was pick-up a poem by Whitman and see what was in store for them if they could get the money from the sale of the Monitors to the Navy. Greene believed Nature had the key to life without war. Easter Island would be their Eden and their rebirth into paradise.

Later, standing on the landing outside his small apartment, Greene read from his adored Whitman and thought about his loved one, Anna, as she awaited his return. They were both like the torn blossoms in the passage:

Tufts of straw, sands, fragments,
Buoy'd hither from many moods, one contradicting another,
From the storm, the long calm, the darkness, the swell,
Musing, pondering, a breath, a briny tear, a dab of liquid or soil,
Up just as much out of fathomless workings fermented and thrown,
A limp blossom or two, torn, just as much over waves
floating, drifted at random.

* * *

Walter held Grace's round face in his large hands. He kissed her eyebrows, one at a time, and then her lips. "I am leaving, Grace," he said. "Time and the devil wait for no man."

Grace's eyes were brimming with tears. "True, I don't know what devil's got inside you, Simon, but I wish you well. Do you suppose you could write me a few lines on your travels? It's a bit of a drudge working this life of mine, you know. You and Mister Whitehead have been the only excitement I've had in this town. I do hate to see you go."

"I promise. I will write to you when I am able to get to sea again. There's something about the sea that brings out the writer in a man. I guess it's the way one feels so small and insignificant next to her magnificence. Just the way I feel when I'm with you, Grace." Walter kissed her again, and they both held each other until the sun went down outside.

Later, after Grace left, Walter took out his assassination accoutrements and knew he would have to devise a new plan to keep his contract with the Confederacy. The Enfield sniper rifle was a possibility if he could find a location where a bead could be drawn down upon the inventor without notice. Walter would scout the area around Ericsson's home on Beach Street. The "Yankee Love Potion" was his late option. If there were a way he could get into the Captain's food supply or into his plate served in a restaurant—wait a moment! The little darkie, Chip Jefferson, from the hotel. Perhaps he was the answer. Walter picked up the rifle and held it up against his cheek, and peered into the scope. Reality took on a simpler aspect when one looked through a spyglass. He was now a spy for the Confederacy, and he knew his time was growing short.

There was a knock at the door. Walter shoved the assassin tools under the bed, but he kept the rifle within his reach. He walked over and stood against the door. "Who is it?" he asked, half-expecting Grace. Perhaps she wanted to stay the night?

"Open up. I have news from Mister Davis," said a deep voice.

This was one of the code phrases for a meeting with his Confederate contacts. Walter took a deep breath and opened the door. The tall, red-haired gentleman who entered was immediately recognizable. He was the same person who came to see him at the Silver Tide Inn in Liverpool. Sitting down in the chair near the window, the Southerner took out his long white pipe and lit it. The room became invigorated with Virginia tobacco.

"We know what happened, Captain Sinclair," he said, puffing energetically. "There are now two men living in your
Penelope's home town, and should you fail in your endeavor, they will be told to take appropriate action."

Walter began to sweat, and he thought about lunging for the rifle beneath the bed, but he knew it would mean they would just kill Penelope when this fellow did not return. "I know, but it was an accident about the ship swerving off course. Her rudder malfunctioned. You know I have enough bloody time to finish the task at hand!"

The gentleman smiled. He looked like he was enjoying this. "Yes, we know. We are aware also of your methods and tools. However, there is another person we want you to work with who has a bit more experience in these matters than you or I."

It was Walter's turn to grin. "You don't say? I suppose it's Dr. Frankenstein, then, is it not? I hear his monster can do these kinds of things with great gusto."

"I'm glad you have your sense of humor during these trying times, Captain. Although, it will do you well to stay focused during these remaining days. You are to meet this gentleman at the Museum of Oddities tomorrow at noon. This man has talents as a chemist and as a master of disguises. You see, he is an actor, and he has been supplying the South with certain drugs we need for our wounded in hospitals. He can help you with your poisons and with your masquerade."

"And for whom am I to ask, pray tell?" said Walter.

"Booth, Mister John Wilkes Booth," said the Southerner.

* * *

Captain Worden slept onboard the *Monitor* that evening, and Chip was allowed to stay on board as well. As he curled up on the rack behind the pantry in the Wardroom, Chip was thinking about whether or not he should tell the captain about what he saw in the water. *I'm* not certain what it was myself. How can I tell him what I don't understand? He would laugh at me, and I could not abide that.

However, Chip believed the inventor and the lieutenant were somehow behind the thing he saw. He vowed to watch them closely to see if he could determine what they were doing. Could they be spies? If they were slave traders, then anything was possible! I will be a spy for my people, Chip thought, turning over toward the bulkhead and closing his eyes. When the time comes, I will tell Captain Worden. But not until I obtain the proof.

CHAPTER TWENTY-EIGHT: ANOTHER LAUNCH

February 17, 1862, Norfolk Navy Yard, Virginia

John Brooke felt newly invigorated as he watched the men put on the last of the wood and iron onto the inclining roof of the behemoth ship, the *Virginia*. The hull was 275 feet long. A roof of wood and iron, inclining about 36 degrees, covered about 160 feet of the central portion. The wood was two feet thick; it consisted of oak planks four inches by twelve inches, laid up and down next to the iron, and two courses of pine, one longitudinal of eight inches thickness, the other twelve inches thick.

The intervening space on top was closed by permanent gratings of two-inch square iron, two and one-half inches apart, leaving an opening for four hatches, one near each end, one forward and one abaft the smoke-stack. The roof did not project beyond the hull, however, and the ends of the shield were rounded.

The armor was four inches thick. It was fastened to its wooden backing by one and three-eighths inch bolts, countersunk and secured by iron nuts and washers. The plates were eight inches wide. Brooke and his men succeeded soon in punching two inches, and the remaining plates, more than two-thirds, were two inches thick. They had been rolled and punched at the Tredegar Works, Richmond. The outside course was up and down, the next longitudinal. Joints were broken where there were more than two courses. The hull, extending two feet below the roof, was plated with one-inch iron; it was intended that it should have had three inches.

The prow "battering ram" was of cast iron, wedged shaped, and weighed 1500 pounds. It was to be about two feet under water, and project two feet from the steam. The rudder and propeller were unprotected.

The battery consisted of ten guns, four single-banded Brooke rifles and six

103

nine-inch Dahlgren's shell guns. Two of the rifles, bow and stern pivots, were seven-inch, of 14,500 pounds; the other two were 6.4 inch (32 pound calibre) of 9000 pounds, one on each broadside. The nine-inch gun on each side nearest the furnaces was fitted for firing hot shot. A few nine- inch shot with extra windage were cast for hot shot. No other solid shot were on board during the fight.

The engines were the same the vessel had whilst in the United States Navy. They were radically defective, and had been condemned by the United States Government. Some changes had been made, notwithstanding which the engineers reported they were unreliable. Brooke was worried about their performance under battle conditions, and this was why he was there to see his craft put into the water.

Brooke watched, as his ship slid down into the Chesapeake. My God! She's going under too deep! He thought, as the water kept rising up the giant craft's superstructure, until the water line was almost to her railing. "Lieutenant Jones! Get those tugs alongside her! We must get her back into dry dock. She'll need several thousand pounds taken from those planks before she can sail safely."

"Aye, Sir!" said Catesby Jones, realizing this would take longer than the Confederate Generals would like. They were worried their early victories would soon turn to losses if they did not have the blockade broken soon. McClellan and his army were moving down the peninsula, and it would be a disaster if supplies couldn't reach their brethren in time. Not only this, but word was that the North had launched their little ironclad, the *Monitor*, and even though she was still being repaired for sea duty, it would only be a matter of time before the *Virginia* would be confronted. "Let's go, men!" Jones shouted, finally getting the feel of his new command after these few days. "We can get her trim as a Southern belle before the end of the week!"

CHAPTER TWENTY-NINE: THE ACTOR

February 28, 1862, New York City

Walter was waiting inside the Continental Club on Broadway. The signs on front of the tavern advertised the appearance of "P. T. Barnum's Famous Siamese Twins, Chang and Eng, with Master of Ceremonies, General Tom Thumb!" The atmosphere was cloudy with cigar smoke, the sound of clinking glasses, and the laughter of New Yorkers who were looking for an escape from the realities of wartime. *I wonder why Booth wanted us to meet here?* Walter was wondering, just as a tall gentleman sauntered up to his table and bowed deeply before him. "Mister Ellwood, I presume?" said Booth, in his eloquent stage voice.

"Yes, I've been expecting you, Mr. Booth. Please be seated." Walter pulled out a chair and motioned for the younger gentleman to sit.

Booth looked both ways across the bar, as if he were being followed. "I think we'd be better positioned back here," he said, moving toward a sheltered table near the rear of the establishment. It had red-velvet curtains in a semi-circle and over the top, to keep the sound inside, yet they could both still watch the stage presentation. Johnny Booth seemed eager to watch, as he squeezed into the cushioned seat and immediately pointed to the little man in the miniature Union Army uniform who was taking the center place on-stage. "Look at that!" he laughed, "General Ulysses S. Grant has come to tell us how badly the North is losing! Oh, but he should change whiskey brands, as it appears he has recently lost some stature."

Walter smiled at the jest. *I'll let him begin. They want me to learn from him, so I'll let him convene.* When the waiter came, he ordered a pint of ale, and Booth ordered a bottle of champagne. The man was an active sort, constantly gesturing and smoking from his long, European cigar. Walter was most impressed by Booth's eyes. They were deep and darkly mysterious, and they had the intense quality of searchlights cutting through fog when they looked at you.

On stage, General Tom Thumb, all of three feet tall, was joking about first meeting the Siamese twins, Chang and Eng. "Chang had joined the Union cause, but his brother, Eng, was a Rebel! No matter how hard they try to separate, these days, it seems they can't break their union," said the little general, and the audience roared with laughter. Everyone except John Wilkes Booth, that is, who was frowning into his champagne glass.

"He's an idiot!" said Booth, twisting his mustache like the villain in a melodrama. "Chang and Eng Bunker are Southern gentlemen who live in Wilkesboro, North Carolina, a slave state! They own at least two hundred slaves between them and run a one thousand acre tobacco plantation!"

When Tom Thumb brought the twins out, they were each wearing uniforms, one of the Union and one of the Confederacy. They seemed to serve as a humorous metaphor for the insanity raging all around. "Well, sirs, will you partake of some whiskey?" asked General Tom.

"Is it Southern whiskey?" asked Eng.

"No, it's a good Yankee potion!" said Tom.

"Then give it to him\ I'll not taste a drop!" said Eng, and Tom handed the bottle to Chang, who immediately began guzzling down the liquid.

General Tom pointed to Eng, and said, "Strange thing about these two. When Chang drinks, Eng gets drunk!"

On cue, Eng began to act inebriated, singing loudly, and trying to get up to dance, but each time he tried to rise, Chang would hold him back in a comedic rendition of "push me, pull you." The audience was enjoying every minute of the act.

Booth, however, had seen it all before, and he chose this moment to begin his lecture. "They did not explain your mission to me, Mister Ellwood, but I am certain it is of extreme urgency to our cause, and I do not ever question my superiors' wisdom in these matters. Therefore, I am going to do everything in my power to assist you in your patriotic endeavor. I am, you see, an actor. My genius is that I can make people believe I am one thing, when, in actuality, I am something quite different. Just tell me your target, and I will assist you with any poison or ruse we will need to develop in order to succeed."

Booth went on to explain how he had been a member of a network of spies and smugglers known as the Knights of the Golden Circle, operating between Richmond and Montreal, Canada. Relentlessly, the group implemented many underground activities, including blockade-smashing efforts along the East Coast and the disbursement of medicines (largely quinine and laudanum) down from Canada, through Union lines, thence to

Virginia. The young actor was ready and willing to assist Walter in his effort to assassinate John Ericsson, and they shook hands and agreed to meet at Walter's hotel room following Booth's appearance in a Broadway play called *The Apostate*.

As Walter left the club with Booth, they stopped to greet Chang and Eng and the little general, who immediately recognized the actor when he approached. "Johnny Booth!

You rapscallion!" said Tom, reaching up to shake the tall man's outstretched hand. "Did you hear? I am courting Lavinia Warren of Massachusetts. Her family name is Bump, and I call her my 'little bump in the road,' but Mister Barnum changed it for her, as he said it sounded ghastly."

"Ah, yes. P. T. Barnum, ever the showman," said Booth. "General, Misters Chang and Eng Bunker, I want you to meet Mister Simon Ellwood of Great Britain."

As Walter shook the hands of the little man and the two joined-at-the-hips brothers, he was thinking about his Penelope, and how she would have been entranced by this experience. Aberrations of Nature were a frequent amusement to her, and she and Walter had once spent an entire fortnight visiting Mister Barnum's circus when it came to London in 1860. Penelope's favorite exhibit was the "Freak Sideshow," and now Walter felt he was an honorary freak. He hoped this young actor of the mysterious Knights of the Golden Circle would not prove to be an anomaly as well. If they did not succeed this time with their plot, then there were some men in England who would pay Penelope a visit, most certainly causing her natural damage beyond repair, and Walter could never stand for that!

CHAPTER THIRTY: THE WOMEN

March 2, 1862, London

Penelope Andrews was living one city block, about 60 meters, from John Ericsson's wife, Amelia Blackstone-Ericsson. In fact, they both shopped at the same stores in the Mayfair District. Their parents had exclusive homes; several servants were on staff, and the two women were fashionable members of the West End society.

Even though Penelope's parents were wealthy, they were not about to give any money to their daughter's beau, Walter Sinclair, whom they knew to be a sailor. Charles Blackstone, 57, was a distinguished member of British Parliament, and a business owner, and he had little use for the sea and for those who came from such wanderlust environs. He considered Mr. Sinclair to be beneath his daughter in all respects, and as far as he was concerned, there would never be a marriage between the two young people.

Penelope Blackstone's love affair with Walter Sinclair was certainly clandestine, and the lovers had gone as far as to use a special post office box at the West End, where Penelope could be seen secretly reading the letters from her lover, who was writing from America. It was just such a day when Amelia came into the post office, and she noticed that the younger woman's envelope had the markings from the States, and this piqued her curiosity so that she approached her.

"Excuse me, but are you corresponding with an American?" she asked, smiling so that her ever-present dimples were clearly visible.

Penelope started, as she was not prepared to discuss Walter's whereabouts with any stranger. However, she knew Amelia from the West End society parties, and she was not about to rebuff her. "Why, yes. I have a good friend over in the Colonies, why do you ask?"

Amelia touched Penelope's arm with the delicacy of a woman in love. "Aren't you Penelope Andrews? I don't mean to be bold, but Margaret Whimple told me you were involved with some pirate or smuggler. Can this be true?"

Penelope laughed in spite of her nervousness. "Heaven's no! Walter Sinclair is a ship's captain doing work in America. He is a legitimate seaman and has never done such criminal deeds. I suppose Margaret Whimple must have quite the imagination. But, I'm afraid, in this particular instance, her comments border on slanderous."

"My husband is also involved in naval work. I am hoping his recent project will make us enough money for me to return to America. I do miss him so!" said Amelia. "Letters can never replace our loved ones, can they?" she added, the tone of her voice falling.

"Oh my! I do believe we've become maudlin. Will you accompany me to the Cheshire Cat for a pint?" asked Penelope. "It is quite a thrill to sit down in a pub, which serves both men and women. Don't say you're not for Suffrage, Mrs. Ericsson. I saw you at a meeting the other night."

Amelia smiled. "Yes, I am a Suffragette. We must stay together, so we shall go over to the pub. I want to hear more about what your young pirate is doing in America!"

* * *

Inside the public house called the Cheshire Cat, Tim Wallach, a tall, sandy-haired Irishman in a dark tweed coat, was sitting at a small table next to the bar smoking a Carolina cigar. When the two women came in, he watched them sit down in the far corner. Tim had been following Penelope Andrews for many weeks, and he was certain she was unaware of his presence. The Confederacy was paying all his expenses, and he was receiving constant coded telegrams about what he should do next. He knew if one particular message came, he was to move in and kidnap the Andrews girl and take her to a warehouse outside Soho. It was all simple and routine. His orders were in place, and he knew his job was secure, unlike many other men whose lives were caught up in the horrors of mortal combat on the front lines. This was easy duty compared to his brother, Albert, who was serving with Beauregard's troops after the attack on Fort Sumter. The two women were becoming more animated as they spoke, and as the waitress brought the two pints of stout to the table, he wondered what they were discussing that was so fascinating.

"I miss John and his perfunctory habits. He would arrange all his suits and shoes in neat, orderly rows. I had to drag him out of his shop to get some fresh air. He was an obsessive laborer, and this was a major reason why I came back to England. He swears it was because of the money, but that wasn't the true reason."

"Yes, I know. Walter was often a frantic beast whenever we spent time in

London. He had no desire to be part of the 'landed gentry,' as he called citizens who worked on shore. However, he was very romantic in his own way. He once blindfolded me and told me he was going to take me to a place where sailors were rescued. He walked me, like a blind woman, up hundreds of stairs until we were inside a room. When he took the blindfold off, we were inside the Old Dungeness Lighthouse in south Kent. They had just installed the first electric light to beam over the sea and save ships from the fog and inclement weather. We spent the evening inside Old Dungeness, as the caretaker had taken Walter's money and left him in charge."

"Oh, my dear! That is quite romantic!" Amelia exclaimed.

"We could see the light as it shone upon the waves, and Walter whispered that I was his guiding light, and would I marry him. But then, before we could arrange our wedding, he left for America."

"I'm so very sorry to hear that, Pen. John was never as romantic as all that," said Amelia, putting her pinky finger inside the stein, pulling out some foam, and delicately licking it off with her tongue.

"I'm worried about Walter. He keeps telling me he's visiting a cousin in New York City, but it has been over two months now. What could he be doing over there with the war on?" Penelope was quite unnerved, and Amelia was the first woman who was truly sympathetic to her, as her husband was also caught up in the Civil War over in America.

"My John keeps me apprised of his personal life, but he won't tell me one thing about what he has to do with the war effort. Ah, but I have discovered, on my own, that he has sold his Monitor to President Lincoln, and that the Southerners are also building their own iron craft," Amelia whispered, conspiratorially.

"Walter won't tell me any details about his business in America. The last I heard, he was trying to negotiate something

with the Confederacy. He won't be in any danger, will he?" Penelope gasped, grabbing tightly onto the older woman's hand.

"John says many people are getting rich at the expense of the Americans and their internal conflict. It's all business to him. He just wants me with him, and he needs money to accomplish our romantic reunion. Truth be known, I really don't care about from which side he gets the money. And you shouldn't care as well! Love is the final refuge of our men, and we shall be their benefactors. Let's drink on it!" said Amelia, and she stood up and raised her stein into the air. Penelope, at first, seemed reluctant; but, finally, she too stood up and raised her ale mug in a toast.

Tim Wallach could hear the women toast, "To love, to honor, to suffrage!" He glowered and got up from his table, shoving his few shillings into a coat pocket and lighting his cigar again. "Women!" he barked, holding the match to the tip of the cigar, puffing in, igniting the tobacco, and blowing out a thick stream of smoke. As he walked by their table he added, "Why don't you go home and tend to your kitchens?"

CHAPTER THIRTY-ONE: THE AMERICAN MUSEUM

March 6, 1862, New York City

The steering problem of the Monitor postponed the ship's departure for Hampton Roads, and the crew was held over for two days. Lieutenant Greene and John Ericsson decided to stay in New York City to attend the Wax Museum, inside the American Museum of Oddities on the corner of Ann Street and Broadway. It was a rather strange gift, as Ericsson had received the two tickets from an "anonymous patriot," who left a note in the envelope saying, "Thank you, kind Sir, for all you have done for our Union cause!"

As they walked down Fulton Street from the Navy Yard, Ericsson began telling the young lieutenant about their trip to Easter Island. The inventor knew he must keep Greene conditioned with the myth, or else, when the time came for the boy to do his duty against the Virginia, he might not have the nerve.

"I've been corresponding with my wife, Amelia, quite often these days. She's rather supportive of our rendezvous. I think you might consider telling your fiancée what we're about." Ericsson adjusted his coat, as the wind from the ocean was quite brisk and cold.

"I'm glad you said that, Sir! I want my Anna to have something to look forward to once this is over. Do you suppose they'll take to the rigors of living under such primitive conditions?" Greene's voice was enthusiastic, and it contained no hint of fear. This pleased Ericsson. The time would soon come when they would have to make their break with civilization, and the missionary zeal of the Swede would be needed to pull off the show without any problems.

"I don't believe our ladies will deter us from our goal. We may have to train them as to the discipline and Spartan abilities required of such an endeavor, but they will thank us for it in the long run." Ericsson tripped over a slab of stone and lurched forward so suddenly that the younger man had to catch hold of him to stop his collapse.

"Whoa! You almost took a frightful fall," said Greene, picking up the elder man's top hat, which had toppled from his head. "Here you are. You'll need this to get into the show."

"Thank you, my boy. Getting on in age is not what my brain wants my body to know. It's nice to have the younger generation along to assist me in this era of turmoil." Ericsson pointed toward the big sign in front of the building just ahead. "There it is! P. T. Barnum's world famous American Museum. Shall we?"

"By all means. You know, Anna and I didn't have time to see the Wax Museum when we visited during my leave. I wish she could be here now," said Greene, walking into the lobby.

There were many people queuing up to the entrance of Mrs. Pelby's Wax Museum portion of the exhibit. Some of the visitors were so stiff and well-dressed that they, too, looked to be waxed manikins. As he stood in line, Greene noticed a sign on the wall that read, "Notice to Persons of Color: In order to afford respectable colored persons an opportunity to witness the extraordinary attractions at present exhibited at the Museum, the Manager has determined to admit this class of people on Thursday morning, next, March 10, from 8 A.M. to 1 P.M. Special performances in the Lecture Hall at 11 o'clock."

As they entered the exhibit, Ericsson was struck by the life-like quality of the wax figures. The first display, a collection of Mexican Generals from the war, looked life-like and realistic, down to the touches of green guacamole sauce left on the beard of General Antonio Lopez de Santa Anna Perez de Lebron, as he dined in his tent with his "Yellow Rose of Texas," the voluptuous mulatto slave, Emily Morgan.

"He looks so authentic one would expect him to break into Spanish!" said Greene, chuckling.

"Yes, I've read that Mrs. Pelby studied under the famous Madame Tussaud in Paris. When I was in Europe, I saw her Chamber of Horrors. It featured quite frightening depictions of notorious murderers throughout history," Ericsson pointed out.

The mechanical panoramic pictures next attracted their attention. The first was a "Vue du Pont Neuf a Paris "-steamers in motion, carriages passing, and omnibuses proceeding to their respective stations-all beautifully represented. The next picture was a steam engine in operation. The third was a scissors-grinder at work. The fourth depicted stonecutters sawing a block of marble. The fifth picture was a railroad bridge, with cars passing over. The seventh showed opera-dancers, with all gayety and beauty. The eighth was the musical concert of monkeys. They noticed the delicacy of the principal performer's touch, the motion of his fingers, the beating of his foot to the tune; the leader was beating time and accompanying the music with his voice.

"How is it these mechanical wonders are so much more entertaining as works of art?" Ericsson asked, as he was an inventor who really had no use for seeing inventions in their reality. " I have always enjoyed the abstract quality of invention more than the final result. I suppose I am more of an artist than an engineer."

"That's fine, Captain. My father is quite similar to you in that respect. I remember his spending fourteen hours designing the decorative display of our Christmas tree, but he spent not one second doing the work!" Greene said.

"I say! Come over here! This display is quite fascinating," Ericsson called to the younger man. He was standing beside the recreation of "The Last Supper of Our Lord, with Disciples." Inside the alcove, the Michelangelo painting was depicted with wax figures for all twelve disciples and Jesus. The figure of Judas was quite striking, and he seemed to be skulking, looking down in obvious guilt.

"And here, they have the trial of Jesus before Pontius Pilate," said Greene, moving up to the next exhibit. Ericsson, still observing the details of *The Last Supper*, finally moved on to where Greene was standing, in the shadows, in front of the trial. Jesus stood on a raised platform, and there were several Roman soldiers also standing to the sides, armed with swords, spears and shields.

"I'm glad we'll be traveling together after this battle. I really believe we will have a much more fulfilling life on Easter Island," said Ericsson, putting a fatherly arm around the younger man's shoulders and looking into his dark, youthful face. There was a look of sublime innocence in Greene's countenance that Ericsson had admired from the moment they first met. It was this innocence that the elder man had lost many years before, but he wanted very much to recapture it.

Greene was staring ahead, observing the trial figures, when one of the figures moved! Yes, he could clearly see it. The wax soldier on the left was moving an arm under his tunic!

Before the gun could be drawn, Greene pushed Ericsson as hard as he could toward the other side of the room. "Get out! He's got a gun!" he shouted, and they both ran toward the exit, about fifty feet away.

"Stop! Traitors!" yelled Booth, pointing at Ericsson and pulling the trigger of his Colt pistol. The bullet ricocheted off one of the columns of granite next to Ericsson's head. Greene pushed the older man down to the ground, and

Ericsson gasped in panic. Others in the room stampeded for the exits, and the women and children screamed in terror.

The second shot hit Ericsson, and he grunted from the impact and the immediate rush of pain. "Christ! I'm hit!" he yelled.

Two policemen were running into the museum, their pistols drawn. The Roman soldier had disappeared behind the curtain on the raised platform. He had knocked down the wax figure of Jesus in his haste to depart.

CHAPTER THIRTY-TWO: HOSPITAL

March 7, 1862, New York City

John Ericsson was rushed over by police carriage to St. Luke's Hospital adjacent to Columbia University that was located at Madison Avenue and 49th Street. Lieutenant Greene rode over with him. The bullet had gone through his left arm, at the elbow, and the blood flow was stopped with a tourniquet. The police found the bullet lodged inside the wall, and they extracted it, hoping they could find a gun to match. Nobody had reported seeing any strangers near the Wax Museum, and there were no witnesses to the shooting other than Ericsson and Greene. Most of the people reacted when the shots were fired, but they did not see who fired.

Greene stood at the side of the bed as the doctor, a tall, thin and graying Union Officer named Laidlaw administered a dressing to Ericsson's arm. "He'll be recuperating for a few days, but he should be fine," said Dr. Laidlaw.

"Thank goodness for small favors!" said Ericsson, sitting up in the bed and scowling. "How am I supposed to be there when my ship gets underway to attack that Confederate monster in Hampton Roads?"

"Don't worry, Captain, we'll take care of everything. You must think of your health," said Greene, gazing out the window at a pigeon cooing on the ledge.

"Oh, you damned Romantic! What do you know about war?" Ericsson burst out, but he immediately regretted what he said. "I'm sorry, my boy. I'm just completely frustrated by being locked-in like this. I'm not used to being confined."

"You'll not get any better by leaving this hospital," said the doctor. "In fact, you might even get worse."

"All right, all right! I shall stay restrained in this mummy costume. Mister Greene, I want you to write to me every day you're aboard ship. I want to know every second's detail about your mission," said Ericsson, pulling at the long sling on his arm, which was attached to a suspension device connected to the wall.

"Don't worry, Captain. I'll give you a detailed report every day. Would you like Teletype messages as well, once we get into the heat of battle?" said Greene.

"Yes, by all means. I want to know exactly how the battle goes," Ericsson responded, and he winked at Greene, hoping to give the young man the inner message.

"I think Captain Ericsson now needs rest. There will be a Union guard stationed outside this door, day and night, until he gets well enough to leave," said the doctor, and he opened the door for Greene to leave.

Greene stood at the door a moment. "Sir, I am so sorry about what happened. I should have jumped in front of you. It's all my fault."

Ericsson laughed, "Nonsense! They were lying in wait for me, and nothing was going to stop that assassin from his duty. This is war, Mister Greene, and it most likely won't be our final confrontation with such devious forces. You stay safe and accomplish your mission. That's all I care about."

"Aye, aye, Sir!" said Greene, saluting and going out the door.

CHAPTER THIRTY-THREE: BUCK THE BERSERKER

March 8, 1862, Hampton Roads, Virginia

Admiral Franklin Buchanan came aboard the Virginia at 0630 hours. As the only veteran in the South who knew how the Union Navy conducted the business of war, "Old Buck" at 62, was a natural selection for the duty he was chosen to accomplish. His tall, Irish presence was immediately felt by the crew as he was piped aboard by the boatswain, one William Ranger, a former shopkeeper from Richmond, who had just that morning discovered what it was like to be aboard a vessel that moved on water. Buck was the first officer chosen to preside over the new Midshipmen's Academy at Annapolis, Maryland.

The crew that day believed they were going to go out to test their new ship, as the newly laid armor was still untried, and the cannons had yet to be test fired. When they saw their new Captain come aboard, they quickly began to rush around to get the ship ready for sea. However, this task was not a very pretty sight, as most of these men had never before served aboard a seagoing vessel. As Buck saluted the boatswain's mate and came aboard, he watched the men as they tripped all over themselves attempting to do the bidding of the petty officers, whose voices rang out with impatience all over the deck. "Get that gun crew amidships! Admiral's come aboard; we've got to heave to, men! Blast it all; what are you doing over there?" Many of the men were slopping grease on the slanted black iron casing, which made the vessel look, from a distance, like the roof of a huge barn that was belching smoke.

The grease was put there to deflect the cannon fire of the enemy.

Buchanan finally found Commander Catesby Ap Roger Jones on the bow, attempting to show a young seaman how to hoist the Command Flag of the James River Squadron. "Give her a pull, Sailor. Hand over hand, like this!"

Jones shouted, demonstrating for the lad.

"Commander, please come with me to my cabin. I need to speak with you before we get underway." Buchanan strode away from the two men, waving his hand forward, as if he were summoning his favorite hunting dog.

"Aye, Admiral! I'll be right there. Sailor, you finish this up. I'll have someone come to check on your work," said Jones, quickly following after his commanding officer who had already entered the side hatch leading to Officers' Country.

Admiral Buchanan was like a man possessed. He knew his plan, as he had spent many sleepless nights going over it in his mind like a repeating dream. He was the only officer who volunteered to command such a ship as the *Virginia*, and he did so because he had spoken with John Brooke, and he had seen his designs for the armor plating and the new rifled cannons to be placed on board. Buck knew it was the chance of a lifetime to command such a ship, and his daring nature drew him to the task with an increased fervor. There had been a terrific storm on March 7th, and Buck's plan to attack had to be postponed for the 8th.

When Commander Jones entered the Admiral's cabin, Buchanan was busy laying out a map of the Hampton Roads harbor. He began drawing a series of lines and "x" marks on the map, looking up at Jones from time to time, a crazed, almost demonic expression on his face. Jones could think of the only comparison he knew. The Flag Officer of the Confederate Navy looked like a Berserker, the Scandinavian warrior who was so ferocious in battle that he often shape-shifted into the form of a wolf, bear and other species of terrible animal. Jones expected Buchanan to morph into said beast at any moment.

"Commander, we will be attacking without mercy. There is no other way to defeat these frigates with our inexperienced crew. They have never experienced the ravages of war, and I'm concerned if they don't get their baptism of fire, then we may not be able to carry on." Buchanan moved his large hand over the first "x."

"This *Cumberland* will be our first victim. She's the only Yankee ship with a gun capable of penetrating our armor. I'm going to ram her, Commander. This will also give our men the baptism they will need. Until they can see what killing means—up close—they will never be any good to us." The Admiral's face took on a hard aspect, like a man who has resigned himself to death long ago.

"Buck, I know you're right about this. You were the head of the Naval Academy, and I trust your judgment about young men. But, don't you think you had better give these boys some kind of a speech before we attack the center of the blockade? They deserve your inspiration, at the least, don't you agree?"

Buchanan stood up straight and gazed steadily into the eyes of his old friend. "You know I wouldn't pass up a good speech, Jonesy. That's why they give us the big responsibilities, am I correct? Muster the men on the gun decks when we enter the harbor. I'll tell them just before we make our run at the *Cumberland*. We are making naval history, and they should never forget our cause."

"Yes, and when we pierce this ship with our fifteen- hundred pound ram, the others will come to her aid. These Yankees don't know the depths of our harbor, Admiral. They'll be grounded on the shoals in no time. They'll be like sitting ducks." Catesby smiled.

"And it's a fine day for Southern duck hunting, Jonesy.
And we've got the guns to blast em!"

* * *

Several foreign ships were anchored in Hampton Roads that day, and the officers aboard the sloop-of-war *Gassendi*, which had been moored there for months anticipating the confrontation between the Monitor and the Virginia, were the first to spot the giant ironclad as she moved past Craney Island. The captain of the *Gassendi* began a betting pool that morning, and most of the wagers were in favor of the giant *Virginia* and against the Union vessel. Rumor had circulated that Napoleon III had rejected the plans for the *Monitor* years before, and this new ship looked as menacing as a "half-submerged crocodile."

The Southern community had assembled along the banks of the Elizabeth and James Rivers to watch the first confrontation between a steam-powered ironclad and wooden ships. Many people were chattering, cheering and pointing at the monster as she moved into view around the peninsula on a clear, mild late-winter morning.

The powerful Federal blockading fleet had no warning that the giant Virginia was approaching. It was "wash day" for the Union Navy, and the ships' crew was blinded by the hundreds of uniforms—blues on the port side and whites on the starboard side—hanging from the rigging of each vessel.

Admiral Buchanan and Commander Jones watched this strange and colorful sight as they steamed into the harbor. Buck knew it was time to call the men to arms. "Commander, have the men assemble on the gun deck on the double!"

"Aye, aye, Admiral!" said Jones, and he gave the order to the Master-at-Arms. Soon, the entire crew, except for the underway watch, was assembled in uneven lines along the gigantic gun deck of the *Virginia*. The Boatswain blew his whistle, and Admiral Buchanan entered the hatch and stood in front of his men. Commander Jones stood at attention next to him.

"Men, this is not a drill. We are going after these damned blockaders and free our new Confederacy from this tyrannical monster! I know most of you have never seen combat on the water, and I am here to encourage you. The enemy would have you forget your families and your friends and give in to their domination. The South cannot exist without the freedom to determine our own destiny! These men we fight want to take this freedom from you, and we cannot permit it! Many men will lose their lives today, but one thing is certain. You have chosen to fight rather than to submit to tyranny. Now, for the sacred honor of our Confederate States of America, and for our families, who look to us for protection, you must now go to your guns!"

CHAPTER THIRTY-FOUR: ATTACK!

March 8, 1862, Hampton Roads, Virginia

The *Virginia's* immediate targets were the *U.S.S. Congress* and the *U.S.S. Cumberland*, both of which were sailing ships, without steam power, and therefore extremely vulnerable. Once Buchanan had disposed of those two, circumstances would dictate where he would strike next. There would be plenty of choices.

Also in the Roads for the Northern blockade were two sister ships of the *Merrimack*, the steam frigates *Minnesota* and *Roanoke*, as well as the steamer *Cambridge*, the store ship *Brandywine*, the sloop of war *St. Lawrence*, three coal ships, a hospital ship, five tugboats, a side-wheeler steamer, and a sailing bark, altogether a large, well-manned squadron mounting a total of 188 guns. Against this powerful force Buchanan had the ten-gun *Virginia*, along with a ragtag assortment of castoffs, including the twelve-gun *Patrick Henry*, the two-gun *Jamestown*, and the *Teaser*, *Beaufort*, and *Raleigh*, all of one gun, for a total of twenty-seven guns.

Buchanan had received a letter from Confederate Naval Secretary Mallory dated March 7 that dramatically expressed the high hopes for the *Virginia* held by the South, and incorporated the worst fears of the North: "I submit for your consideration the attack of New York by the *Virginia*. Can the *Virginia* steam to New York and attack and burn the city? She can, I doubt not, pass Old Point safely, and in good weather and a smooth sea she could doubtless go to New York. Once in the bay she could shell and burn the city and the shipping. Such an event would eclipse all the glories of all the combats of the sea, would place every man in it preeminently high, and would strike a blow from which the enemy could never recover. Peace would inevitably follow. Bankers would withdraw their capital from the city, the Brooklyn navy-yard and its magazines and all the lower part of the city would be destroyed, and such an event, by a single ship, would do more to achieve an immediate independence than would the results of many campaigns. Can the ship go there? Please give me your views."

This one letter had given Buck the impetus he needed to plan his attack. Now, as he crossed the waters of the Hampton Roads harbor, he momentarily had visions of completing the Secretary's request. However, he also knew that there was another threat from the Yankees that was probably on its way at that very moment. John Ericsson's craft, the *Monitor*, was also an ironclad, and she was fast enough and small enough to maneuver the Roads much easier than his bulky giant. The North had put her money into developing a ship that had a revolving turret instead of many guns, and this frightened Buck. He had taught Physics at the Naval Academy, and he knew his ship was too low in the water to be able to do anything to counter a revolving cannon. His only hope would be to destroy the blockade before the *Monitor* arrived, and then see about getting the *Virginia* into Norfolk to be outfitted for a possible run up to New York.

As the sailors on board the Cumberland saw the giant ship coming at them, they really didn't know what was happening. Their superiors had not prepared them for what they now saw. The first lookout to spot her, after the U.S.S. Congress, which was passed on the way, fired a warning signal, said to his officer-of-the-deck, "Will you look here at this, Sir? Don't she look like some half-submerged crocodile comin' at us?"

When the *Virginia* struck the starboard superstructure of the *Cumberland*, just under the fore rigging, Admiral Franklin Buchanan began to shout and pace the gun decks, urging his men forward. The daring assault had opened a seven-foot-wide wound in the Union ship's side. "We've got her now, men! Keep firing! She'll go down!"

Smoke from the cannon fire exchange enveloped both ships, but on board the *Cumberland*, men were being burned alive; slipping in the blood and gore and screaming, they flung themselves off the ship by the dozens, small, momentary phoenixes in the waters off Newport News. The Union cannon fire blew the ironclad's launches away, riddled its smokestack and shot off its anchors as well as the muzzles of two of her guns, but they could not penetrate her armor. And, amidst it all, Buchanan kept up his relentless cry, "She's almost done for, men! Keep firing!"

Panic began to sweep the crew of the *Virginia* when the ram would not pull out of the hull of the *Cumberland*. "We're all a-gonna drown!" a young seaman yelled, and he left his post at one of the cannons, and attempted to desert ship. Commander Jones ran over to him and shouted, "Get back to your gun, sailor, or I'll have you arrested!" The sailor, more frightened of his commanding officer, did what he was told, but the *Virginia* seemed to be stuck for good inside the sinking enemy vessel.

The greased sides of the *Virginia* were so hot from the ricocheting shells that the men could hear the iron plates crackle and pop. She literally seemed to be frying, from stem to stern.

One sailor took a big whiff of the odor and said, "Jack, don't this smell like hell?"

"It sure does, and I think we'll all be there in a few minutes," said another.

Just when it seemed both ships were going to go under, a huge tidal swell hit the ships, and the resulting motion broke the ram off inside the *Cumberland*. When this happened, the *Virginia* was released from her death-grip, and was free to pull back from certain destruction.

"Back her down slowly," Jones yelled to the enginemen, below decks. Gradually, the giant ironclad pulled away from the sinking *Cumberland*, until she was again back in the channel. Sailors on board the *Virginia* watched, in stupefied rapture, as the former champion of the United States Navy slipped slowly under the waves, settling to the bottom of the James River just after 3:35 PM. At least 121 sailors died with her, including many wounded who went down with the ship.

Commander Jones was right about the other ships getting stranded in the shoals. As the Virginia turned around to attack, she confronted what looked like a row of wounded geese stuck in the shallows of Hampton Roads. In addition to the Congress, which was stranded off Newport News Point, the frigates *Minnesota*, *Roanoke*, and *St. Lawrence* had all run aground at Hampton Flats while attempting to come to aid of their stricken sister, the *Cumberland*.

As she was unable to bring any but her stern guns to bear, the nearby Congress became the *Virginia's* next victim. Once again, Buchanan began to urge his men on. "We'll get us another one, men! Get to those guns and be ready to fire at my command!" The ironclad then made her slow journey toward the waiting frigate, trapped in the mud of the flats.

"Fire at will!" yelled Buchanan, and the cannons began to blast out their fury on the hapless Congress. For a solid hour, the wooden frigate was unable to return any fire, and the damage was tremendous. Many fires were ignited, and men were diving from the ship in flames. Finally, the ship's captain raised the white flag of surrender.

Two Confederate gunboats, seeing the Congress's flag of capitulation, moved next to the ship to remove the Union wounded and take them prisoner. Suddenly, without warning, a unit of Federal soldiers onshore began shooting at the sailors from the gunboats as they tried to rescue the survivors on the *Congress*. Several sailors fell over the railing, shot to death.

Buchanan was furious! He pushed his way through the smoke and sailors to the top of the *Virginia's* deck, so he could better see what was happening. "Destroy that ship!" he shouted, going berserk. "They're firing on her white flag!" Admiral Franklin Buchanan was still cursing from the shot-riddled railing when a musket ball from one of the guns of the onshore Union soldiers struck him in the right thigh.

"Jonesy! It seems as though we've ruffled those ducks' feathers. They're now firing back!" said Buchanan, and he slumped to the ground. Two sailors rushed to his aid and dragged him to safety. As he was being dragged, Buck shouted to his executive officer, Catesby Jones, "Plug hot shot into her and don't leave her until she's afire!"

Jones carried out his orders swiftly, and, in minutes, the *Congress* was an inferno. Then, with less than an hour of daylight remaining, Jones backed the *Virginia* off and headed toward the last duck on the pond: the *Minnesota*.

However, the same bad luck that captured the *Congress* in the mud with nowhere to turn, had turned to fortune for the *Minnesota*, as the Union frigate was now trapped off Salter's Creek, and when the *Virginia* attempted to approach, Jones quickly realized he could never get close enough to the Yankee ship to inflict mortal damage. The giant ironclad was too heavy in the water.

Thwarted by the coming darkness and the ebbing tide, Jones fired upon the *Minnesota* for several minutes, from a distance, but he then broke away and headed back toward Sewell's Point. The tide would come again tomorrow, and the frigate would still be there. Hopefully, Jones thought, he would be able to send her to the bottom before that blasted new ironclad, the *Monitor*, showed her colors in the Roads.

That night, Jones counted his losses at two men dead and nine wounded, including Admiral Franklin Buchanan. Nearly 100 indentations from the enemy's cannons pockmarked his vessel's armor. The Union, on the other hand, suffered more than 280 casualties all told, as well as the total destruction of two of the most important ships blocking the South's central tactical harbor. Jones was proud of his men, and he was proud of the Confederate States of America.

CHAPTER THIRTY-FIVE: PANIC IN WASHINGTON AND LONDON

Washington, D. C., March 8, 1862

The telegraph lines to Washington, D. C. were buzzing with the news about the attack on the Union blockade in *Virginia*. The horrible loss of the two big ships in a few short hours demonstrated the awesome power of the South's new super weapon. Secretary of War Edwin M. Stanton, who heard the reports early Sunday morning, prepared to have barges sunk in the Potomac River for the protection of the capitol. In a gloomy meeting with President Lincoln and his cabinet, Stanton said, "The whole character of war has changed."

Several times during this meeting, Lincoln and Stanton went to the window and looked out over the river. "Mister President, the danger is clear and present. This giant *Virginia* could send a cannonball through this window at any moment."

Secretary of the Navy, Gideon Welles, had a calmer demeanor and a cooler head. "Our intelligence says this craft was carrying too much armor to finish off the *Minnesota*, which had run aground at Salter's Creek. How can this ship make it up the Potomac? She would run aground before she could get out of Hampton Roads."

William Seward, the vain Secretary of State who had been defeated by Lincoln in the Republican primaries, agreed. "Yes, we have more problems with France and England. They were observing the battle in Virginia and were going to give the South assistance, depending on how well this ironclad fared against us. If the Rebels get aid from Europe, then we will surely have more trouble than we need right now."

Lincoln picked-up the little model of the *U.S.S. Monitor* from his desk, stood up and walked to the window again. "Where is our little ironclad right now, Gideon? This *Monitor*," he said, gazing out at the Potomac, and turning the tiny turret gun around and around in small circles.

Welles perked up. "She was held up in a storm, but if all goes well, she should arrive at Hampton Roads tomorrow morning, Mister President."

Lincoln smiled. "My bones tell me our cheese box on a raft will stop this *Virginia*. Admiral Buchanan was wounded and is no longer calling the shots on the *Merrimack*. This Catesby Jones knows little or nothing about our secret ironclad. Could be this Ericsson's Folly just might run up *Virginia's* skirt and whistle Dixie!"

* * *

London, England, March 8, 1862

Penelope Andrews was taking a bath when Amelia Ericsson burst into the house. She ran right past Smythe, the family butler, and opened the door. She was quite out of breath, and her chest was heaving. "Pen, you've got to come with me! John's been shot, and he's in hospital in New York. Somebody tried to assassinate him!"

Penelope sat up in the tub and took a towel from her friend. She stood up and wrapped the towel around her dripping torso. "What? Who would do such a thing?" she asked, as she stepped gingerly out of the water.

"The bloody government wouldn't tell me much. They just said John had been shot, and he would be recuperating at the St. Luke's Hospital of Columbia University. Oh, Penny, I must go to John. I would never forgive myself if something were to happen," her voice trailed off, and she began to sob deeply. "I've been such a horrible wife! I should have stayed with him in America, but I am spoiled rotten!"

Penelope Andrews took her friend by the arm and led her over to the couch inside the spacious lavatory. "Come, sit. Yes, of course I'll go with you to America. It shall be our adventure! It's time I tracked down my Walter and see what he's up to. We'll have a grand time together, Amelia!"

The younger Penelope comforted the older woman for some time, and they both made a decision to book the first passage to America they could arrange. War could not stop their love, and it most certainly would not come between them and their men. However, they knew they would have to proceed clandestinely, as their parents would not be cooperative. These were dangerous times, and two British women alone in a country under siege was not what parents desire of their only daughters. But, to the two young women, this was an escapade of a lifetime.

CHAPTER THIRTY-SIX: THE ARRIVAL OF THE IRON MAIDEN

March 9, 1862, Hampton Roads, Virginia

Chip Jefferson had enjoyed the trip down to Hampton Roads—even the storm—and he was quite excited about the prospects of being in battle against the giant Confederate ship, the *Virginia*. He followed the Captain around like his shadow, and he asked him many questions about what would happen when they confronted the enemy. Captain Worden was very patient, and he answered Chip's questions with tolerance and kindness. In fact, the Captain was a bit concerned with having such a young man on board during these dangerous times.

This concern hit a high point when Chip picked up a telegram from the War Department that lay on the Captain's wardroom table. The contents discussed what had happened in Hampton Roads on March 8, and Chip's eyes grew wide with wonder as he read about the "Union ships sunk and hundreds of men killed," and his imagination became infused with pictures of his own body being torn in two by a gigantic cannon shell that had a face that looked like John Ericsson's. Chip still believed the inventor was up to no good, and he was keeping up his surveillance of Lieutenant Greene and his whereabouts on the ship.

Mister Greene was the Executive Officer, and his combat duty was to command the revolving turret guns, the first such inventions to be used in war. The South had only one, 11-inch Dahlgren in all of Hampton Roads, and their little *Monitor* had two sitting inside her turret. However, Greene also knew that the key to his escape to Easter Island was how well he could keep those guns from hitting anything on the *Virginia*, which would deliver a deathblow. He had stayed up every night on the way down from New York, trying to plot his methods, and he at last believed he could pull it off without anyone getting suspicious. The final test would be combat, and Greene also believed anything could happen when the firing began. Captain Ericsson had told him to "stay focused on your purpose," and so Greene behaved in a very focused manner. He was brief and direct with his men, and he was also without any humor, and this made him an unpopular sort aboard the small vessel. Gone were his volumes of Whitman and Emerson, and he no longer wrote in his journal. Instead, he had become a man on a mission, and his job was a totally private one, known only to him and to John Ericsson.

When they arrived at their battle station, at eleven p.m. on March 8, the crew of the *Monitor* was nervous, and they also knew they had to stop this *Virginia* from doing any more damage. Captain Worden had called them all to general quarters on the previous day, in order to explain their purpose for being at Hampton Roads.

"Men, events in history call us to action. Today, the combined forces of the rebellious Confederacy attacked us, and two of our Union's frigates, the *Cumberland* and the *Congress*, have been destroyed. It is the worst day in American naval history, and our duty is to see to it that no more ships or lives are lost to this juggernaut of insanity called the *C.S.S. Virginia*.

I need all of your mental and physical attention to do this job. We shall overcome for the sake of our United States of America, and for the sake of freedom from slavery!" All the men cheered, and Chip felt proud to be serving under such a distinguished captain.

However, between one and two a.m., on March 9, 1862, as the little *Monitor* was sailing into Hampton Roads, the aft weapons magazine on board the *Congress* blew up, sending thousands of luminous missiles into the gloomy sky. It almost looked like a Fourth of July celebration, if the crew had not known about the Rebel ironclad and what she had done to the *Congress* that morning. The men did not sleep much at all that evening, as they were anchored beside the last remaining frigate, the *Minnesota*. All those aboard the Union blockade's guardian knew that they were the only hope of protection for this ship against the demon giant, the *Merrimack*.

* * *

Captain Catesby Jones was now commanding officer of the *Virginia*, and as he steamed out of the protection of Sewell's Point, he remembered the tale of his old Surgeon, John Mason, aged 62, who reported seeing the little *Monitor* the previous night when the *Congress* blew up. "She was like a black cat crossing in front of that exploding Yankee ship. I've never seen a stranger looking craft! She reminded me of the torture instrument used in Nuremberg, Germany, called the Iron Maiden. I expect inside that black ship there are men who are being suffocated or torn apart by metal spikes. I wouldn't put it past those Yanks to torture their own men!"

That evening, at officers' mess, Doctor Mason treated the group with his after-dinner tale about the medieval torture device, the Iron Maiden, described in a novel he had in his possession called *The Blood Countess*. Doctor Mason read to the other men from the book, and they wondered together in transfixed attention. "Sharing the room with the rack wheel at the Thurzo was an iron maiden, a metal statue of a woman. This was a great example of this sort of object, a unique construction from one of Germany's greatest clock makers. She had breasts, arms, legs, and two faces, one in front and one in back. The front face was round, with oval eyes that peered down with a look that could be alternately filled with pity and enigmatically amused. The small mouth was finely etched with hair-thin wrinkles. The eyes in the back face were closed, but the mouth was slightly open, as if she was about to whisper something. Long fine blond hair covered her head and came down in two braids over her ears, past her waist. She was dressed in a ballooning dress of worn velvet folded thousands of times, spilling over her feet. Her bare breasts were round and shiny from the generations of furtive schoolchildren who had rubbed them on visits to the museum. Two strands of pearls and a gold necklace with a black stone on the end were draped about her curved swan's neck. She opened from the front... along a seam between her breasts that was invisible when she was closed. The trigger that caused her to open was hidden in the black stone at the end of the gold chain. When the stone was pressed, her hands moved to embrace the person who had set off the hidden mechanism. When she opened, she revealed a hollow interior with sharp iron spikes. Her arms pulled in her victim, and then she closed up, piercing her prey."

Jones stood up after the reading, stretched, and addressed his fellow officers, "I'm turning in now, gentlemen. If the Union is sending us contraptions like this, then I'll need a good night's rest to greet such a woman!"

When he and his crew retired that night, they hoped to accomplish a lot the next day. The *Minnesota* was aground, the *Roanoke* and *St. Lawrence* had retired below Old Point, and the enemy was greatly demoralized. This *Monitor* was but a rumor, but the purpose was clear for Jones. If he did not destroy the rest of the blockade, then the cause of the South would be set back, perhaps indefinitely.

It was now 0800 hours, and the James River Squadron was under weigh. Jones steered his vessel directly toward the *Minnesota*, closely attended by the *Patrick Henry*. The little black demon was about a third of a mile distant when it began to fire. Jones decided to confront her, as he could not get a clear broadside to fire at the *Minnesota*. The blasted Ericsson contraption was blocking the way!

* * *

Greene could see her from his vantage point inside the gun turret. The iron pressing in upon him from all sides, the booming backfire of the two cannons splitting his eardrums, and the heat from the pressure build up were all combining to make him lose focus. *I can't let them hit the ship*, he thought, gripping onto the bulkhead for dear life.

* * *

On the previous day, Greene had written in his journal, for the first time, in order to maintain his focus on events: It was at the close of this dispiriting trial trip, in which all hands had been exhausted in their efforts to keep the novel craft afloat, that the *Monitor* passed Cape Henry at 4 P. M. on Saturday, March 8th. At this point was heard the distant booming of heavy guns, which our captain rightly judged to be an engagement with the *Merrimack*, twenty miles away. He at once ordered the vessel stripped of her sea-rig, the turret keyed up, and every preparation made for battle. As we approached Hampton Roads we could see the fine old *Congress* burning brightly, and soon a pilot came on board and told of the arrival of the *Merrimack*, the disaster to the *Cumberland* and the *Congress*, and the dismay of the Union forces. The *Monitor* was pushed with all haste, and reached the *Roanoke* (Captain Marston), anchored in the Roads, at 9 A. M. Worden immediately reported his arrival to Captain Marston, who suggested that he should go to the assistance of the *Minnesota*, then aground off Newport News. As no pilot was available, Captain Worden accepted the volunteer services of Acting Master Samuel Howard, who earnestly sought the duty. An atmosphere of gloom pervaded the fleet, and the pygmy aspect of the newcomer did not inspire confidence among those who had witnessed the destruction of the day before. Skillfully piloted by Howard, we proceeded on our way, our path illuminated by the blaze of the *Congress*. Reaching the *Minnesota*, hard and fast aground, near midnight, we anchored, and Worden reported to Captain Van Brunt. Between 1 and 2 A. M. the *Congress* blew up, not instantaneously, but successively; her powder-tanks seemed to explode, each shower of sparks rivaling the other in its height, until they appeared to reach the zenith —— a grand but mournful sight. Near us, too, lay the *Cumberland* at the bottom of the river, with her silent crew of brave men, who died while fighting, their guns to the water's edge, and whose colors were still flying at the peak

* * *

The dreary night of March 8 dragged slowly on; the officers and crew were up and alert, ready for any emergency. At daylight on Sunday the Merrimack and her consorts were discovered at anchor near Sewall's Point. At about half-past seven o'clock the enemy's vessels got under way and steered in the direction of the *Minnesota*. At the same time the *Monitor* got under way, and her officers and crew took their stations for battle. Captain Van Brunt officially reported, "I made signal to the *Monitor* to attack the enemy," but

Captain Worden required no signal.

The pilot house of the *Monitor* was situated well forward, near the bow; it was a wrought iron structure, built of logs of iron nine inches thick, bolted through the corners, and covered with an iron plate two inches thick, which was not fastened down, but was kept in place merely by its weight. The sight-holes or slits were made by inserting quarter-inch plates at the corners between the upper set of logs and the next below. The structure projected four feet above the deck, and was barely large enough inside to hold three men standing. It presented a flat surface on all sides and on top. The steering wheel was secured to one of the logs on the front side.

Captain Worden took his station in the pilot house, and by his side were Howard, the pilot, and Peter Williams, quartermaster, who steered the vessel throughout the engagement. Lieutenant Greene's place was in the turret, to work and fight the guns; with him were Stodder and Stimers and sixteen brawny men, eight to each gun. John Stocking, boatswain's mate, and Thomas Lochrane, seaman, were gun-captains. Engineering Officer Isaac Newton and his assistants were in the engine and fire rooms, to manipulate the boilers and engines. Webber had charge of the powder division on the berth-deck, and Joseph Crown, gunner's mate, rendered valuable service in connection with this duty.

The physical condition of the officers and men of the two ships at this time was in striking contrast. The *Merrimack* had passed the night quietly near Sewall's Point, her people enjoying rest and sleep, elated by thoughts of the victory they had achieved that day, and cheered by the prospects of another easy victory on the morrow. The *Monitor* had barely escaped shipwreck twice within the last thirty-six hours, and since Friday morning, forty-eight hours before, few if any of those on board had closed their eyes in sleep or had anything to eat but hard bread, as cooking was impossible; she was surrounded by wrecks and disaster, and her efficiency in action had yet to be proved.

Worden lost no time in bringing it to test. Getting his ship under way, he steered direct for the enemy's vessels, in order to meet and engage them as far as possible from the *Minnesota*. As he approached, the wooden vessels quickly turned and left. Captain Worden, to the astonishment of Captain Van Brunt (as he stated later in his official report), made straight for the *Merrimack*, which had already commenced firing; and when he came within short range, he changed his course so as to come alongside of her, stopped the engine, and gave the order, "Commence firing!" Lieutenant Greene moved up the port, ran out the gun, and, taking deliberate aim, pulled the lockstring. The *Merrimack* was quick to reply, returning a rattling broadside (for she had ten guns to the *Monitor's* two), and the battle fairly began. The turret and other parts of the ship were heavily struck, but the shots did not penetrate; the tower was intact, and it continued to revolve. A look of confidence passed over the men's faces, and they believed the *Merrimack* would not repeat the work she had accomplished the day before.

The fight continued with the exchange of broadsides as fast as the guns could be served and at very short range, the distance between the vessels frequently being not more than a few yards. Worden skillfully maneuvered his quick-turning vessel, trying to find some vulnerable point in his adversary. Once he made a dash at her stern, hoping to disable her screw, which he thought he missed by not more than two feet. Shots ripped the iron of the *Merrimack*, while the reverberation of her shots against the tower caused anything but a pleasant sensation. While Stodder, who was stationed at the machine, which controlled the revolving motion of the turret, was incautiously leaning against the side of the tower, a large shot struck in the vicinity and disabled him. He left the turret and went below, and Stimers, who had assisted him, continued to do the work.

As the engagement continued, the working of the turret was not altogether satisfactory. It was difficult to start it revolving, or, when once started, to stop it, on account of the imperfections of the novel machinery, which was now undergoing its first trial. Stimers was an active, muscular man, and did his utmost to control the motion of the turret; but, in spite of his efforts, it was difficult if not impossible to secure accurate firing. The conditions were very different from those of an ordinary broadside gun, under which the crew had been trained on wooden ships. The only view of the world outside of the tower was over the muzzles of the guns, which cleared the ports by a few inches only. When the guns were run in, heavy iron pendulums, pierced with small holes to allow the iron rammer and sponge handles to protrude while they were in use, covered the portholes. To hoist these pendulums required the entire gun's crew and vastly increased the work inside the turret.

* * *

Later, Dana Greene wrote in his letter to John Ericsson: The effect upon one shut up in a revolving drum is perplexing, and it is not a simple matter to keep the bearings. White marks had been placed upon the stationary deck immediately below the turret to indicate the direction of the starboard and port sides, and the bow and stern; but these marks were obliterated early in the action. I would continually ask the captain, "How does the *Merrimack* bear?" He replied, "On the starboard- beam, " or "On the port-quarter," as the case might be. Then the difficulty was to determine the direction of the starboard-beam, or port-quarter, or any other bearing. It finally resulted, that when a gun was ready for firing, the turret would be started on its revolving journey in search of the target, and when found it was taken "on the fly," because the turret could not be accurately controlled. Once the *Merrimack* tried to ram us; but Worden avoided the direct impact by the skillful use of the helm, and she struck a glancing blow, which did no damage. At the instant of collision I planted a solid one-hundred-and- eighty-pound shot fair and square upon the forward part of her casemate. Had the gun been loaded with thirty pounds of powder, which was the charge subsequently used with similar guns, it is probable that this shot would have penetrated her armor; but the charge being limited to fifteen pounds, in accordance with peremptory orders to that effect from the Navy Department, the shot rebounded without doing any more damage than possibly to start some of the beams of her armor-backing. The *Merrimack*, also, had only shells——no solid shot— and had either of us had such ammunition, the result would have been quite different!

* * *

During the battle, Chip was called to the pilot house to deliver a message to Captain Worden. Chip's imagination took off as he braved his way on deck. He could see the giant enemy ironclad looming above them, like a fantastic metal horror from his dreams, and he could hear the cannons firing at them, shells hitting nearby and whizzing on top of the water toward him. *Oh Lord, if you get me out of this, I swear, I will go to church with Momma and Daddy every Sunday!* Chip thought, as he neared the hatch leading into the pilot house. It was at that moment, when he was just about to enter that a large shell from the enemy hit the top of one of the slits in the pilot house bulkhead. Chip could hear a scream from inside, and when he entered, and the smoke cleared, he saw a sight that would haunt his memory forever after. Captain John Worden, his protector, the protector of Freedom for his race, was blinded——covering his eyes, dripping with blood—yelling, like a man possessed!

* * *

Later, Dana Greene wrote about the event, in more detail, in his letter to Ericsson: "When that vessel rammed the *Cumberland* her iron ram, or beak, was broken off and left in that vessel. This ram was of cast-iron, wedge-shaped, about fifteen hundred pounds in weight, two feet under water, and projecting two and a half feet from the stem. A ram of this description, had it been intact, would have struck the *Merrimack* at that part of the upper hull where the armor and backing were thickest. It is very doubtful if, under any headway that the *Merrimack* could have acquired at such short range, this ram could have done any injury to this part of the vessel That it could by no possibility have reached the thin lower hull is evident from a glance at the drawing of the *Monitor*, the overhang or upper hull being constructed for the express purpose of protecting the vital part of the vessel

"The battle between us continued at close quarters without apparent damage to either side. After a time, the supply of shot in the turret being exhausted, Worden hauled off for about fifteen minutes to replenish. The serving of the cartridges, weighing but fifteen pounds, was a matter of no difficulty; but the hoisting of the heavy shot was a slow and tedious operation, it being necessary that the turret should remain stationary, in order that the two scuttles, one in the deck and the other in the floor of the turret, should be in line. Worden took advantage of the lull, and passed through the porthole upon the deck outside to get a better view of the situation. He soon renewed the attack, and the contest continued as before.

"Two important points were constantly kept in mind: first, to prevent the enemy's projectiles from entering the turret through the port-holes, — for the explosion of a shell inside, by disabling the men at the guns, would have ended the fight, there being no relief gun's crews on board; second, not to fire into our own pilot-house. A careless or impatient hand, during the confusion arising from the whirligig motion of the tower, might let slip one of our big shot against the pilot house. For this and other reasons, I fired every gun while I remained in the turret.

"Soon after noon a shell from the enemy's gun, the muzzle not ten yards distant, struck the forward side of the pilot house directly in the sight-hole, or slit, and exploded, cracking the second iron log and partly lifting the top, leaving an opening. Worden was standing immediately behind this spot, and received in his face the force of the blow, which partly stunned him, and, filling his eyes with powder, utterly blinded him. Only those in the pilot house and its immediate vicinity knew the injury. The flood of light rushing through the top of the pilot house, now partly open, caused Worden, blind as he was, to believe that the pilot house was seriously injured, if not destroyed; he therefore gave orders to "put the helm to starboard and sheer off." Thus the *Monitor* retired temporarily from the action, in order to ascertain the extent of the injuries she had received. At the same time Worden sent for me, and leaving Stimers the only officer in the turret, I went forward at once, and found him standing at the foot of the ladder leading to the pilot house.

"He was a ghastly sight, with his eyes closed and the blood apparently rushing from every pore in the upper part of his face. He told me that he was seriously wounded, and directed me to take command. I assisted in leading him to a sofa in his cabin, where he was tenderly cared for by Doctor Logue, and then I assumed command. Blind and suffering as he was, Worden's fortitude never forsook him; he frequently asked from his bed of pain of the progress of affairs, and when told that the Minnesota was saved, he said, 'Then I can die happy.'

"When I reached my station in the pilot house, I found that the iron log was fractured and the top partly open; but the steering gear was still intact, and the pilot house was not totally destroyed, as had been feared. In the confusion of the moment resulting from so serious an injury to the commanding officer, the *Monitor* had been moving without direction. Exactly how much time elapsed from the moment that Worden was wounded until I had reached the pilot house and completed the examination of the injury at that point, and determined what course to pursue in the damaged condition of the vessel, it is impossible to state; but it could hardly have exceeded twenty minutes at the utmost. During this time the *Merrimack*, which was leaking badly, had started in the direction of the Elizabeth River; and, on taking my station in the pilot house and turning the vessel's head in the direction of the *Merrimack*, I saw that she was already in retreat. A few shots were fired at the retiring vessel, and she continued on to Norfolk I returned with the *Monitor* to the side of the *Minnesota*, where preparations were being made to abandon the ship, which was still aground. Shortly afterward Worden was transferred to a tug, and that night he was carried to Washington."

* * *

At the end of the day, both sides believed they had won. However, in New York City, Inventor John Ericsson had received a cable from Assistant Naval Secretary G. V. Fox. In it, the details of the battle were observed, but it was also stated that it had been the poor construction of the pilot house by Captain Ericsson that led to blinding of Captain Worden and the resulting escape of the *Merrimack*.

Ericsson, afraid that his contract for more *Monitor*-class ships would be lost, and with it the return of his Amelia, dashed off a letter explaining the real reason for the Monitor turning tail after the Captain was blinded. In it, Ericsson offered up his innocent lamb, Lieutenant Samuel Dana Greene:

My Dear Sir:

No one knows better than yourself the shortcomings of that fight, ended at the moment the crew had become well trained, and the machinery got in good working order. Why? Because you had a miserable executive officer, one Lieutenant Samuel D. Greene, who, in place of jumping into the pilot house when Worden was blinded, ran away with his impregnable vessel. The displacements of the plate of the pilot house, which I had designed principally to keep out spray in bad weather, was really an advantage, by allowing fresh air to enter the cramped iron walled cabin—certainly that displacement offered no excuse for discontinuing the fight.

John Ericsson, New York City

* * *

When Dana Greene received word of the letter from Ericsson, he was crestfallen. He was now the captain of the Monitor, but he was also gradually retreating back into his private world of Whitman and the Transcendentalists. One evening, he called Chip into his cabin and read to him his new philosophy of life. "Son, I want you to understand that all of the eternal heavens are contained inside you! Isn't that fantastic? Wherever we go, the entire universe goes with us. Listen to this passage about it from the poet, Walt Whitman, as he teaches us: 'Abstract yourself from this book; realize where you are at present located, the point you stand that is now to you the centre of all. Look up overhead, think of space stretching out, think of all the unnumbered orbs wheeling safely there, invisible to us by day, some visible by night . . . Spend some minutes faithfully in this exercise. Then again realize yourself upon the earth, at the particular point you now occupy . . . Seize these firmly in your mind, pass freely over immense distances. Turn your face a moment thither. Fix definitely the direction and the idea of the distances of separate sections of your own country, also of England, the Mediterranean Sea, Cape Horn, Easter Island, the North Pole, and such like distant places.'"

Chip stared at his new captain for a moment, and then he smiled. "Thank you, Mister Greene. I think I understand you. I have been doing that since I was a little slave boy. You see, we needed to keep our imaginations on higher things than in this here life."

Greene closed the book, put his arm around the youth's shoulders, and they both went to dinner. Chip, in contrast, was thinking, Now I know you're a crazy man, and I'll be keeping my eye on you! You ran away from battle, and now you 're talking crazy about the stars. I want Captain Worden - Ishmael— not you, Mister Starbuck!

CHAPTER THIRTY-SEVEN: ACCIDENTAL MEETING

New York City, April 2, 1862

Penelope and Amelia landed at New York Harbor on the *H.M.S. Europa*, of the Cunard Steamship Line, and immediately took a Hansom cab to Columbia University. They chatted continuously all the way there, wondering about John's health, speculating as to the whereabouts of Walter, and gazing out the window at the wartime streets of America. When they arrived at St. Luke's, Penelope was going on about a man on the voyage who kept spitting brown tobacco juice in her presence during dinner. "It was quite disgusting! When I told the gentleman to desist, he simply twirled his mustaches, winked, and said, 'I sell tobacco to all your countrymen, Madame. If I were to desist, then I would not be an ambassador tradesman of the Carolinas!' I wanted to report him to Captain Early, but then I recalled that Walter was running tobacco for those men in the South, and thus I kept to myself."

Inside the hospital, they discovered that John had checked out two days prior, and he was now back at his lodgings on Beech Street near Canal, and they told their driver as much. He took off in a flurry of hooves and dust. Amelia was distressed about John leaving the hospital without waiting for her. He knew she was to be arriving, as her ship was on schedule, and she wondered whatever could have caused him to leave so abruptly.

On the ride over, the cab passed a tavern on Broadway called the Union Blockade. Penelope noticed a man coming out of the front entrance, and she shouted up at the driver, "Stop! Driver! It's Walter, my fiancé! Oh, please, stop!"

The two horses came to a halt, and Penelope sprang from the coach like a woman possessed. She ran up to the tall young man and turned him around.

"Walter?" she asked, but when he turned, she saw it was not he. It was another, less distinguished gentleman, who was obviously quite inebriated. "You're not Walter," she said.

"Hey, little lady. Can you spare some change for a man in need?" said the drunk.

Penelope opened her purse and handed the man a pound note, forgetting that she had yet to exchange her money for American currency. However, as he was too drunk to really notice, he took the bill and staggered back toward the tavern entrance.

When Penelope was back inside the hansom, she looked embarrassed. "I was certain it was my Walter. I suppose it's all the fatigue from our voyage and stress about his being over here.

"Driver, you may proceed to Beech Street!" Amelia directed, and the cab took off once more.

* * *

"Darling!" Amelia gasped, as she entered John Ericsson's residence on Beech Street. John was in his workroom, his usual domain, and his Lead Draftsman, Charles McCord, was there also. Ericsson turned from his bench and a look of pure joy filled his tired features as he gazed upon the woman for whom he had been working so hard for these many months.

"Amelia! You've come, at long last!" he said, taking her diminutive waist into his hands and pulling her toward him. He could smell her Parisian essence, and the softness of her cheek against his muttonchops was like an elixir of life to his aging body. John held her at arm's length for several moments, and then said, "You shall never have to leave again, my dearest. I've done it! The United States Government has agreed to purchase 500 *Monitor*-class ships from me, and we were busy working up the plans before you became the luscious frosting on our celebratory cake."

Amelia was overcome with delight. "Oh, John, I told you it would all work out. Didn't I? You were always such a pessimistic soul. You need me around to keep you in high spirits!"

"You didn't tell me your husband was such a genius. And a very handsome gentleman as well!" said Penelope.

Amelia's face turned crimson. "Oh, Pen! I'm so sorry! John, this is my best friend and confidant, Penelope Andrews. She has been very kind to me these last few weeks, giving me solace in the West End, as this horrid war rages on over here in the colonies. Her fiancé, Walter Sinclair, is also over here in some kind of business with the war. We hope to look him up for dear Pen, as she is almost as lovelorn as I," Amelia said, and she kissed her husband warmly.

John walked over and took Penelope's hands. "Any friend of my Amelia's is immediately a friend of mine. How was your voyage, my dear?"

"We had an uneventful voyage, Captain. There do seem to be many men making enterprise from this war, however. I dare say you have been one of the lucky ones to profit from this tragic circumstance. Does this cause you any ill feelings?" said Penelope, in her usual audacious manner.

"My, Amelia! I do like your new friend. She gets right down to business. No, Penelope, I have long ago given up my ill feelings about such things as man's inhumanity toward man. However, I do believe in finding one's own place on this earth, where it is possible to live in moderately safe and healthy splendor. This war boon has provided my wife and me with the means to become castaways from these ill feelings. It shall now be only a matter of planning and of patience. The time is at hand for us to find our own paradise. Isn't that our plan, Amelia?" asked John.

"Yes, when John was shot, we agreed to escape from this insanity as soon as we could muster the resources. If we can find passage, we shall travel away to our island in the sun. It shall, indeed, be our own paradise! I love you so much, John," she said, both of her white arms winding around Ericsson's wide waist like a young girl hugging a trained bear.

"Captain, why don't we stop working and take these fine ladies out on the town for dinner?" Charles McCord spoke for the first time.

Penelope brightened at once. "Yes! I am certainly up for a pint of something and a big, juicy, American steak! I've heard about these prime cuts from every man on board the *Europa* coming over. Now I shall taste for myself!"

John laughed. "Well, well! It seems your friend has a good cultural grasp of these American cousins of yours, Amelia. Let's all go to a place Charles and I have frequented many times over the months. It's called Fox Cave. The poet, Walt Whitman, has read there many times, and he has even been in fist fights with patrons when he began arguing his fierce patriotism for the Union cause. It's all quite jolly, and I think you ladies will enjoy yourselves. Yes, and we can obtain quite a large American steak there. I believe they're called New York sirloin, is that correct, Charles?"

"Right you are, Captain. New York seer-loin she is! Penny here will have a great task to get her choppers around this piece of meat!"

Penelope made a face with bulging eyes, and mimicked a huge bite in the air, and they all laughed uproariously. However, as they were about to leave, a tall man in an overcoat approached the front entrance. He was, at first, in the shadows. But, as he came closer, and came into the gaslight of the front porch, Penelope screamed. "Walter! What are you doing?" she asked, staring in incomprehensible horror at her fiancé, who was standing in front of them pointing a long, black pistol.

"Am I interrupting something?" said Walter, smiling, in spite of the fear in his stomach. "I think we should go back into the house," he said, making a brushing motion toward the inside with the Colt in his hand.

CHAPTER THIRTY-EIGHT: THE CAPTAIN RETREATS

Hampton Roads, Virginia, April 2, 1862

Chip Jefferson was keeping a sharp eye on his new captain, Lieutenant Samuel Dana Greene, and the way the gentleman was behaving made Chip certain something was wrong. Mister Greene began to request meatless meals because, he said, "One should value the peaceful serenity of the vegetarian existence." Greene also began staying up late into the night reading from his beloved Emerson, Thoreau and Whitman, and he received old issues of the Transcendental Movement's magazine called *The Dial*, which he read to Chip as if he were reading scripture. It was quite strange, indeed!

The *Monitor* had not confronted the giant enemy again since that infamous day in March, but word had it she was going to come out again "to play" pretty soon, and the ship's company was constantly practicing battle drills, although the new captain did not seem to have his heart in the exercises. Chip often found his captain locked inside his cabin, reading poetry and writing in his journal. After that letter came written by Mister Ericsson, the mood of the captain began to get worse. Chip was certain Ericsson was doing something to the young man's mind. Chip's family had an old cousin named Josie who purportedly knew the ways of the African witch doctors, and she could put people under her spell. It certainly looked to Chip that Greene was under just such a spell by this evil inventor, John Ericsson, with his brusque manner, his talk of the slave trade, and his fixation with Easter Island. It was this fixation that made Chip think Ericsson was as crazy as Captain Ahab, and he was using this young Samuel Greene the same way Ahab used Mister Starbuck. *Only, this time, Mister Greene was star-struck*, thought Chip, and he chuckled to himself, as he picked out the beef in the stew for the captain's mess. Inside, he

141

could hear his captain reading to himself, and he pushed the door open with his foot while holding the tray of food. "Evening, Captain. Sorry to bother, but I have the latest from the cook. Brunswick Stew without the meat." He set the tray down on the table.

The young captain looked up briefly from his reading. "Yes, indeed. Stew. Thank you, Chip. You may go now."

Chip was about to leave when he spotted the title of the book in Captain Greene's hands, *Easter Island: The Rapaniu Speech and the Peopling of Southeast Polynesia*. Chip wondered at the title. Then, he had a flash of insight. Certainly, that was it! That's the way all the slave traders did their work. First, they learned the language and the tribal customs so they could negotiate with the tribal leaders. His father told him about this himself, as this was how his own family was negotiated for in Africa. Mister Greene was learning about Rapaniu speech so he could trade for slaves!

"Aye, Captain. You have yourself a nice meal," said Chip, and he closed the hatch behind him.

* * *

After the young Cabin Boy had left, Captain Greene began to write again in his journal:

It's all clear to me now. Captain Ericsson was using me all along for his own selfish interests. I have seen it with the clarity of vision that my new life's regimen has given me. As a Transcendentalist, I can commune with Nature and see into the hearts of scoundrels like John Ericsson. He has lied to me all along, just so he could get a big contract for more ships. There is no paradise at Easter Island. And there is only one way I can get my revenge on this man. He does not know about life aboard his own invention! We have nearly exploded and sunk twice from the heat and infernal noise and confusion this craft engenders. Combat is not like sitting in a neat drawing room sipping brandy. No, it is much more sinister, Mister Ericsson. And, I will show you just how sinister I can be once this assignment is done!

CHAPTER THIRTY-NINE: THE NEGOTIATION

New York City, April 2, 1862

I've been after you for several months, Captain Ericsson. It's now time we had a talk." Walter was still pointing his revolver, and the women were clutching each other and staring at him in disbelief. Ericsson and McCord were seated on the divan, wondering if this madman were going to kill them all. Was it some love triangle? Did he seek revenge?

"Walter, what's happened to you? Have you lost all your senses?" Penelope's voice was shaking with emotion.

"I was contracted by the Confederate Government to kill this gentleman," said Walter, twitching the barrel of the pistol at Ericsson. "Indeed, I was supposed to destroy his infernal invention as well, but as with many enterprises in my life, I was unable to complete the mission."

"You told me you were doing business over here, Walter. I thought you might have been running the blockades with your ship, but you said nothing about such horrors!" said Penelope, making a motion to approach her fiancé, but his stern look made her stop. "Why didn't you tell me?" she asked, holding out her arms in a pleading gesture.

"Tell you? My dear Pen, these American rebels said they would kill you if anybody else ever discovered my plan. In fact, both of our lives are in danger right now, unless I can kill this bastard and bring them the drawings of his ironclad. Do you understand? We are as good as dead while this man is still alive!"

"You can't be serious, Walter Sinclair," said Amelia, walking up to him with no fear in her eyes. Walter pointed the gun at her, but she did not flinch. "You will hang for murder, and then where will poor Penelope be?"

"If I might be so bold, Sir, but I believe I have a stake in this discussion," said Ericsson, adjusting his necktie.

Walter turned his gun on the inventor. "Yes, I suppose you do. Make your peace quickly, as I do not have much time."

"This woman is quite correct, you know. Even if you do kill me and take my plans to the enemy, do you suppose they will fulfill their end of the bargain? I doubt it. Even if they do, where will you go? The Union and the Confederacy would not want you here. And, if you did return to England, you could be arrested," Ericsson pointed out, in his matter-of-fact, scientific manner.

"They told me you were a tricky one that they did. They gave me quite a small fortune to accomplish this job, and I am to receive the other half when it's completed," said Walter, trying to keep the confidence in his tone, although he was becoming more doubtful every moment.

"Listen, Mister Sinclair, I have a proposition for you. It may solve all of our problems at this juncture. The Union Government has just negotiated for a contract worth quite a bit of money. I dare say it is quite a bit more than what the Confederacy has offered you."

Walter was listening intently, although he still kept the gun on his prey.

"I want to make a rather lengthy and dangerous voyage to Easter Island. My partner, Mister McCord, and I have some new ideas about how to outfit a ship to make the journey without too much difficulty. However, I need a ship and a captain. If you'll assist me, Captain Sinclair, I will promise you a safe passage to an island where you and your betrothed can live out your lives in peace."

Sinclair looked over at Penelope with concern in his eyes. He understood what Ericsson was saying, and, deep down, he trusted this Swede. They would be better off leaving what was left of civilization to try another world. It could prove dangerous, but there would be more danger if they stayed here.

"I say, love, what are your thoughts on this?" Walter asked his fiancée.

Penelope walked over to him and took his two large hands into hers, staring deeply into his brown eyes. "Walter, I am attracted to you because you are an adventurous man. This would simply be another chance for us to live dangerously!"

"Then, it's settled? We can discuss the trip over dinner," said Ericsson, picking up his hat and coat once again.

"Look! There's someone at the window!" Amelia shouted, pointing to the dark shape moving past the bay window.

Sinclair and McCord ran out of the house to apprehend the intruder, with the women and Ericsson following close behind. Huddled down behind a hedge, Sinclair pulled forth the skinny body of the little orderly, Chip Jefferson.

Ericsson frowned. "What are we to do with this fellow?" he asked, beginning to worry about too many complications in his flight for freedom.

Walter brushed the front of the boy's shirt, which had become dusty from his sleuthing around the house. "Your Mister Greene can take care of the lad, Captain. We can't risk his going to the authorities, now can we?"

"I'm afraid you're correct, Mister Sinclair. We'll take him with us to Easter Island," said Ericsson.

Chip's eyes grew wide with horror. "Oh, no! Captain Ahab! I will not go with you slave traders to Easter Island!"

Amelia walked over to the boy and put a soothing arm around his narrow shoulders. "Now, my boy, we are not slave traders. Didn't John tell you? We're going to live in Nature's paradise. It will be a wonderful adventure!"

PART III: RETURN TO PARADISE

December 29, 1862 - September 2, 1863

CHAPTER FORTY: ANCHORS AWEIGH

New York City, December 29, 1862

The months passed, and the British blockade-runner had been thoroughly transformed into an oceangoing vessel with many new inventions, thanks to the genius of one John Ericsson. In addition, the little Captain's Orderly, Chip Jefferson, had been convinced by the ladies that the adventure awaiting them all was far more exciting than the dangers of this Civil War. As a result, Chip went back to the *Monitor* to tell Captain Greene about the plan and to try to convince him that the journey to Easter Island was their only way to stay safe. Chip knew he could not tell his parents about leaving the country, as they would never understand. His father would be especially angry, as he believed the world was teeming with slave traders and profiteers, but Captain Ericsson and Sinclair had convinced the boy that Easter Island had been preserved from this kind of activity. "Most of the stories in books and articles are written to sell copies, my boy," said Ericsson. "This island still possesses the charm and character of a natural paradise."

Walter added, "We'll be the top dogs on that island, that's for sure. With Mister Ericsson's genius at invention, we just might be considered gods!" That was enough for Chip's imagination to take over, and he resigned to keep the trip a secret from everybody, including his family back home in New York.

John Ericsson and Walter Sinclair personally supervised the reconstruction and loading of the *H.M.S. Caine*, as they wanted to be certain that all the right cargo was brought on board, and they needed to be extremely cautious about not disclosing their destination. The women were being kept at the hotel in Brooklyn until they were ready to sail, and Charles McCord was watching after them, although Sinclair was distrustful of McCord and insisted that the Irishman not be permitted any alcohol until they were underway.

Before they began their long journey of over 11,000 miles, they had to first get Lieutenant Greene. He was soon to be relieved of his command aboard the *Monitor*, and Ericsson thought it best they pick him up at the Bachelor Officers' Quarters at the Brooklyn Navy Yard when he arrived from his deployment in Virginia. Captain Ericsson was still under the assumption that Greene was anxious to live out his life in peace on Easter Island, but Chip Jefferson had stated "the new Captain was recently acting mighty strange onboard the ship."

As Chip Jefferson and Dana Greene would soon be, in effect, kidnapped by this adventurous group, the dangers would continue to plague them on this journey. The United States Government would not be happy to see its top naval inventor and two war heroes going "absent without leave." Ericsson believed, however, that the Union would be too busy with the war to notice a British ship escaping New York Harbor. As a British citizen, Captain Walter Sinclair had all the necessary papers for the Caine, and they had acquired permission to leave port on April 5, two days hence, presumably to head toward their final destination of Liverpool, England. They, of course, would not be going to England, as their trip would be a long and dangerous voyage around Cape Horn and on out into the South Pacific to the islands that had been termed "the navel of the world."

The two women, Penelope and Amelia, would be traveling the long voyage without the usual formal attire and civilized accoutrements to which they were accustomed. They believed it to be a great adventure, however, and so they decided they would wear the clothing of sailors and pitch in with the work as best they could.

The war was going at full force, and as the ship was being loaded, two United States Marines, accompanied by a naval officer, came over to the berth where the *H.M.S. Caine* was a beehive of activity. Captain Sinclair met the young officer and his men at the gangway, whereupon two men were busy loading cargo onto the ship. "Good day, Lieutenant," said Walter, affecting his best military bearing.

"Are you the captain of this vessel?" the officer asked.

"Yes, indeed I am. We're pulling out at 0800 hours on January fifth. Did you want to see my papers?" Sinclair smiled.

"No, I'm just checking for possible unauthorized cargo. My men need to go through some of that freight you're loading." The tall lieutenant motioned for the two marines to stop the workers and have them bring the boxes back down the gangway and onto the pier where they could be examined.

"Certainly, Officer! Heave to, men! Get that gear back down here for these kind gentlemen," said Walter.

The two marines opened the cartons to reveal mostly hardtack, or sea biscuits, and bully beef, or beef jerky. Two other cartons contained nuts and dried beans. The Lieutenant, seemingly satisfied, had his men close the cartons back up. "Your food seems to be the sort used on long voyages, Captain. I thought your manifest said Liverpool."

"These are times of war, Officer. I'm bringing these quality preserves to our own naval forces in jolly England. We have also been inconvenienced by your little dispute. We can no longer obtain all the fresh quality foodstuffs we once enjoyed from our colonies," said Walter, smiling broadly.

The young lieutenant became a bit irate at this. "Yes, we know all about war, Captain. My brother was killed this week when one of your countrymen ran his ship through a blockade. He was sliced in two as the runner rammed his frigate broadside."

"I'm terribly sorry to hear that, Lieutenant. The war has made bitter enemies of brothers, and some of my countrymen have seen to profit from your miseries. On behalf of the British who only want the war to end, I salute you and your brother for your noble sacrifice."

The young officer smiled. "Very well, Captain. You may carry one with your loading. Good luck with your trip."

"Thank you, kind sir! I, for one, shall spread the word of Union hospitality to all my mates in England. It's been an honor doing business with you!" Sinclair motioned for the dockworkers to get on with their duties.

The sun was beginning to go down on another day in port, and

Walter was happy to be finally getting back to his true home, the sea. Ericsson and Greene would have to listen to him once they were underway, and he relished the chance to be in charge. The several inventions installed by Ericsson and his "genius" were hindrances, to Walter's way of thinking. A flush toilet! As long as a man knew which way the wind was blowing, who needed the likes of such a contraption? A hot-air engine and a screw propeller on his stately warship? Ericsson said they would need these when they rounded Cape Horn. Walter had made it three times before without the aid of such devices. The one invention that Walter did concede was a miraculous contrivance, one that would make their trip a true possibility, was the desalting apparatus. Sinclair watched, as this tank was able to turn a gallon of seawater into fresh water——drinkable, unsullied water! Walter knew, from experience, that the most valuable commodity on long ocean voyages was fresh water. This invention would allow them to travel on without risking the danger of exposing themselves to strangers at sea. Pirates, or even slave traders were roaming the South Pacific these days, and with their little water device, they would not need to ask for any assistance. However, there was still a distance between them, and Walter resigned himself to be wary of the genius Swede. For genius had a way of turning into power, and power was often the most corrupting influence of all. As for the adventure, Walter needed it as much as the ocean needed the fish in her depths to be complete. It was the romance of adventure that kept Walter alive, and this was bound to one fantastic gamble!

* * *

Hampton Roads, Virginia, December 29, 1862 On board the U.S.S. Monitor

Captain Dana Greene, eating a strict vegetarian diet, was down to 110 pounds in his stocking feet, and he was spending each morning, before chow was served, performing an elaborate ritual, reading from Whitman, stripping down naked, and asking the Oversoul to guide him in his daily duties. He also asked the gods to forgive him for, what he believed, was a disgraceful defeat against the enemy. The *C.S.S. Virginia* had become a monster in Greene's dreams, taking on mythic proportions. Instead of a ship of iron, this was a gigantic steel wall, over a thousand feet high, standing in front of the little *Monitor*, as Greene looked up and grew more frightened by the moment. In his dream, Greene could not stop his craft from speeding straight for the wall, and inside the wall, there were thousands of men, their bodies set on fire from some infernal menace inside this gigantic metal Jericho, and these bodies were leaping out into space, falling hundreds of feet to their deaths. And Greene and his little metal boat would race toward this wall of doom, passing the screaming men who were bobbing, like cadaver corks, in the waves around him. Just before slamming into the gray steel wall, Greene would awaken screaming.

Chip walked in on the Captain several times during their eight months tour of duty down in Virginia, and what he saw was enough to frighten any young man. Chip had once before seen a young slave become this obsessed with tobacco in the fields. One day, the slave began smoking the leaves, right in front of the master. The slave had secretly rolled giant cigars inside his cabin. He did this because the master smoked them, and the field hand thought he could endear himself to the owner by smoking in front of him. However, the opposite occurred, as the slave was beaten until he could no longer work in the fields, and he eventually died alone, smoking away until his dying breath. Chip did not want to watch his new Captain starve himself to death, so he began telling him about the trip to Easter Island. Chip, in his own imagination, over the months of standoff against the *Virginia* (as President Lincoln himself had ordered the *Monitor* not to attack) had concocted quite a splendid picture, and he wanted the young lieutenant to begin to see that their redemption could be just around the corner.

Gradually, day-by-day, Captain Greene began to come out of his stupor. Dana was beginning to return to his normal, romantic self, and Chip was very pleased with himself. They spent hours talking together, in secret, while the other sailors went about their plan of the day. They talked about living in a world where you could fish for your dinner and pick your drinks out of trees. Where young women ran around half- naked, with no shame, and where color was not a badge of disgrace. Chip even told the young lieutenant about what Captain Sinclair had told them about becoming gods to these natives.

"Do you believe they'll think we're superior beings, Captain?" Chip asked, his eyes wide with expectation.

Dana smiled. "Well, we will have one of the most ingenious

men in the world in our company. I suppose we'll be able to show them a thing or two. There are many superstitions in these native tribes. If we show them a kindness they've never before experienced, then I can imagine we will become quite popular."

"My Daddy says these poor folks have already suffered from cannibalism and from slave traders. I guess we will look like Santa Claus and his elves next to all that!" Chip laughed at his own joke.

"We had better go down and get some dinner, or I'll be Santa Stick to them!" said Greene, and they walked off, laughing to themselves.

CHAPTER FORTY-ONE: OFF THE CAPE

December 30, 1862, off of Cape Hatter as, North Carolina

Lieutenant Greene's ship was prepared for its new deployment. The Navy Department had replaced Greene as captain with Lieutenant Thomas O. Selfridge, Jr., and the Monitor was to be transferred to another blockade and would be traveling south down the Atlantic seaboard. The turret was "keyed up" and a plaited tarred hemp gasket was placed between the turret and the brass deck ring in the recess. The gun ports had their huge iron pendulums secured in position. Wood bucklers were bolted to the outside of the turret covering the open gun ports and then caulked tight. The turret was revolved so the gun ports were abeam, and then it was set down on the gasket. Everything loose inside of the turret was secured or stowed below for rough seas. The two massive 11-inch Dahlgren shell guns were slid to amidships, their carriage compressors tightened, and all tackle drawn tight and secured. A temporary helm was rigged on top of the turret and tested.

Greene was to serve as the first lieutenant while they traveled down the coast, and he was in charge of securing the ship for sea. On deck, the pilothouse view slits were caulked shut. There was no doubt that the ocean was going to roll across her low deck and right up the angled sides of the pilothouse. The deck lights over the officers' quarters and the Wardroom had their iron covers secured in place. Every opening on deck would be inspected and secured before the ship head out to sea. The *Monitor* was under tow of the 236 foot, side wheel steamer U.S.S. Rhode Island. They were part of a four-ship flotilla along with the *U.S.S. State of Georgia* and the new ironclad *U.S.S. Passaic*.

Chip was serving at his captain's side at the helm when the storm clouds came. He could see them forming to the starboard side. They all knew the waters off Cape Hatteras were known to experience extremely inclement weather conditions, but Chip had never before seen storm clouds like these. They looked like gigantic, black demons approaching the ship, cracking out lightening and booming thunder, until Chip had to cover his ears. He could feel the whole ship shake, uncontrollably, when the thunder erupted, and, when the rains began to fall, it was as if the seas had been turned upside down upon them.

About eight o'clock, while Chip was taking a message from the captain to the engineer, he saw the water pouring in through the coalbunkers in sudden volumes as it swept over the deck. About that time the engineer reported that the coal was too wet to keep up steam, which had run down from its usual pressure of eighty pounds to twenty. The water in the vessel was gaining rapidly over the small pumps, and Chip heard the captain order the chief engineer to start the main pump, a very powerful one of new invention. The was done, and Chip saw a stream of water eight inches in diameter spouting up from beneath the waves like the blow from a whale.

About half-past eight, the first signals of distress to the *Rhode Island* were sent by lantern. She lay to, and the *Monitor* rode the sea more comfortably than when it was being towed. The *Rhode Island* was obliged to turn slowly ahead to keep from drifting upon the smaller ship and to prevent the towlines from being caught in her wheels. At one time, when she drifted close alongside, Captain Selfridge shouted through his trumpet that his ship was sinking and asked the steamer to send her boats to rescue the crew. The *Monitor* steamed ahead again with renewed difficulties, and Chip was ordered to leave the helm, and he was ordered by Selfridge to be his messenger. The chief engineer reported that the coal was so wet that he could not keep up steam, and Chip heard the captain order the engineer to slow down and put all steam that could be spared upon the pumps. As there was a danger of being towed under by the *Rhode Island*, the tow-lines were ordered to be cut, and Chip saw James Fenwick, quarter-gunner, swept from the deck and carried by a heavy sea, leeward and out of sight. Fenwick was attempting to obey the captain's order. The daring boatswain's mate, John Stocking, then succeeded in reaching the bows of the vessel, and Chip then saw him, too, swept by a heavy sea far away into the darkness. It was as if some hidden sea monster, with powerful tentacles, were grasping these brave men and pulling them away from the ship!

About half-past ten o'clock the *Monitor's* anchor was let go with all the cable, and it struck bottom in about sixty fathoms of water; this brought the ship out of the trough of the sea, and it rode more comfortably. The fires could no longer be kept up because of the wet coal. The small pumps were choked up with water, or, as the engineer reported, were "drowned," and the main pump had almost stopped working from lack of power. This was all reported to Captain Selfridge, and he ordered Chip to see if there were any water in the wardroom. This was the first time Chip had been below the berth-deck in the storm. He went forward and saw the water running in through the hawse-pipe, and eight-inch hole, in full force, as in dropping the anchor the cable had torn away the packing that had kept this ship tight. Chip reported to his captain, and at the same time he heard the chief engineer report that the water had reached the ash-pits and was gaining very rapidly. The captain ordered the engineer to stop the main engine and turn all steam on the pumps, which, Chip noticed, soon began to work again.

The clouds now began to separate, a moon about half size beamed out upon the sea, and the *Rhode Island*, now a mile away, became visible. Signals were being exchanged, and Chip felt that the *Monitor* would be saved, or at least that the captain would not leave his ship until there was no hope of saving her. Chip was sent below again to see how the water stood in the wardroom. He went forward to the cabin and found the water just above the soles of his shoes, which indicated that there must be more than a foot in the vessel. Chip returned to the bridge and reported this to Captain Selfridge, who ordered all hands to begin baling out the water, and it seemed they were baling out the entire ocean, but the goal was to employ the men, as there now seemed to be danger of panic among them. Chip kept working most of the time, taking the buckets from through the hatchway on top of the turret. The buckets seemed to have no more than a pint of water in them, however, the balance having been spilled in the passing from one man to the other.

Although the weather was clear, the sea did not cease rolling, and the *Rhode Island*, with the two lines wound up in her wheel, was tossing at the mercy of the sea, and she finally came drifting against the sides of the little *Monitor*. A boat that had been lowered was caught between the vessels and was crushed and lost. Some of the seaman aboard the *Monitor* bravely leaped down on deck to guard the ship's sides, and lines were thrown to them from the deck of the *Rhode Island*, which now lay her whole length against the ironclad, floating off astern, but not a man would be the first to leave his ship, although the captain had given orders to do so. Chip was sent again to examine the water in the wardroom, which he found to be more than two feet above the deck, and he realized he was the last person to see Engineer S. A. Lewis, as he lay seasick in his bunk, apparently watching the water as it grew deeper and deeper around him. He called to Chip, as the boy passed the door, and asked if the pumps were working.

"Yes, for now," said Chip.

"Is there any hope?" asked Lewis, who was almost as young as Chip, and whose fate was in the balance.

Chip felt moved at seeing this young white man, as innocent as Chip had been before his duty aboard this ship, so he tried to give the fireman something to live for, "As long as there's life there's hope," Chip said.

"Hope and hang on when you're wrecked," said Lewis, repeating an old saying among sailors.

Chip left the wardroom and learned that the water had gained so much as to choke up the main pump. As he was crossing the berth deck, Chip saw the ensign, Mr. Fredrickson, hand a watch to Master's Mate Williams, saying, "Here, this is yours. I may be lost." The watch and chain were both of unusual value.

Williams received them, then, with a hesitating glance down at the timepiece he said, "This thing may be the means of sinking me," and he threw it down on the deck. There were three or four cabin boys, pale and prostrate with seasickness, and the cabin cook, old Robbins, an African Negro, who was under great stress.

"You men are crazy!" Robbins shouted, picking up the watch and giving it back to its owner. "Go about your duty, and don't be crazy!"

As Chip climbed up the turret ladder, the sea broke over the ship and came pouring down the hatchway with so much force that it took him off his feet. At the same moment, the steam broke from the boiler-room, as the water had reached the fires, and for an instant, Chip seemed to realize that all was lost. The *Monitor's* fires were now out, and Chip could hear the water blowing out the boilers, so he ran up to report this to Captain Selfridge. As he was doing this, he saw a boat pull alongside. Selfridge again gave the orders for the men to leave the ship, and fifteen, all of whom were seamen and men in whom Chip had placed his confidence, at one time or another, but now they were the ones who crowded the first boat to leave the ship. Chip was disgusted to witness such a cowardly scramble, and, not feeling in the least alarmed, resolved that he, a freed slave, would stick to the ship as long as the officers did. It was then Chip saw three of these cowardly seamen swept from the deck and carried leeward on the swift current, never to be seen again.

Baling was again resumed, and Chip occupied the turret all along, and he passed the buckets from the lower hatchway to the man on the top of the turret. He took off his coat—one that he had received from home only a few days before—and, rolling it up with his boots, drew the tampion from one of the huge guns, placed them inside, and replaced the tampion. A black cat was sitting on the breech of one of the guns, howling one of those hoarse and solemn tunes that no one can appreciate who is not filled with the superstitions, which Chip had been taught by the sailors, who are always afraid to kill a cat aboard ship. Chip would as soon touch a ghost, but he caught her, and, placing her in the other gun to be safe, he replaced the wad and tampion. But Chip could still hear that distressing yowl. As he raised his last bucket to the upper hatchway, no one was there to take it, so, Chip scrambled up the ladder and found that he had been deserted. He shouted to those on the berth-deck, "Come up! The officers have left the ship. A boat is alongside!"

As Chip reached the top of the turret, he saw a boat made fast on the weather quarterdeck, filled with men. Three others were standing on deck trying to get on board. One man was floating leeward, shouting in vain for help. Another, who ran by Chip and jumped down from the turret, was immediately swept off by a breaking wave and never rose. Chip was excited, feeling that it was his only chance to be saved. So, he made a loose line fast to one of the stanchions, and he let himself down from the turret, the ladder having been washed away. The moment he struck the deck, the sea broke over it and swept Chip, as he had seen it sweep his shipmates. He grasped one of the smokestack braces and, hand-over-hand, crawled up, to keep his head above water. It required all his youthful strength to keep the sea from tearing him away. As the smokestack brace swept out from the vessel, Chip found himself dangling in the air nearly at the top of the smokestack. He let himself fall and succeeded in reaching the lifeline that encircled the deck by means of short stanchions, and to which the boat was attached. The sea again broke over the ship, lifting Chip upward, and he still clung, in desperation, to the lifeline. He thought he had measured the ocean, but when he felt the ship turn, as his head rose above the water, Chip was somewhat dazed from being so nearly drowned, and he spouted up, it seemed, more than a gallon of water from his lungs. Chip was about twenty feet from the other men, whom he saw to be the captain and one seaman. The other man had been washed overboard and was now struggling in the water. The men in the boat were pushing back on their oars to keep the boat from being washed onto the *Monitor's* deck, so that the boat had to be hauled in by the painter about ten or twelve feet. First Lieutenant Greene, and then other officers in the boat, were shouting, "Is the captain on board?" and, with severe struggles to have their voices heard above the roar of the wind and the sea, they were shouting, "No," and trying to haul in the boat, which was finally accomplished.

The captain, ever caring for his men, requested that Chip and the seaman get aboard, but both of them, in the same voice, told the captain to get in first. The moment he was over the bows of the boat, Lieutenant Greene cried, "Cut the painter! Cut the painter!" Chip thought, Now, or I am lost, and, in an instant, exerting all the strength that his slim body could muster, he jumped, caught on the gunwale, and was pulled into the boat with a boat-hook into the hands of Mister Greene, who put him in a seat next to one of the oarsmen. The other seaman, Thomas Joice, managed to get into the boat in some way, Chip could not see how, and he was the last man saved from the ill-fated ship. As they were cut loose, Chip saw several men standing on top of the gun turret, apparently afraid to venture down upon the deck, and it may have been that they were deterred by seeing others washed overboard while Chip was getting into the boat.

After a fearful and dangerous passage over the frantic seas, they reached the *Rhode Island*, which still had the tow-line caught in her wheel and had drifted perhaps two miles to leeward. They came alongside under the lee bows, where the first boat, which had left the *Monitor* nearly an hour before, had just discharged its men. However, the men in the second boat found it a more difficult task getting on board the *Rhode Island* than it had been getting from the *Monitor*. They were carried by the sea, from stem to stern, for to have made fast would have been fatal; the boat was bounding against the ship's sides; sometimes it was below the wheel, and then, on the summit of a huge wave, far above the decks; then the two boats would crash together; once, while Surgeon Weeks was holding on to the rail, he lost his fingers by a collision which swamped the other boat. Lines were thrown to them from the deck of the larger ship, which were of no use, for not one of the men could climb a small rope. The men who threw them would immediately let go, in their excitement to throw another, and Chip found himself hauling in rope instead of climbing.

Two vessels, lying side by side, when there is no any motion to the sea, move alternately; in other words, one is constantly passing the other up or down. At one time, when the little boat was near the bows of the steamer, they could rise upon the sea until they could touch her rail, then, in an instant, by a very rapid decent, the men in the little boat could almost touch her keel. While they were rising and falling upon the sea, Chip caught a rope, and, rising with the boat, managed to reach a foot or two of the rail, when a man, if there had been one, could have easily hauled him on board. But they had all followed after the boat, which at that instant was washed astern, and Chip hung, dangling in the air over the bow of the *Rhode Island*, with Ensign Norman Atwater handing to the cat-head, three or four feet from Chip, and like him, with both hands clenching a rope and shouting for someone to save him. Their hands grew painful and all the time weaker, until Chip saw the young ensign's strength give way. He slipped a foot, caught again, and with his last prayer, "Oh God!" Chip saw Atwater fall and sink into the deep, never to rise again. The ship rolled, and rose upon the sea, sometimes with her keel out of water, so that Chip was hanging thirty feet above the sea, and with the fate of the ensign before him, which no one else had seen, the youth still clung to the rope with aching hands, calling in vain for help. But Chip could not be heard, for the wind shrieked far above his voice. At that very moment, Chip lost hope, as he believed he could hold on no longer, and he began to see his parents fading from his mind. While in this state of confused abandon, within a second of releasing his grip on the rope, the sea rolled forward, bringing with it the boat, and just when he would have fallen into the sea, it was there, like a miracle, and Chip could only think about what the old black cook, Robbins, said as the young lad fell into the bottom of the boat beside him, "Where in the hell did he come from?"

When Chip finally became aware of what was going on around him, he saw that no one had succeeded in getting out of the boat, which by then lay just forward of the wheel-house. The *Rhode Island* captain ordered his men to throw bowlines, which was immediately done. The second one Chip caught, and, placing himself within the loop, was hauled on board. He then assisted in helping the other men out of the boat, and the rescue boat continued back to the *Monitor*.

It was half-past twelve, the night of the thirty-first of December, 1862, when Chip stood on the forecastle of the *Rhode Island* with Lieutenant Greene. They were watching the red and white lights that hung from the pennant-staff above the turret, and which now and then were seen as both ships would rise on the sea together, until at last, just as the moon had passed below the horizon, the lights were lost, and the *U.S.S. Monitor*, the iron maiden, was seen no more.

The *Rhode Island* cruised about the scene of the disaster for the rest of the night, and until the following noon, in hopes of finding the rescue boat that had been lost. She then returned to Fort Monroe, where Chip and the other survivors arrived the next day with their sad news.

CHAPTER FORTY-TWO: GREENE AND CHIP COME ABOARD

January 2, 1863, Brooklyn, New York

Lieutenant Dana Greene and Chip Jefferson came aboard in the morning, and the ladies were there to greet them and to console them after their tortuous ordeal. Anna Cameron was joining their crew in the afternoon, and Penelope and Amelia were busy fixing up their quarters for the new woman. Captain Sinclair gave the ladies his cabin, as it was the largest, and he bunked with the men in the Crew's Quarters. The Captain's Cabin was now a frilly place, with laced pillowcases, curtains over the portholes, and several watercolors of English country scenes hanging from the bulkhead. The women, however, refused to wear female attire aboard ship, as they chose, instead, the regular seamen's wear of blue gabardines.

Their journey would take them over 11,000 nautical miles, and Captains Ericsson and Sinclair were well aware of the hazards and potential dangers of such a bold venture. However, now the combined courage and will power of these undaunted souls would be tested far more than the endurance required for the travel. They came from different worlds, both in the psychological and in the physical senses, and these differences, more than any other, worried Captain Ericsson the most. He had never planned to have so many people along with him on his escape to Easter Island. Certainly, he wanted the young lad, Lieutenant Greene, and his young fiancée, Anna Cameron. They reminded him of him and his wife, Anna, when they were young and full of adventure. But, Sinclair and his fiancée, and the Negro orderly, Chip Jefferson, they were impending storms on the horizon. Sinclair had actually sailed to the South Pacific before, and the little former slave knew far too much for his own good.

* * *

January 3, 1863, at sea

Ericsson decided he was going to challenge everybody on the voyage by having each person keep a journal of his or her adventure. He called a meeting on the first night at sea, and he addressed them all at the captain's table, his glass of port raised high, his eyes gleaming with emotion. "We are making history, ladies and gentlemen. Just as our forefathers sailed to the New World to make their mark, we, too, will be voyaging to our paradise to establish a new existence. However, we shall be keeping our existence simple. Our purpose will be to maintain a peaceful, harmonious bond with Nature, and we will make all of our duties and daily plans reflect this purpose. With this in mind, I want all of you to keep a daily journal of our progress. Future historians will want to read a chronological record of our story, and this will give them what they need to judge us. Thus, you will each receive a ship's log, and in this log, each of you will write down what he or she needs to express in the way of personal discovery. You may write any ideas or reflections you may have about your daily activities, and your record will remain sacred and secret, until such time as we all agree to turn these records over to the authorities for publication. Is this acceptable?"

"Are you certain these will remain secret?" asked Penelope, who was already beginning to complain about the shipboard lifestyle. "I don't mind telling everyone that this little 'adventure,' as you call it, seems more appropriately called 'misadventure' every day."

Anna Cameron laughed. "Right you are, Pen. I believe we will all have a great deal to say in our journals, and we should have them remain secure. As a young girl, I know that my diary was one of my most secret and prized possessions. If someone were to read it, I would have been traumatized beyond repair!"

John Ericsson cleared his throat. "Now, ladies. You will each have a locked safe in which to store your journal. The key will be yours to keep around your beautiful necks. Nobody will have access to your journals but you. That's a promise."

"I think it's a grand idea!" said Chip Jefferson, reaching over to grab another cinnamon roll from the platter. "It's the way a free democracy should permit it. Each person has freedom of expression."

"Well stated, young man," said Dana Greene, as he smiled broadly at the young lad. "I agree. Historians will be able to better evaluate our progress, as a whole, with these different journals from which to choose. We can also explore ideas for new inventions in our new paradise. I, for one, plan on beginning a new life, with my love and with my new friends,

and this journal will be my record of this journey to freedom. We will all remember our deeds, and we can thus begin to separate ourselves from the hell on earth back in the States."

"Then, it's agreed! Let's drink on it!" said Ericsson, lifting his wine glass, as the others also stood up with their glasses and lifted them up to seal the pact of their new constitution.

CHAPTER FORTY-THREE: AMELIA ERICSSON'S JOURNAL

January 4, 1863, at sea

The first day at sea we are struck by inclement weather. We are all retching violently from the constant motion by the ship, and I became ill just watching the furniture slide across the room, until that little Negro, Chip, pokes his nappy head into my cabin and announces that "Dinner is being served." Luckily, I have a large porcelain bowl next to my bed, so the instantaneous regurgitation is released into a proper receptacle. Chip then carries it out to be tossed overboard, sloshing the contents back and forth, until my stomach feels another wave of nausea, and I have no place to vomit! I soon retain another bowl, and thus I am prepared for the worst.

Captain Sinclair, Lieutenant Greene and my husband are the only members of our expedition who do not get ill from bad weather. They boast to us of their "sea legs," and their cocky behavior is enough to make one sick all over again. I once left my husband because of his poverty, and this voyage is not endearing itself to my Epicurean nature. It is my husband's bold personality that has caused him problems in the past, and I can see it becoming a problem on this adventure. I hope I am not correct in this assumption, but when I see him parading around the ship, issuing orders and discussing the "new philosophy of paradise" with the other men, I begin to suspect we are in for some inclement psychological weather as well.

For example, at dinner tonight, Mister Greene began the meal with one of his ghastly readings from his god-poet, Walt Whitman. John, my husband, encourages the young man, and thus we are trapped before dining, under a canopy of romantic images and tired leaps of unreal imaginings. As I was still quite queasy from the weather, these poetic musings added to the nausea, until my face must have turned an emerald-yellow color, quite amusing to the others at dinner.

I do love my John, and if I must endure this as a punishment for my rather spoiled upbringing in London, then so be it. The others are quite encouraging, and full of humor, so my personal misgivings are often buffered. Penelope, in particular, is my best bulwark against this masculine environment, and we often share little jokes between ourselves, to soften the impetuous philosophies of our men. "Wait until the weather is back to normal, Amelia," says my darling Pen, lifting her eyebrow with coquetry. "We shall again hold sway over the parlor and the bedroom!"

We let little Anna Cameron in on our joke, but she is rather indifferent, as she is still too young to understand how we older women have learned to control our men. However, Penelope and I are both certain, after this voyage has come to its destination, we will have convinced Anna that it is much better to join our ranks than it is to follow her quixotic husband into some inauspicious escapade. Her Mister Greene often looks to me to have the gaze of some young bull in the pasture that has been struck by Cupid's arrow, and he thus begins to sniff flowers, instead of snorting and grinding his hoof into the earth. Penelope's Mister Sinclair, on the other hand, is all bull, through and through, and I have often wondered about his handling of Pen in the boudoir. My Dear John, heaven knows, must be drugged into a state of romance, and even then he has often fallen asleep before I am able to seduce him!

This shall be a long voyage, and I hope we are all able to get to know each other better. If we are to be living under primitive conditions on this Easter Island, then we indeed must learn to survive together. Even though I may come from austere surroundings, I am a fighter. We British have been able to conquer many foreign shores, and we can bring about a change that will make our reputations known all over the world. I plan to carry on this tradition of my relatives, and so does Pen, and thus our affiliation has begun! We secretly call our order, "The Amazon Women," although every time I utter the title, Pen begins to giggle uncontrollably.

CHAPTER FORTY-FOUR: CHARLES MCCORD'S JOURNAL

January 6, 1863, at sea

I've been off the liquor for over two weeks now, and I don't really crave it, although it was quite a bit of a rough going there for a few days. I experienced some strange hallucinations, some of them telling me I was being kept prisoner aboard this ship by the devil himself. That's correct; I even tried to strangle my fine friend and employer, Captain John Ericsson! The other men pulled me off of him, as I was quite out of my senses, and I was immediately sedated with some laudanum. When I awoke, I apologized profusely to the good Captain, to his wife, and then to the entire ship's company and I have been keeping myself busy ever since.

Captain Ericsson and Mister Greene are two of the most brilliant inventors I have ever worked for, that's to be sure. They have outfitted a large sanctum aboard the ship, and I am able to put in a good day's work at the drafting board, designing the new devices these men have created for our new home on Easter Island. The inventions range from a cocoanut harvester to a device to catch fish with a mechanical net. They have even developed some contraptions for the ladies, including a privy that allows one to shower inside a tent under a heated stream of water, and a steam-powered booster ladder, that pushes the rider up to a higher level, in case the ladies need to exit the ship or a smaller boat with little discomfiture. I am certainly happy to keep busy at the drafting board, as my mind can stay concentrated on the work and not on the sugarplum visions of whiskey bottles floating above my head at odd times in the day, mostly in the evenings.

I have no doubts that we will arrive safely at our destination. Even though, I am told, it will take well over eight months to reach Easter Island, the company I keep is good, and we will certainly have some of the most talented and beautiful people in the world to establish this new existence of ours. I must say I have taken to praying to Jesus, Mary and Joseph these days, as I need to get my spirits in some way. Most of these people are not of a religious nature, except for the little Chip lad, and he told me he is of the Protestant faith. Mister Greene says he is a believer of something he calls the "Over soul" or "overalls" as I like to jest with him. He reads Emerson incessantly, and when he reads at dinner, I quietly make the sign and say my own prayer to the Lord. Captain Ericsson has assured me we will be able to practice the religion of our choice on our island, even though the natives are yet to be converted to any of our known religions.

We also have an armory on board, and Captain Ericsson has appointed me the Master-at-Arms. I consider it an honor, and I spend a few hours of my day cleaning the rifles and pistols we have stored in there, and this is when I also take the time to write in this journal. It was a good idea the Captain had about writing our own journals. I was never much for writing, but the women have shown me the dictionary, and I take time to correct my grammar, as much as I can, and it gives me some amount of satisfaction to know that someone might be reading my thoughts about our journey sometime in the near future. It's rather like the people must have felt in the Bible when they had their stories written down. It's a real honor, I must say, and I will do my best to keep up with this writing work, in addition to my other chores. This sobriety has given me a great deal of extra time, and I enjoy staying busy. It's now time for dinner, and I must get these rifles stored back in their proper closet. Did I mention, dear journal, that I am also the salad maker? Mrs. Ericsson is the chef, Mrs. Sinclair is her assistant, and I am their salad man. My nose is still a bit bulbous and red, and Mrs. Sinclair has called me "Charlie Tomato" during some of our lighter moments in the galley, bless em' all!

CHAPTER FORTY-FIVE: ANNA CAMERON-GREENE'S JOURNAL

May 23, 1863

Now that we are married, I believe I am a changed woman. As I watch all the others making plans for life on the island, all I can write down is my desire to have a child! Dear Journal, I cannot relate these feelings to anyone, as yet, as I know they all believe we will be living an adventure that will be quite different from our lives back home in England and America. It is difficult to explain, but the moment Captain Sinclair pronounced us "man and wife," I became fixed upon the desire to have a child. Perhaps it is my personal adventure. So be it. Isn't this a woman's true calling, after all? What more adventure can there be than having a child in the wilderness, with no doctor and no hospital to ensure one's safety? Can this be any less daring than any of these men's exploits during war or on the high seas? Alas, every time I speak about the prospects of having children, the other women just laugh and tell me I had best talk with Mister Ericsson about such matters.

I did speak with Captain Ericsson. I must say, his ideas about our New Republic were quite shocking to me! Where is the romance in having children in common? When I registered my disapproval, he just patted my hand in a most condescending manner, and said, "My dear lady, you shall have your children, but having a common parentage will give these children of ours a noble purpose. Not knowing their mother or father will make all of us their mothers and fathers. Thus, our Republic will be their parents." I can't imagine it! It's too horrid to imagine. How can a child be nurtured properly without the special care only her mother can give?

I spoke to Dana about what Captain Ericsson told me, and he was also very patronizing. "Captain Ericsson is planning our new government, Anna, and we must not question his authority."

Dear Journal, I do so want to be a good wife and good citizen, but something inside me is repelled by the thought of giving my child over to the masses. Captain Ericsson says it will free me to go out and be something much more than a "mere" doting mother. He says I can be a huntress or warrior. Humbug, I say! Is it so criminal to want to wear fine things and be a mother to one's child? Is it too much to ask? Apparently it is. However, I will bide my time, and when the right moment comes, and it shall come, I will get my own way. I remember the Biblical stories about women who were able to overcome the same masculine pride and control, and I am no less of a woman! I, too, can be a noble Tamar, who was able to trick her father-in-law and have her own way. If I must use my sexuality to get my way, so be it! We shall be cast out onto this uncivilized land, and perhaps it will take uncivilized actions to succeed! Ah, a woman's adventure is never-ending!

CHAPTER FORTY-SIX: DANA GREENE'S JOURNAL

February 12, 1863, at sea

Anna and I are back together again, and I suppose this should be enough, but the transition to life aboard ship again has been a bit strenuous for me. My last days with the Monitor were quite horrendous, and I was actually looking forward to time away from the sea. Alas, this is not meant to be, so I shall make the best of my situation. We certainly cannot go back to our relatives. My father would disown me as a coward, and the Union Government would, most likely, imprison me. It is true; we have gone over this journey thousands of times. Ericsson and I have had our plan ready for months, but now we have some new additions that make me uncomfortable. This Captain Sinclair and his wife are not, in my opinion, worthy citizens for our new island life. They both seem too autocratic and inflexible, and they are not the type of people to understand the reality of life in Nature. Certainly, Captain Sinclair understands life at sea, but it is the understanding of the competitor and not of the assimilator. One must learn, as the Transcendentalists have taught us, to harmonize with Nature and become open to the power of the Over-Soul. Here, I have it! Dr. Emerson says it better than I can:

Behold, it saith, I am born into the great, the universal mind. I, the imperfect, adore my own Perfect. I am somehow receptive of the great soul, and thereby I do overlook the sun and the stars, and feel them to be the fair accidents and effects that change and pass. More and more the surges of everlasting nature enter into me, and I become public and human in my regards and actions. So come I to live in thoughts, and act with energies, which are immortal Thus revering the soul, and learning, as the ancient said, that 'its beauty is immense,' man will come to see that the world is the perennial miracle which the soul worketh, and be less astonished at particular wonders; he will learn that there is no profane history; that all history is sacred; that the universe is represented in an atom, in a moment of time. He will weave no longer a spotted life of shreds and patches, but he will live with a divine unity. He will cease from what is base and frivolous in his life, and be content with all places and with any service he can render. He will calmly front the morrow in the negligency of that trust which carries God with it, and so hath already the whole future in the bottom of the heart.

I plan to live my new life with this profoundest of philosophies steadfast in my mind. The war has led me to this place, it is true, and I can be something greater if I can overcome the curse of being fractured by division. I am not simply a part of a single government, a single people, and a single marriage. I am part of the universe, a child of the One, and I will see to it that my life continues to expand, as Nature envelopes me in Her totality!

CHAPTER FORTY-SEVEN: JOHN ERICSSON'S JOURNAL

March 10, 1863, at sea

My grand experiment is going smoothly, even though the addition of Sinclair and his wife has caused me to change some of my plans. I have had time to reflect and to read, and it has been Plato who has been my ultimate salvation. His *Republic* has given me the inspiration to design my plan so that it will serve us well in our new environs. Combined with my exploration into the characters of my passengers, this philosophical treatise will become the bedrock upon which we will build our community on Easter Island.

First off, Plato's understanding of the human soul has been of great assistance to me in my own designs for the future. He believed that each of us could be categorized according to our class and according to our interests and virtues. And, beneath our surface life, there is the motivation of the soul. My chart of Plato's teachings helps me to plan my own Republic on Easter Island.

I note, with pleasure, that I can place each of my new citizens into one of these three categories. For example, Sinclair and Greene are perfect candidates for the Warrior Class. They have the spirit and courage that is demanded of these "Guardians of the

Republics" Plato calls them. I know that Greene has been aspiring toward something he believes is knowledge, but the Transcendentalists are not true philosophers. Emerson never lived in Nature, about which he preaches so profoundly. And Greene has been truly fooled by the chimera of unity. It will not take me long to put him back into the class upon which his soul is truly based, the warrior of spirit and courage! As for Sinclair, he is the epitome of Platonic spirit. He even saw the South as men who were fighting for honor, and thus he became a compatriot for their cause. Sinclair will be easily swayed by the manipulations I will use on him.

The Commoner Class shall, of course, be the natives on the island, as well as Mister Charles McCord, the Catholic. Even though McCord fools himself onboard ship, once he gets out into this pleasure-seeking wilderness, he will become his old self again. We will work on his temperance.

The rest of the group will be groomed to serve, with me, as the Philosopher Kings of our island paradise. Together with the Warriors, we will be the Guardians of Justice. We shall live in poverty, as an example to our public that we hold their best interests in mind. In addition, we will hold all our wealth in common, as well as our wives and our children. Children will be raised in common and will not know who their real parents are. These children will not be randomly conceived. They will be bred deliberately to produce the best offspring. As Plato suggests, we will keep the breeding process secret from them. Every year after the breeding committee, or whatever I will choose to call it, secretly makes its choices, there will be a kind of fertility festival. Everyone will choose names by lot, and the name he or she draws, or no name, will be the choice of the gods for them. This is the kind of thing that Plato called a "noble lie"; the lottery is to be rigged by the breeding committee. Everyone will actually draw the name designated for him or her; those who draw a blank will simply be undesirable for offspring. I have already spoken to Amelia, and she has agreed to serve with me on our breeding committee.

There will be no racism or class imperative, as I have chosen young Chip to be in our Philosopher Class, and most of the women are also chosen, except for Greene's Anna. This poor girl is too caught up in the pleasures of the world, and even though I have agreed to marry them before we land, I will soon, thereafter, announce our New Republic.

Socrates said that he hesitated to make an issue out of it, but that, yes, there will be women Guardians. Women have all the same parts of the soul and so all the same interests, virtues, and personality types as men. Since children will be raised in common, individual women will not be burdened with the task of child rearing and will be free to take their places in their proper occupations along with the men. If the warrior women are not as strong as the men, then they may not be at the forefront of the battle, but they should be at the battle. This equality even extends to athletics, which is somewhat shocking, since Greek athletes went naked. Words like "gymnasium" and "gymnastics" both derive from gymnos "naked." The Greeks rather prided themselves on not thinking that it was shameful or ridiculous to go naked, as all the "barbarians," their neighbors, thought. But Socrates says that nothing is ridiculous except what is wrong, and that in time people would get used to naked women athletes just as at one time they got used to naked men. I am certain the natives on Easter Island will find our ideas quite acceptable. And, over time, so will my public.

In addition, if any of the natives is seen to be a possible candidate, we will certainly honor his or her attributes and potential with the schooling necessary for members of our class. All will stand a chance to become Philosopher Kings, make no mistake, and our new Ericssonville will stand the test of the future to come!

CHAPTER FORTY-EIGHT: PENELOPE SINCLAIR'S JOURNAL

April 6, 1863, at sea

aptain Ericsson performed the wedding ceremony, and it was a wonderful affair! Anna wore one of my French gowns, and Mister McCord let us imbibe in one of the bottles of champagne that Captain Ericsson has locked away. I know of McCord's problem with alcohol, having witnessed the incident in the dining room when he attacked Captain Ericsson, and I specifically asked him if our celebrating with champagne bothered him. He smiled rather balefully and said, "No Mum, I'll just let you drink your little fizzy water. It will have no effect on me, as long as I stay on this side of the room." I must say, he did look a bit downcast, especially when we began to dance following the wedding ceremony. But, as I am one to keep a party going, I dragged him off his feet and we danced a good while, even though my feet were not fit for walking when he finished stomping on them. Mister Greene even composed a song for his new wife, Anna, and Anna sang it to my husband's harmonica accompaniment. Afterward, I was so intrigued by the groom's little tune that I inscribed it to add to this journal:

Our love will go on, like the heat of the sun, And your moonchild eyes will haunt my soul, Until dawn fuses with dusk, and snowflakes burn, Let me kiss your lips, and feel your hands, Patiently waiting, for our hearts to become one.

That young man has quite a romantic nature! Amelia and I often discuss the possibility of educating our husbands into the ways of romance, but we know their hearts are not in it.

"After all," says Amelia, "they're still young. The bloom will soon be off the rose." However, the young Greene is quite handsome, and when he is making love to his young wife, I often get pangs of envy that creep over me, like rabbits loose in the Garden of Eden. I love it when Mister Greene talks about our new life to come on Easter Island. When he mentions that we shall perhaps "turn native," and "wear little or nothing about our bodies," I can see my poor Walter's face cringe in a distasteful way. But, I must admit, my heart begins to race at the thought of cavorting in the tropical wilderness with the likes of young Mister Greene about! Am I so evil, dear journal, to want both romance and adventure? Dear Walter, he has always been so strong, and I love him dearly. However, when I see him next to Mister Greene, I can't help but see what I have missed. When we have all arrived at our new paradise, I am anxious to let Nature take hold. Things should be different, and my own passionate nature will be given a much wider berth.

Until then, I shall play the doting wife, and secretly write in this journal to confess my heart's desire. The things I tell you, I shall not tell another soul! I am, after all, a liberated woman.

I can learn from the dark side of humanity by watching young Chip Jefferson. He reads his novels and books, and I wonder what bold ideas he concocts inside his black brain? Does he lust after us? Walter has told me these slaves have an insatiable desire for the white woman that often boils over into criminal acts. I suppose Chip will revert to his primitive state once we land. They are so close to being monkeys, or so say many of the scientific books. Monkey see, monkey do. He sounds intelligent, too, and that's what amazes me the most.

Amelia says his slave owner, a woman who believed these Negroes could learn basic skills, educated him. I must admit, he is a novelty, especially when he recites his knowledge of Easter Island. He sounds so professorial, I laughed out loud the first time I heard him. He just looked embarrassed until Captain Ericsson bid him to continue. I don't say a thing, anymore, when he does it. I know Chip shall revert to his wild nature when the time comes. And, so shall I! Won't it be grand?

CHAPTER FORTY-NINE: WALTER SINCLAIR'S JOURNAL

May 18, 1863, at sea

We've had some rough seas the last week, as we sailed around Cape Horn, and most of them have been walking past me like ghosts, hanging onto the rails, weaving down the passageways, spewing forth at any mention of victuals being served in the galley. I expected as much from the women, but even the men have been under the weather, except for Greene and his little darkie. I suppose they were in some rough weather when they were sailing around Cape Hatteras in the *Monitor*, and that's enough storm surges to give a two-year-old toddler his sea legs. I decided we had to put to shore at Tierra del Fuego, as the storm on the 17th of May was especially tumultuous. We would most certainly have gone under if I hadn't made this decision.

We made it into the strait of Le Maire at noon, and I held the ship close to the Fuegian shoreline to stay away from the currents. At about three that afternoon we finally anchored at the Bay of Good Success, and the storm at last began to subside, although the clouds still hung above us like gloomy bugbears. As Captain Ericsson advised us, this was the same spot that Charles Darwin and his *Beagle* landed in 1832, and the others seemed quite impressed. I had been here once before, in 1860, running some slaves from the South Pacific to Nassau.

A group of about fifty natives were on shore when we arrived, and the men of the tribe approached us, with the gray and grizzled elders staying in front, with sagging breasts and animal skins wrapped around their loins. I knew their ways, so I brought along some tobacco, and they smiled broadly when I handed it to them. They also talked their chirping gibberish, with those infernal clicking sounds deep in their throats. They sounded rather like Bedlam lunatics, but Ericsson seemed quite taken in by their antics. When they motioned to their younger folk to come up and begin dancing, in our honor, I would suppose, Ericsson immediately began to imitate their prancing, whooping leaps. However, what appalled me the most was when the women and that little black shoeshine boy, Jefferson, all began to sing and dance with them as if they'd been at it for many years!

Was this what it was going to be like once we landed at our "paradise" Easter Island? I certainly hope not! My fiancée, Penelope, was especially strange when all this native paganism was taking place. She kept dancing around young Mister Greene, as his obvious shyness seemed to be a lure for her to embarrass him with her leg kicks and shrill screams. I must say, I wonder if dear Pen has lost a bit of her English reserve? I must talk to her about decorum when we have a few moments alone together.

The storm finally let up, and we all bid adieu to our friends the Fuegians. Captain Ericsson pointed out that "our" natives on Easter Island would be much more isolated, with practices that would probably fascinate us even more than these "primitives."

CHAPTER FIFTY: CHIP JEFFERSON'S JOURNAL

January 7, 1863, at sea

I am really happy to have a secret place to write down my thoughts about what is going on around me. My Papa always told me that literacy was what separated the classes in a democratic society, and so I was taught at an early age to read and to write. I was taught, even though we were slaves, because our masters were much different than most of the owners in the South. Mrs. Sims was always reading to me and teaching me how to read and sound out the words. It's kind of a magic way of seeing the world through symbols, and now that we will journey to our "new world," I will no longer be looked at as strange because I can read and write. Some of the men aboard the Monitor were nice to me, and I would often read them letters from home, and I was even paid to write love letters, although the quartermaster got angry when his lady friend severed their relationship after getting one of my epistles. However, many of them thought I was very strange, and even called me names, just because I could read and write! They said "our people" should not have this skill because we would never do anything except the low-class jobs.

As the youngest aboard this ship, I am given the duties of a cabin boy, but Captains Ericsson and Sinclair have promised me that once we land on Easter Island I will be free to establish my own livelihood, and I will no longer be considered a subordinate. Even at home I did not feel totally free, as my parents, even though they loved me, were also quite a burden.

My friends in the Navy, on the contrary, were very supportive of our race's fight for independence, and now I can finally establish a new life on my own. I no longer distrust Captains Ericsson and Sinclair, or Lieutenant Greene, as they have told me that they were never slave traders. In fact, as they now tell me, we shall never allow slavery or any type of indentured servitude at our new city-state on Easter Island. Just last night, at dinner, Captain Ericsson showed us all his written constitution, and, sure enough, there was an amendment that said, "No slavery or any type of racial servitude will be permitted at Ericssonville." Captain Sinclair laughed at the name our good leader had given the new city, but we all agreed, since it had been Captain Ericsson's idea in the first place, then the least we could do was to allow our city to be named after him. Perhaps one day, if I can become as intelligent and productive as these gentlemen, then I, too, will have a place on Easter Island named for me. Until then, I will continue reading and studying the books Captain Ericsson and Lieutenant Greene have given me, and work hard to earn their respect. Papa always told me that we had to perform much better than the white folks, because we would never be considered equal to begin with. I am hoping, with my complete being, that things will be different on our new island.

Captain Sinclair and his wife are not as friendly as the others. I suppose it's because they are English, and many of the English have taken sides with the Rebels in the South. Mister Sinclair never teaches me anything about being a sailor. Captains Worden and Greene, and even Captain Ericsson will always point out something for me to learn on board ship, but this Sinclair always tells me he's too busy, and he often just laughs in my face, as if he finds it much too absurd that I should be asking him such questions. I shall endeavor to stay away from him in the future, and I will try not to get in his way on the island. In the meantime, the others will help me learn. I still love the sea, and our voyage is quite exciting. Captain Ericsson says we shall stop at Pitcairn Island before we finish our journey to Easter Island. This is where the mutinous crew of the *H.M.S. Bounty*, led by Fletcher Christian, was able to establish another home, free from the hangman's noose. We, too, would most likely be hanged or sent to prison if we stayed in America. This is our only refuge and our only solace. I owe my life to these men, and I will experience my new one thanks to their kindness.

CHAPTER FIFTY-ONE: ARRIVAL AT PITCAIRN ISLAND

May 24, 1863

At 1,400 miles to the west, Pitcairn Island would be their closest neighbor, and John Ericsson wanted to find out how these descendants of the British Navy mutineers on the *H.M.S. Bounty* had survived these many years, since 1790, devoid of contact with civilization. Walter Sinclair, who had visited the island once, in 1858, told Ericsson and the others what little he knew about the present settlers and their history. Walter knew they could not dock in the only bay on the island, Bounty Bay, as it was guarded by treacherous reefs, where many ships before them had grounded and sunk. Thus, the only way they could go ashore was for the men on the island to come out to them in longboats and escort them to the main village, Adamstown, named after the lone survivor of the mutineers, John Adams.

"John Adams was the man responsible for the survival of Pitcairn Island and its population," said Walter, puffing on his after-dinner pipe, standing at the helm, on the night before their arrival at Pitcairn. Captain Ericsson, Chip Jefferson and Dana Greene were on the bridge with him, and they listed earnestly to his story:

"Fletcher Christian, the man who had led the mutineers to this remote island, was a son of the Coroner of Cumberland and of Manx descent on his father's side. He had been to school with the poet William Wordsworth, was well educated and, in the words of a friend, mild, generous and sincere. Certainly his energy and cheerfulness drew both respect and affection from his fellows and, although he died a few years after landing at Pitcairn, he is still remembered as the founder and first leader of the settlement."

"Wordsworth you say? What an esteemed Romantic poet!" said Greene, picturing himself as a modern Fletcher Christian.

"Of the other mutineers, Midshipman Edward Young was also well connected and was devoted to Christian, whom he succeeded as leader; reckless Jack Adams, later to become Patriarch of Pitcairn, was a Cockney orphan; Mills, Brown, Martin and Williams were killed by the Polynesians within four years of arrival; and of the other two, the Scotsman William McCoy and the Cornishman Matthew Quintal little good can be said, except that they were neither better nor worse than the average seaman of the time. On arrival the mutineers made themselves rough leaf- shelters where the village of Adamstown now stands, but the tiny community did not settle down without friction and, indeed, murder. The Tahitians were treated more as slaves than as fellow human beings and their revolt led to the slaying of some of the mutineers and, finally, to their own deaths. By 1794 only Young, Adams, Quintal and McCoy remained of the male settlers, leading households of ten women and children."

Sinclair looked directly at Chip, when he spoke about how the Tahitians were treated, and Chip visibly flinched at the word "murder," as if he had been struck.

"The next four to five years were peaceful except for occasional outbreaks by the women, including an abortive attempt by some to leave the island. Gradually the men and women grew reconciled to their lives and to each other, and all might have remained harmonious had not McCoy, who had once worked in a distillery, discovered how to brew a potent spirit from the roots of the ti plant. By 1799, Quintal had been killed by Young and Adams in self-defense, and McCoy had drowned himself. Then, in 1800, Young died of asthma, leaving John Adams as the sole male survivor of the party that had landed just ten years before."

Ericsson was thinking about what Sinclair had told them, and he realized that his own crew of men and women had much in common with these first mutineers. They even had their own inebriate, Charles McCord, and so John made a mental note to keep his Irish draftsman away from any distilling devices on their island.

"As leader of the community of ten Polynesian women and twenty-three children, the former able seaman, John Adams, showed himself to be as capable, kind and honest as he had formerly been loyal and helpful to Christian and Young.

"Each family had its own house and most, but not all, of them were within the village, planned in English style around a common and fenced to keep the chickens in and the hogs out. Solidly built of local timber, some of them with bedrooms on a second floor, the island homes owed little to Polynesia except their thatched roofs.

"The women had brought their own utensils from Tahiti, which were handed down from mother to daughter, and the men landed tools and other implements from the *Bounty* and fashioned more as necessary. Food cooked in Polynesian stone- lined ovens, consisting mainly of yams, taro and bananas with coconut cream and an occasional pig, bird or goat was in Polynesian style, served twice a day, at noon and nightfall. Clothes were at first made out of sail cloth from the *Bounty*, but they were later replaced by loin cloths and skirts of tapa, the traditional Polynesian fiber cloth. In brief, European and Polynesian ways mingled in complete isolation from the rest of the world."

"You see, gentlemen? The inventiveness of these settlers was key to their survival!" Ericsson pointed out, lighting up his own pipe and puffing away like a locomotive. "Continue, Captain, this is all quite interesting indeed."

Walter motioned for Greene to take the helm, which the young man did, and then Sinclair sat down at the chart table's chair to address them with his full attention.

"John Adams was no scholar. He read with difficulty and could hardly write, but he was essentially a gentle man who humbly discharged his responsibility for the community he headed. Such was his manner that all took pleasure in obeying his example, which he patterned on virtue and piety and regulated by the *Church of England's Book of Common Prayer*, on Sunday services, family prayers and grace before and after every meal. And to ensure everybody's well-being, Adams saw to it that the young people cultivated the land, cared for the stock and were not allowed to marry until they could support a family."

Walter Sinclair had told his story to this point with some amount of satisfaction. He was pleased with what Adams had accomplished, and that's why he remembered. Adams was a man, like himself, who was almost illiterate, but who had understood the simple skills of human survival. Walter also believed his own survival skills were going to prove just as important to their expedition on Easter Island, despite the two Union "inventors" and their brash little darkie.

"What happened to them next?" asked Chip, as his dark eyes had been riveted on the tall Captain as he told his tale. Chip's own reflections were about how he would fit into their own island life in the near future.

"As he grew old, Adams worried about the future of his flock, but his appeals to the British Government and missions for a successor to lead and educate them were not met, and it was to voluntary exiles that succession fell.

"The first was John Buffett, a shipwright from Bristol who landed with John Evans, a Welshman, in 1823. Both married island girls and founded families, and Buffett taught the children and took over the church services.

"The population had now risen to 66 from the 35 of 17 years earlier, and Adams, believing the land was yielding less, seeing the supply of timber decreasing and concerned that the erratic water supply would be insufficient for the growing population, sought the community's removal to Australia.

"Meantime, in 1828, another settler arrived. George Nobbs, alleged to be the illegitimate son of a marquis, was well educated and had served both in the British and Chilean Navies. He was a strong character and soon ousted Buffett from the role of schoolmaster and pastor. Then, in March 1829, John Adams, venerable and corpulent, died at the age of 62. He left behind a community which, though it originated in mutiny and had suffered misery and murder, was to form the basis of countless future sermons. The dramatic regeneration was virtually Adams' work alone, and he was mourned as 'Father', the name by which he had been known to every member of the community."

To Sinclair, this was the end of the story. Anything that

followed the death of John Adams was anti-climactic at the least.

"Well? What happened after Adams passed on?" Greene asked.

"I really don't know. I wasn't interested in what more this Mister George Nobbs had to tell me. Besides, we left the next morning to continue our voyage." Ericsson cleared his throat and hit his pipe against the side of his palm to empty the burnt tobacco. "I will inquire as to the rest of this history as soon as we dock tomorrow morning. We can learn from their history, and this story is not half told. You must not be so eager to resolve things, Walter, as we shall have a long time to plan our new civilization. I want to have as much information I can get to do the planning."

I can do the planning, thought Walter, in disgust. *What gives you the right to do our planning, old man? We'll see who leads the survivalists on Easter Island. Inventions of yours will do little good when it comes to establishing a daily routine. It shall be me, Captain Walter Sinclair, who will take on the role of John Adams for our little group!*

Dana Greene stretched his arms out wide and yawned. "I don't know about you, fellows, but I'm going to turn in. Wake me for the next watch, Captain," he told Sinclair.

"Right," said Walter, as he took the helm back from the young lieutenant. *You need to be awakened from your dreams, all right!* Sinclair thought, as he watched the dark ocean swell before him, like an invitation to adventure. *We'll see who shall be king of Easter Island!*

CHAPTER FIFTY-TWO: THE HISTORY OF PITCAIRN

May 25, 1863

When they all arrived at Adamstown, the women were so overjoyed to at last have access to a proper bath that they did not hesitate to ask to use the facilities. Mr. and Mrs. Young, who were the leaders of the small group living on the island, escorted the three women to a sheltered, palm frond covered shack where there was a tub installed. Hot water was brought in to allow the women, one by one, to enter the tub and clean themselves with the tallow soap made from coconut milk and pig fat. "This tub was on board the *H.M.S. Bounty* when she arrived here in 1790. Before the ship was burned, the survivors brought this tub and many other supplies on shore," Mayhew Young explained, motioning for two of his sons to fetch the hot water. "We hope you ladies enjoy your bath. I'll return with some of your towels. It was so very kind of you to bear these as gifts for our small community. When we arrived here from Norfolk Island, we discovered there was no cloth at all on the island, and the French had been here during our evacuation years. We have not had cloth material since 1856."

John Ericsson was discussing the recent history of Pitcairn

Island with Moses Young, the other leader of the small group of 16 who now lived there. Ericsson believed he had much to learn from this group, as they had decided to return to Pitcairn after only two years living on Norfolk Island, 3,300 miles west of Pitcairn.

"By 1850, the population was 156 and increasing rapidly. Our friends in England and the Pacific were again discussing the question of emigration, for it was feared that land would soon become insufficient, and fish had deserted the coastal waters since the landslides caused by the great storm of 1845. As we did not wish to experience the devastation of our emigration to Tahiti in 1831, when we lost 10 of our tribe to disease, we decided that an uninhabited island would be much more suitable to our needs. Thus, as the British Government had recently decided that Norfolk Island could no longer serve as a penal colony, we were told that we could use the island for our new home."

"What do you suppose caused your discomfort in Tahiti? I would think being with a larger community would be invigorating," said Ericsson, seeing his own group's situation as analogous, as they were also headed to a native community of Polynesians who were not used to having outsiders in their midst.

Moses, who was obviously the group's historian, responded with some admirable examples. "Queen Pomare IV and her people treated the Pitcairn Islanders with great generosity and kindness. Land was made available for the islanders to build their own homes and a large house was offered for their temporary lodging in Papeete. The Pitcairners, however, did not feel at home and could not adjust to this different way of life. We had become on the one hand too European in our ways and, on the other, stricter in morals and sexual behavior than our hosts. We longed to return to our own habits in our own island, all the more so when infectious diseases, to which we had little immunity, began to kill us."

"Ah, I see! No immunity from the diseases of these Tahitians was your ultimate downfall," Ericsson said, all the while thinking about how his own group would fare on their own island retreat.

"Yes, disease was quite devastating to the group. On 21 April, within a month of arrival in Tahiti, Thursday October Christian I, the son of Fletcher Christian, the first child born on Pitcairn, died. His death was followed by the youngest, Lucy Anne Quintal, and during the next two months there were 10 more deaths and only a single birth. Attempts to arrange for their return to Pitcairn failed, until Captain William Driver of the Salem whaler *Charles Doggett* arrived at Papeete and offered to take the remaining 65 survivors back to their island home for $500. The local community immediately organized a subscription; the Pitcairn Islanders, anxious to return, contributed to this by selling blankets and other necessities. Captain Driver sailed with them from Papeete on 14 August 1831, and reached Pitcairn on 3 September."

Ericsson realized that he would have to invent some way to protect his group from the diseases of Easter Island. But first, he needed more information. "Did the Pitcairn Islanders eat and socialize with the natives while they lived there?" he asked, as an idea was beginning to hatch in his brain.

"Why, yes. We learned to eat together in their ritual and sacred meals. We have a copy of James Morrison's book about the religious customs among the Tahitians. He was the Boatswain's Mate aboard the Bounty, and he chose to stay in Tahiti after the crew mutinied, and Fletcher Christian and his group continued on to Pitcairn. I'll let you read our copy. It was given to us by a visiting American whaler by the name of Paul Sanderson." Moses Young extracted a black, wide, and hand-written journal from the shelf behind him and handed it to Ericsson. "Take care, Captain, as this contains important information about the sacred rituals of Tu Nui e A'a i Te Atua, King Pomare I, paramount chief of the Pare-Aue region. I shall require its return before you leave the island."

"Certainly, sir!" Ericsson said, standing up. "I believe we should find the others now and take your guided tour of this island. We would enjoy hearing about how you were able to survive after your return from Norfolk Island. We can learn a lot from you, I am certain."

"I'll do my best to inform you, Captain. We get so few visitors; it is an honor to share pleasantries with you."

Outside the hut where the women were bathing, two boys, of about ten and twelve years of age, were peeking inside the bath chamber from between wooden planks. As Anna Cameron-Greene was lowering her naked form into the tub, she spotted them, and she screamed. The boys ran from the hut, more frightened than Anna, and this was the end of the bathing for the three women. They later met with the men inside the dining room next to the Young's shack, which stood next to the tallest palm tree on the island. It overlooked the bay and was sheltered by the rising hills of

Adamstown.

For dinner that evening, the guests from the *Caine* were fed sea bass and pork in the conventional European manner, with dishes and cutlery given to the islanders as gifts from shipwrecked sailors who wanted to show their gratitude. Moses Young pointed out that they were able to survive from these gifts because there were many shipwrecks on the treacherous reefs surrounding Pitcairn, and the Pitcairn Islanders used their two longboats to rescue the survivors and bring them ashore. The community fed and clothed the shipwrecked sailors who, after they returned home to relate their adventure, rewarded their rescuers with gifts of crockery, clothes, flour, books and even an organ.

After dinner, Miriam Christian entertained everyone with a tune on the organ. She played several American favorites, and Dana Greene danced with his wife, Anna, and even Walter Sinclair and John Ericsson tried their dancing feet with their women, although with much less success. In fact, Penelope enviously watched Dana Greene's wife, as she was spun, around and around, and they all laughed uproariously to the tune of "Yankee Doodle Dandy." I'll soon have your doodle dandy, my lady, thought Penelope, as she trudged around the floor with Walter. There will be time enough for me to attract the likes of Dana Greene!

Before leaving Pitcairn, John Ericsson gave Moses Young the gift of a fifth of Irish whiskey, and they both sat before a roaring fire on the beach to drink it. Ericsson, however, pretended to drink, and as Young would raise his cup to down the liquor, the captain would fling the contents of his cup into the sand. Thus, as his host became increasingly inebriated, Ericsson remained stone sober. The goal of his plan was to get Young sufficiently drunk so that he would forget about the book he had given John.

The trick worked splendidly, and John Ericsson was able to journey back in the longboat without the company of one Moses Young, who was recuperating with a horrible hangover. John knew this book would assist him in developing a plan to gain control over the natives on Easter Island. He needed the trust of these people in order to keep the power base he needed to establish his Platonic Republic. Sinclair and Greene were potential rivals for control over the island, and Ericsson wanted to gain the upper hand before they landed.

John also knew that many of the problems of the Pitcairn

Islanders stemmed from the women, and he therefore wanted a way to keep his own women out of mischief. He had already seen Penelope's wandering eyes upon young Dana Greene, and this would not do in his new republic! Indeed, Ericsson realized he was in part to blame for the romantic notions Greene had about Easter Island, but now was the time to stop the young man's wild imaginings before they became a hindrance.

After they all arrived back on board the Caine, Ericsson told everyone he was going to his quarters and that he should not be disturbed. He said he "needed to plan for their arrival at Easter Island," and he put Sinclair in charge. It would take another week's voyage to reach their final destination, and Ericsson's planning was to be about how their new government would be set-up, to be certain, but it was also going to be about forecasting to stop potential uprisings amongst the citizens and tribal members. He already had a few inventions in mind that could keep his new society in line, and he was not afraid to use them.

CHAPTER FIFTY-THREE: ON TO EASTER ISLAND

May 26, 1863

Behind his locked door and under his copper gas lamp, John Ericsson opened the journal of *Bounty* crewmember, James Morrison, and began reading. The text, although it was filled with grammatical and other erroneous passages, proved to be quite enlightening. Two hours later, when he had completed his analysis, he was especially interested in a passage in the journal which read:

> *Turban bound on with Secred leaves a Breastplate (Calld Tawmee) on their Breast and their Cloaths bound on with a Sash or Girdle of Braided hairor Cocoanut Fibers neatly platted of a Great length, and Made up in Bights or doubles, with a Tasell at each end. The Provisions brought to the Morai must be dressd on it, and near the House, where Baskets are kept for keeping it in, should it last three or four days.*
>
> *They always wash themselves before, and after they eat, and should a Dead lizard, Mouse or rat toutch them they would wash before they handled any Food and should they happen to find one in or near their oven or toutch any of their Culinary Utensils they would use them No More. Notwitshtanding which the[y] will eat a Hog which has died if they know of No disorder which might be the Occasion of his Death.*
>
> *If any person toutches a dead body except of those killd by War, or for*

195

Sacrafice, is rendered unclean and can toutch no provisions with their hands for one Month, during which time they must be fed by another. If the Man killd in War be toutched by a relation they must undergo the like but otherwise Washing is sufficient. If any person have a running sore or large Ulcers they are toutchd by no person else and if they die the House wherein they lived is burnt with evry thing belonging to it. When Mourning for the Death of any relation they Shave the Fore part of their heads and sometimes the hind part together with their Eye brows & beards and Cut their heads with Sharks teeth in excess of Grief or Joy. See the Mourning Ceremony. They always Venerate the Grey heads, and are kind to Strangers, and protect the Fatherless & the Widow. A Child may Curse its Father, Mother, Uncle or Aunt but it would be Blasphemy for them to Curse it. The Child may not Curse its Grand Father, Grandmother, Brothers or Sisters but the Grand Father or Grandmother may Curse their Grand Children with Impunity, but it is Death For any Man to Blaspheme or revile the Gods or the King.

John believed he understood why the Pitcairn refugees in Tahiti had contracted diseases. There was much cutting of the skin by these natives, and it was a medical fact that disease was often spread through infections contracted from open wounds. Moses Young had pointed out that the Pitcairn settlers in Tahiti made a point of taking up all the practices of the natives, and if they did the things described in Morrison's journal, well then, it was obvious that disease and infections could have run rampant amongst their group, resulting in the deaths of so many

Ericsson understood it to be his duty to keep his people away from such blood-letting practices, but he also knew he must perform the obligatory worship, or else he would never gain an upper hand with these primitives. However, he had with him certain vaccines against the modern plagues, and these would help inoculate the natives as well as his passengers. As he read on, Ericsson saw where he could perform some practices that were less dangerous but still important to the tribe's cultural traditions:

War in this Country often happens from mere trifles; however what we may think a trifle may seem to them of Great Consequence —— The Districts have all a parting or Boundary line, frequently a river, which separates their lands from each other. If any dispute happens the party Who happens to be the Occasion of it are Calld upon to make good any damage or defeciency which if they refuse to do war is declared in this Manner ——

The Priests and the head Men of the Contending Party being Assembled near their Bounds, and having consulted the Preists — if they give a Favourable answer War is then the Word and the party who think themselves most Injured send out a

Slinger to the Boundary line, where having Charged the Sling he discharges it over the Heads of the Opposite party Crying out 'W"affwa te Vye ay O' which Signifies the War is declared but litterally The Water has borne down its banks'. This is answer d by a Slinger from the other side who slings a Stone and Calls out in the same manner; they then Cry out to each other 'Yowrye t 'Eatooa te Tamye ra' — 'God save you in your War' — they then return home seemingly in peace, and make a War Feast, killing a Number of Hogs for the Warriors, and sometimes make a human Sacrifice & Next morning repair to the Appointed Ground. They are always attended by inspired priests who before they come to the Charge encourage them to Fight manfully and there is no fear of Victory and Spirits them up by blowing their Conch Shells which they always use on these Occasions having a bamboo tube which they blow through like a Trumpet. They always send or offer conditions of Peace to those which are deemd the weakest party which if they refuse & they are Worsted they are drove from their posessions and the Conquering Chief puts a Subordinate Chief of his own in to Command the Conquered Country and if the Vanquishd people will promise to pay obedience to the New Chief they are permitted to remain and enjoy their lands as before, but this they seldom will do, they having so great an affection for their Chiefs that they had rather partake of his disgrace and loose their Estates then enjoy their property under another. Should

they act otherwise they would be very meanly lookd on, be made a by word among their Countrymen, and their lives be a torment to them afterwards.

They take No Captives nor give any quarter, unless a man falls in with one who has formerly been His adopted friend, a breach of which they were never known to make —— they are not forced to Fight any longer then they please, and a man never obtains the Name of a Warrior tho he kills his Man, should he receive any wound himself, as they think that a Man Who suffers himself to be wounded does not know how to defend himself, and tis more Honor to return with whole bones then broken ones. Tho they are not Imediately under the Authority of the Chief in Battle, yet they Fight furiously knowing that in case of being Vanquishd they loose all their posessions. Yet tho this seems of small account where it is but ask and have, yet they all prefer the having to give then being forced to receive ——

197

and when they make a present, it is so freely done and so graceful that Christianity may blush at the action and be ashamed to be surpass'd by those whom we Call Savages —— This is the Chief reason that a Taheitean has to Fight for and in Some of their Sea Actions Much blood has been shed as they Frequently lassh Bow to bow & fight it out, when the Strongest party generally get the day and the Weaker are forced to save themselves by Jumping Overboard.

Their Weapons are Spears of 12 or 14 feet long pointed with the Stings of the Sting Ray —— Clubs of 7 or 8 feet, both of which are Made of Toa a hard heavy wood, Slings made of the Platted fibers of the Cocoa Nut; they have bows and Javlins for Sport but never use them in War.

Some of their War Canoes are very large, and carry from one to Three Hundred Men; they have often one Hundred paddlers all of which have heaps of Stones and each man a Sling besides Spears & Clubbs, and when the one party becomes too strong for the Others they are forced to Fly and the Conquerors Carry off their prize in Triumph — Such was mostly the Fate of o 'Toos Fleet after Captain Cook left him, and since that time his Navy has gone almost to ruin, tho he has still been lucky, and often Conqueror yet he always prefers peace to War.

They always bring off the Dead if they can, by any means, as all that they leave are Carried to the Morai where the body being offered as a Sacrafice, the lower Jaw bone being Cut out and placed in the Morai as a Trophie and the Body is interrd in the Morai. The Man who kilid him now takes his Name. This being the only Method by which they attain to the Charracter of a Warrior they must bring off their dead which is often severely disputed by the living and especially the Friends of the Fallen Warrior who fight more furious to protect the body when dead then they did to assist him while living — If the Conqueror Should prevail and Maintain his conquest he takes the Name of His Adversary as a Title of Honor — after the Peace is made the relations of the Deceased Warriors soon find out the Men who killd them and each Family send a present to the Man by Who their Freind or Relation was kilid & hire a Set of Urre Heiva or a Sort of People somthing similar to our Morris Dancers and a Principal part is acted by the Daughter or Nearest Female relation of the Deceased Warrior in a Dance at the House of the Man who killd him. The Dance being Finished the Cloth, Matting & Dresses are all presented to Him and He Now entertains all the Deceaseds Relations, sumptuosly for Several days and they Declare that they [do not] Owe him any Grudge or animosity for killing their Relation and their Sorrow is now turnd to Joy and evry thing is most amicably Settled and the Conqueror, to Make the

Friendship more Firm on his part, adopts the Nearest relation of the Deceased as his Friend, and by bearing his Name becomes one of the Family and is ever after Treated as such and is as much beloved in the Family as if he had been born in it.

These passages in Morrison's journal would prove to be quite valuable to him. He now understood the culture of war amongst the natives of the Pacific. It was this knowledge, he believed, that would give him the method of control. Without a thorough understanding of his people, he knew he could never invent the machines and war tools that would make him their king. He would, at last, fulfill Plato's dream of establishing a republic, headed by an authentic philosopher king!

CHAPTER FIFTY-FOUR: THE ARRIVAL

June 15, 1863

It had taken them longer than they had planned, as the weather in the South Pacific was unpredictable, and they met with two storms. However, as Captain Sinclair was an experienced seaman, the ship was able to maneuver through the rain and giant waves, but they were driven off course for several days. Finally, back on course, Sinclair steamed the rest of the way. The women were quite excited about their landing, and they spent many hours talking about what they would do once ashore for the first time.

Visiting the village and doing some primitive shopping were foremost in Anna's mind, as she was getting quite irritated with life aboard ship and with the seaman's attire they had to wear, day in and day out. The other women also wanted to get new clothes and other items to make their habitat more attractive and livable, and they had some unique ideas about how to decorate.

Chip ran around packing things for all of them, and the men kept busy with the arrangements of a more technical nature. Ericsson knew he must establish a quick connection with the natives on the island so he could set-up his new colony without problems. He planned to seek out the priests of the tribe, as he was prepared to show them some feats of spectacular genius. He knew fishing and land cultivation would be most beneficial to his cause, and he had two inventions to show them that would be most valuable to his cause.

Captain Sinclair knew the local harbor to land, Hanga Piko, which was sheltered from storms, but it was very difficult to navigate. Therefore, Sinclair had procured a map from another British captain that instructed him how to navigate amongst the treacherous currents and volcanic rocks. The main population lived at Hanga Roa, but the swell there was quite dangerous to any anchored ships. Ericsson wanted to land at Hanga Piko because he said it would serve their interests best, as they would need access to their ship in order to construct the new Ericssonville colony.

As they came into the harbor, the sight that greeted them was not to be believed. Instead of a lush, tropical paradise, filled with waving palms and greenery, what they saw was a barren land of eroded, sand-like dirt and scattered shrubs. Captain Ericsson stood with the other men on the beach at Ovahe, which was said to be the place where the first King of the island, Hoto Matua, landed in his double-hulled canoe in around 400 A.D. Ericsson was certain the books had said that this land was a paradise, but the sight he now saw was far from Edenesque. What had happened? What had caused this land to become so barren and forsaken?

It was Dana Greene who spoke first. "I suppose we need to push on inland to see what else she has to offer, right mates?"

Sinclair laughed. "So, this is Ericssonville? Indeed, I can see the resemblance, Mister Ericsson. She's as nearly as bald as you are!" The Brit ran his big hand over the elder Swede's shining head.

The wind picked-up at that moment, and a dark cloud appeared overhead. Ericsson knew it rained almost every day in this climate, and he also knew they needed to get things unloaded despite the approaching downpour. "Get to work, men! We need to establish a small beach colony here, and I want at least two tents pitched over there by those caves in the side of the cliff," he ordered, pointing to the several hundred feet of volcanic ash cliff that bordered the white, sandy beachfront property.

Six hours later, the two tents were in place, and the women were busy cooking stew on a large, cast iron pot over a coal fire. They had brought over 200 pounds of coal with them from America, and it was good thing, judging from the sparse fuel all around them. Only Anna seemed to be out of composure, as she had become quite seasick during the storms, and she was still not in a good mood. The harsh living conditions were not what she was expecting out of life on "their island," and she told her husband as much. Dana told her he was going inland with Captain Ericsson to see if they could make contact with the natives. He assured her that they would soon find comfort, and then he gave her a hug and a kiss. "Anna, we can't go back there. I am a deserter, and they would hang me or put me into prison for the rest of my life. We will find our new life right here, I promise you."

Dana's assurances were somewhat comforting, but Anna was still out of sorts as she stabbed at a potato before slicing it sideways and then tossing it into the pot. "I say we should visit the natives' village ourselves, ladies—tomorrow," she said, a smug tone coming into her voice.

Penelope poked at the coals and laughed, "I say, perhaps you should strip down and do a little fertility dance to initiate us into your tribe!"

Amelia Ericsson raised her eyebrows in exasperation. "Let's not have any of that! You know how the Captain is about our new civilization. We can't have any pagans running about and causing mischief. There will be no unescorted shopping visits without the men going with us."

"Oh, Amelia, I thought we were in agreement about Women's Suffrage?" asked Penelope, realizing that her friend had become much more conservative since they had voyaged to their New World. "Why shouldn't we have the same rights to explore as those men of ours?"

"I'm not saying we shouldn't have the same rights. I'm just saying that we don't know what dangers lurk out there. We may be equal in mind and spirit, but we certainly don't have the martial skills that our men do!" Amelia responded.

Dana Greene and John Ericsson came into the "cooking cave" and inhaled deeply. "My, that smells delicious!" said Dana, putting an arm around Anna's waist.

"Yes, but we must wait to eat, my boy. Ladies, we shall be going out for some time to explore the island. The other men will be in shortly. Feed them, and keep some aside for us, if you would. I will address the group when we return."

"Yes, my dear. We shall certainly save you both hearty

portions," said Amelia, wiping her hands on her apron.

The two men picked-up a gas lantern and a compass and turned to leave. "Welcome to Ericssonville!" the Captain proclaimed, putting an arm around Greene's shoulders as they stepped out into the gathering dusk.

Drizzle was coming down in a fine mist, and it reminded Dana of the night the Monitor had sunk. He was happy to finally be ashore. "Right, Captain. We've finally arrived. May I read something appropriate from Mister Emerson at tonight's gathering? I believe it would be a nice touch."

"Certainly, you may! The time has come for our new civilization to understand our role amongst the natives. That's why I wanted us to go out tonight. I want to show you a spot that will be quite valuable to us in the coming days."

"What spot is that, Captain?" asked Dana, excitement in his voice.

"You shall soon see, my boy, you shall soon see."

Standing just inside, on the shadow side of the cave, Walter Sinclair watched the two men as they walked over the sand and into a break in the volcanic cliffs, as the rain increased, and they soon disappeared, leaving him to raise his collar and mutter before stepping out after them, "Yes, we shall all see!"

CHAPTER FIFTY-FIVE: FATHER PEREZ

June 15, 1863

Captain Ericsson and Dana Greene arrived at a cave near the base of the Crater called Rano Cao after walking for two hours in the rain across the island. Ericsson had learned about the priest, Father Adolpho Perez, from Moses Young on Pitcairn Island. Father Perez had journeyed to Easter Island from Chile in 1856, ostensibly to convert these "savages" to Christianity. He was a member of a group of ten Catholic missionaries of the Jesuit order, who landed by ship, and he was the only one who stayed. Four died of smallpox, and five left by boat, in 1857, when their efforts to convert the natives proved futile. Father Perez remained on Rapanui because he had been converted by the natives to their new religion.

When Ericsson and Greene entered the cave that night, they met a man who was a far cry from the Catholic order of Jesuits. Indeed, he was almost naked, with sealskin wrapped around his loins and sandals made from polished driftwood on his feet. He was seated in the corner of the cave at a small desk, with an overhead torch lighting his work on several tablets, which were stacked all around him, like so many Hebrew Commandments. His hair was wild and black, and around his sun-bronzed neck was the figure of a wooden carving that appeared to be in the shape of some kind of bird creature.

Ericsson, who spoke Spanish, addressed the priest. He planned to keep what he found out from this gentleman all to himself for possible use at a later time. He told the priest that they had arrived to establish a colony and to work with the local natives to improve their lot.

Father Perez began to laugh maniacally, tears running down his sun-baked cheeks. He told Ericsson about the sad history of Easter Island. The population had once been large, seven to nine thousand, and the clans were formed on various parts of the island. However, there evolved a centerpiece for their pagan religion, and it was the carving of the huge moai statues. The father explained to John that it was this cult of statues that eventually created the environmental destruction that they saw today all over the island.

"The Hanau Eepe and Hanau Momoko had a war, or so legend tells it. Hanau Eepe means fat and Hanau Momoko means thin. All but one of the Hanau Eepe was killed. The creation of the moai destroyed the many thousands of palms and sweet potatoes which grew all over the island at that time," said the priest.

"How did that occur?" asked Ericsson.

"They used up the trees transporting the moai all over the island. They greased the rollers with sweet potatoes, and pushed the statues until they could be raised in a ceremony. The clans competed and began fighting over the diminishing resources. There was even cannibalism!" the priest whispered, as if he could negate the fact simply by making it less audible.

"What sort of government exists today?" asked Ericsson.

"Most of the clans have moved up onto Rano Kau volcano. They live in the village called Orongo. I am their priest, the only one from below who is allowed to go up there. It is the place where heathen rituals are practiced! The god of fertility, Meke-Meke, rules up there, and none of the clans living elsewhere on the island is allowed to go up there. However, when the Bird Man has been appointed, after the great contest, the island becomes possessed!" the priest's eyes grew wide, and Ericsson understood that he had to counter this demonic cult in some way, or this island's population would never see civilization again.

Walter Sinclair stood just outside the cave, and he could hear the priest speaking to Ericsson and Greene. Sinclair could also speak Spanish. He learned it in his travels to Spain for English merchants. The idea of this fertility cult intrigued him immensely. This would be a perfect way to seize power over the natives and over Ericsson and his ideas of law and order. If this Bird Man were given power over the island, then he would find out what it would take to win the contest! Sinclair left the cave, and he secretly vowed to visit Orongo as soon as he could figure a way to get there. Perhaps this priest could get him up there, he thought, and he put his hand on the revolver tucked inside his belt. The gun felt cold and securely persuasive.

* * *

After returning to the encampment, Ericsson told the others what he had learned from the priest, Father Perez. Of course, what he told them was not the truth, as he did not want any of them being tempted by the pagan rituals on the volcano.

He knew he needed to act before the contest began, and he also knew that if the others knew about this Bird Man cult, then they might be tempted to participate. Therefore, Ericsson told them about the poor, crazy priest, who had been broken by the harsh elements of the island. He said it was their job to teach the natives how to restore the island to natural wealth, and he had brought the implements to do just that. "Soon," said Ericsson, puffing out his chest, "this will be Ericssonville, and these people will be civilized!"

CHAPTER FIFTY-SIX: HANGA ROA CLAN

July 21, 1863

Ericsson learned there were two major clans, or mata, on Rapanui. The surviving clan at Hanga Roa numbered about 200 natives, led by their tribal leader, King Maurata, to whom Ericsson was introduced in a grand ceremony. King Maurata was the fifty-seventh king going back to the founding king of the island, Hotu Matua. Maurata's clan, together with the high priest, named Kannon, was gathered all around the two men, as they discussed the restoration of the land to agricultural pursuits. The natives wore castoff clothing from the ships of war that had visited, and many seemed to enjoy sporting brass buttons. Many were also ornately tattooed, and the women had intricate patterns drawn on the skin below the waist, and the lines were fine, like lace- work, and from the thigh to the knee the appearance was that of silk tights. Others wore clothing made from the branch bark of the Hibiscus that grew near the village. Some of the women were bare-breasted, as they collected in chattering bunches all around the men, and they also wore cast-off women's hats and dresses.

King Maurata spoke to Ericsson through pictures he drew on an elaborate picture board, similar to the rongo-rongo tablets the priest had shown him. King Maurata told John Ericsson about the other clan, the Fainga, who had formed after the island became deforested during "the Moai Wars between the long ears and the short ears." There was no clan leader of the

Fainga's 600 native members. Instead, the Bird Man cult formed the ritualized basis for their existence, and, of course, for the yearly contest to see who would earn the right to become Bird Man and rule the island. King Maurata told Ericsson that his clan had never won the Bird Man contest. In fact, they were most often subjected to the most horrendous degradations. Many of their women were taken off to become "love slaves" to the Fainga, and their clan had to pay great donations from their sparse supply of chickens, rats and their only crop, sugarcane.

Ericsson asked the chief what life had been like before the Moai Wars, and King Maurata drew pictures of giant palm trees, swimming dolphins and large canoes. Obviously, there had been a disastrous ecological failure of some kind, and Ericsson supposed it had to do with the construction of the moai, and the resulting competition between clans, as the renegade priest Father Perez had suggested. He also knew his inventions could bring this land back to its original splendor, and this would be his method to establish himself as a leader in their midst.

First, Ericsson showed the clan the seeds of the Chilean wine palm, the giant plants that grew to be over 60 feet tall. He had gathered over 200 of these seeds during their visit off the coast of Tierra del Fuego. He also showed them the steel plow, the device that would till the rich, volcanic earth of Easter Island, so the palms could be planted. Ericsson explained how he would build a network of canals and irrigation waterways, so they could supply the necessary water to their new crops of breadfruit, corn, yams and lettuce. He also explained that they could build canoes once more and harvest fish and their eggs along with crustaceans, which could be farmed inland, within salt water tide pools. They would also visit Motu Motiro Hiva, the uninhabited island 260 miles away, where they could gather eggs from the wild birds that nest there by the thousands.

At the mention of the birds' eggs, there was an uproar from the assembled natives. Egg collection was the province of the warrior clan of the Bird Man, and the Fainga would kill any person who attempted to gather eggs before the competition. King Maurata explained that the annual contest took place in the summer, when the strongest men of the clans would gather at the cliffs overlooking the tiny islands of Mutu Rau Kau and Muto Nui, where the Sooty Terns would arrive to lay their eggs. Only King Maurata and the young men who were competing were allowed into the village of Orongo for the Bird Man contest. King Maurata's last honorary job was giving the ceremonial "go!" to the men as they plunged down the side of the cliffs on their way to swim across the shark-infested waters to retrieve the first egg and return it and become crowned "Bird Man" for the coming year.

Otherwise, the warrior cult held dominion over the island, and King Maurata did not believe Ericsson's "gardening" tools would do much good against the spears and knives of the Fainga. It was at that moment that Ericsson motioned to Dana Greene, who had come with him, and the young man uncovered the invention of one Dr. Richard Jordan Gatling, a close friend of Ericsson's.

Greene, with some reluctance, fed cartridges into the top hopper of the gun. The Gatling gun was a hand-crank-operated weapon with six barrels revolving around a central shaft. The cartridges were fed to the gun by gravity through the hopper mounted on the top of the gun. Six cam-operated bolts alternately wedged, fired, and dropped the bullets, which were contained in steel chambers. The Gatling used the six barrels to partially cool the gun during firing. Since the gun was capable of firing 600 rounds a minute, each barrel fired 100 rounds per minute. One can imagine the commotion that ensued once Greene began cranking this weapon. There was no doubt in any of the assembled natives' minds that they were about to experience the dawn of a new civilization.

CHAPTER FIFTY-SEVEN: FAINGA CLAN

July 21, 1863

Walter did not use the gun on Father Perez, as the priest was more than happy to take him to the village of Orongo, on the outer rim of the Rano Kau volcano. The crazy priest even sang songs in Spanish as they made their way up to the top. Once there, Walter noticed that the soil was much more fertile, and there were many green ferns growing wild all over the rim and down into the valley of the volcano itself. Rano Kau was one of three volcanoes on the island.

Easter Island was born out of the ocean by volcanic eruptions, and the island had a triangle shape that was formed by the three large volcanoes located at the corners. The highest volcanic cone on the island was Maunga Terevaka in the northeast corner, which rose to 1,674 feet. Rano Kau volcano, the second largest, had fresh water inside its long dormant center, one of the few sites on the island for fresh water. The breezes at the top of the volcano were comforting to Walter, and he could see, off in the distance, his ship anchored in the harbor at Hanga Piko.

The houses at Orongo were not made from bulrushes, as were the design of the huts in the village below. Instead, this warrior caste had constructed stone dwellings inside the volcanic cliffs, rising from the sea, overlooking the two small islands of Mutu Rau Kau and Muto Nui.

The priest noticed Walter staring at the houses. He spoke to him in Spanish, "*Las casas de las mortes, señor.* These are the death chambers. Men who fall down the face of the cliffs during the contest usually wash up on the beaches. They put their bodies inside these houses as an honor. To die during the competition for the Bird Man is a great thing!"

Walter understood the logic of that. He had risked his life many times for different causes. Going after Ericsson and his attempt to sink the Monitor were contests to him, just like these young men who wanted to be the Bird Man. He also knew what Ericsson and Greene were up to down in the village. The Gatling was certainly a nice touch. However, Walter knew where the ammunition was stored, as he was the captain. The Bird Man clan sounded like his kind of chaps. Fertility rights? What was that coming toward them?

Sinclair and the priest stood still as a crowd of young, completely nude women surrounded them, giggling, and draped flowers around their necks as they stood in front of the main hut. This was the "communal hut," where the Fainga clan met to dance and to bloody raise hell! Sinclair ducked his head as he entered the small entrance to the low hut. Inside, he could hear the sound of drums, and he could make out an altar where a man in a feathered costume sat. The big torches stood on either side of his throne, and several of the nude women were lounging, in a variety of alluring poses, at his feet, on rugs made from the flag of a Peruvian merchant ship.

The priest pointed to the Bird Man. "The birds have laid their eggs, and soon the contest will begin. This man will be replaced by the new victor."

"Ah, and this new Bird Man gets to rule the roost, correct?" asked Sinclair.

"Yes, but not until they have sacrificed this man to the fertility god Meke-Meke."

"What? You mean they kill the Bird Man?" Walter was surprised. However, a plan was forming in his mind as he heard this new fact.

"Yes, it's considered a great honor to die at the peak of one's power. You see, we have been raided recently by Peruvian slave traders. Over five-hundred of our people were taken prisoner, and several were shot as they tried to escape. Therefore, this contest has taken on a bit of a desperate purpose."

"I see. There is something I want you to do for me before the games begin. In return, I will guarantee you receive all the food and liquor you need from my ship's store." Sinclair put his arm around the priest's shoulders.

"Of course! What is it you need, senor?"

"I don't want any of my fellow travelers to know about what happens to the Bird Man. Can you see that this happens?"

The Bird Man stood up as a group of natives took him by his arms and guided him out of the hut. This was the sacrificial escort, and the young man held his head high with pride as he was marched outside. The feathered headdress waved in the breeze as he bent down to fit through the narrow opening.

"I will not tell any of your compadres. Also, I don't think there will be a problem with the natives telling them about this ritual, as it is sacred and is not mentioned. Even if they did speak of the fate of our Bird Man, it would not sound as if their words meant what they, in fact, do mean."

"What are you suggesting?" asked Sinclair.

"Their word for the ritual sacrifice of the Bird Man is fekitoa, which means 'a gathering of two men.' You see, the natives believe that after the Bird Man is sacrificed his spirit immediately is met by the Great Spirit, Meke-Meke, and they both go up into heaven to frolic together forever and ever. Thus, even if a native did tell your friends about the sacrifice, it would not imply what it, in fact, actually means."

"That's excellent! I say, do these women also like to frolic?" asked Sinclair, smiling.

"Oh, yes! Why do you think I gave up my religion?" said Perez, and he led Walter over to a couple of voluptuous handmaidens. The women giggled and covered their mouths.

"Wait until the other men discover what the Bird Man wins," said Sinclair, lustfully gazing at the nude women. "You say the natives must do whatever the Bird Man requests of them?"

"Yes, he is a king for the year," said Perez.

"Then we shall have a new king. God save the king!" Walter laughed, and the women also laughed, as Sinclair chucked them playfully under their olive chins.

CHAPTER FIFTY-EIGHT: THE BIRD MAN

July 22, 1863 to September 2, 1863

When Chip Jefferson heard that any male on the island could compete to become Bird Man, he was immediately transfixed with hope. Even though the other, older adults were mostly disappointed by life on the island, Chip was charged with new energy. After all, he was now 17, and his body was fully developed. Walter Sinclair, who had gone up to the village of Orongo, told the group all about the Bird Man contest the following evening after dinner. Lieutenant Greene right away said he was going to compete, and when Chip also volunteered, Sinclair thought Chip's entry was a splendid idea.

"Good show, young man! I see you have the courage needed to win. In fact, I am so impressed by your bravado that I am going to personally supervise your training. I have learned a few techniques from the natives in Orongo, and you shall be the beneficiary of my research and my knowledge of tactics."

Captain Ericsson also saw the whole ritual as a challenge, so he vowed to assist Greene. "I will do some research of my own, Sinclair. It's quite obvious why you would want to win the Bird Man contest, but what I want to know is what you will do with the Bird Man power if you were to acquire it?"

Sinclair smiled. "I believe we have a difference in philosophy, John. Whereas you have your Greek rubbish about philosopher kings, I rather fancy Machiavelli. You see, you are not the only learned fellow on the island. Let me read to you the passage that addresses your question about what I plan to do with my power. You have voiced your plan to create a Platonic Republic. Machiavelli has something interesting to say about how one should handle republics. Let me read it to you, "But when cities or countries are accustomed to live under a prince, and his family is exterminated, they, being on the one hand accustomed to obey and on the other hand not having the old prince, cannot agree in making one from amongst themselves, and they do not know how to govern themselves. For this reason they are very slow to take up arms, and a prince can gain them to himself and secure them much more easily. But in republics there is more vitality, greater hatred, and more desire for vengeance, which will never permit them to allow the memory of their former liberty to rest; so that the safest way is to destroy them or to reside there."

Sinclair put the book down on the dining table. "So, you see, gentlemen. I will train my young prince to become the victorious Bird Man. And, as to your republic? I believe the Fainga have answered this question quite nicely. The old prince has been banished from power, and the power lives on in Orongo, with the Bird Man religion. I shall endeavor to continue this tradition of power and my new prince will help me secure it."

After this exchange, Chip decided to commit to a vigorous regimen of training under Captain Sinclair to get into shape for the Bird Man competition. He still did not trust Ericsson and Greene because of their use of the Gatling gun to

frighten the natives, and the prospect of becoming the "prince" of the island was quite attractive to him. The religion based on youth and strength was quite appealing to Chip, and he saw the contest as a great opportunity to gain favor amongst these white people who had seen him as a lowly former slave and ship's orderly. He only wished his father were there to see him train. It would have made him quite proud.

Captain Sinclair instructed Chip to go on a diet of protein to increase his strength. He also put him on a rigorous exercise routine that included running, lifting, and swimming. Sinclair told Chip he would tell him some of the secrets he had learned from the natives in Orongo. However, he would save this information until just before the competition. "I don't trust those others," said Sinclair, "if I told you now, they might find some way to get the knowledge out of you." Even though Chip assured him that he would never divulge such secrets, Sinclair remained steadfast. "In due time, my boy. In due time. Fact of the matter is how am I going to be able to trust you?"

As the days progressed, Chip began running all over the island. He enjoyed the freedom it gave him, the pulsing rhythm of the earth beneath his feet, the throbbing of blood through his system, and the joy of learning that his body could be put to such a trial. Gradually, the more he ran and swam, he felt his strength increase, and his lungs expand, until he began to believe he could win the contest. It was a joyful feeling that gave him a hearty appetite, and Captain Sinclair provided him with a bountiful supply of meat and potatoes from his ship. It would soon be time to test his abilities, and Chip began conditioning himself for the mental effort it would require. He believed if he thought of himself as a prince it would justify his victory. Sinclair explained to him that he would be able to run the island in any way he wished, and, he whispered, in a conspiratorial tone, "You'll get your choice of the ladies in Orongo!" The thought of having such a chance to be in such a powerful position gave Chip's demeanor an added gusto. He whistled, he made jokes, and he took long baths in the water near the ship, imagining he was the prince of Easter Island. It was quite a grand vision, and Chip shared his vision with the Priest, Father Perez. Together, they discussed a new plan based on what the priest knew about the rongo-rongo tablets. The real adventure was soon to be upon them all.

* * *

King Maurata stood at the top of the Rano Cao volcano in the village of Orongo. He held up his spear, ready to drop it for the start of the Bird Man Race. Around him, the villagers were whooping it up and dancing all around the fifteen men, who were lined up at the starting line, ready to begin. No other member of the king's clan was allowed, although the Americans were present to see the competition. The women from America were quite shocked by the nakedness of the other females, except for Penelope Sinclair, the wife of Walter Sinclair. She was imagining herself dancing in front of Dana Greene, who looked strong and handsome as he stood near the end of the line of male competitors.

The only other American to compete besides Lieutenant Greene was Chip Jefferson. The young lad was in outstanding shape, as Sinclair had drilled him—almost constantly—since the competition had been announced. Sinclair knew his only chance to take over the island was riding on this young man's strong shoulders. As the Bird Man, he would be able to confiscate the weapons of Ericsson and Greene and put them into his ship's armory. He could also keep the rest of the Americans under control so he could begin his new regime. The young Chip, of course, would be offered up as a sacrifice after he served his purpose, and Sinclair would begin his plan to ethnically cleanse the island of its dark-skinned, inferior races.

As Chip stood at his place at the beginning of the race, he looked down the row of men who were also competing. There were thirteen strong island men and Mr. Greene, of course, and then there was he. He believed this was perhaps his only chance to become a respected member of this new society. He would no longer be the former Southern slave who fought for the Union back in America; he would be the Bird Man, and the entire island would have to do what he told them to do. The prospect of this power sent a chill down his spine, and he remembered the dream again, and then the old chief dropped the spear, and he was off!

Since the goal of the race was to cross the dangerous waters of the sea between Easter Island and the tiny islands of Mutu Rau Kau and Muto Nui, it was Sinclair's plan to have Chip strike out for Muto Nui, the smaller of the two islands. To ward off shark attack, Sinclair had bathed the boy's body in dead shark oil. This was known by fishermen to be one of the best repellants ever used. In addition, Sinclair had taught the lad how to go down the cliffs with rapid decent by using a grappling hook and rope he had rigged up for the occasion. Chip wore it around his waist and he would extract it when the time came. This would likely add minutes to his time over the other men, even though they were more familiar with the terrain. In addition, Sinclair knew Ericsson and Greene would probably have a few tricks up their sleeves for the occasion, but he did not worry.

Dana Greene watched the others compete from his place on the side of the cliff. It was a small cave that Ericsson and he had found earlier in the week. In it, he could see the progress of the contest without being seen, and he could use the spyglass Ericsson had given him. Ericsson and Greene did not care who won the event because they had the Gatling machine gun. If their agricultural plan did not impress the people, then they would resort to force. As Greene watched Chip Jefferson swim ahead of the others on his way out to the tiny island, he was happy for the young lad. If they could not win the war against the Rebels in America, then it would be a small but satisfying victory to see the young orderly become the Bird Man and show that his kind were quite capable of performing as well as any white man could. However, the Bird Man Cult would be civilized, and Chip would be the key to their new societal order.

The egg of the Sooty Tern was now inside a pouch on Chip's waist. She had nipped at his finger, but he was able to extract the egg from the nest. He took one final look around him, gazing off into the vast stretch of ocean, wishing his father and mother could see him in his moment of triumph. Then, he plunged down the side of the island's cliff, taking great care not to hit his pouch against the rocks. When he hit the water, he swam with all his strength for the shore of Easter Island and his new title of Bird Man.

Sinclair was thinking he would allow the colored lad his few moments of triumph. Perhaps he would even lose his virginity during a night of celebration. However, he would also keep him under close watch. Tomorrow, after the festivities and the coronation of the new Bird Man, Sinclair would begin his new plan to take over the island.

Chip Jefferson ran across the finish line with the bird's egg, and he was declared the winner of the Bird Man competition. Orongo Village leaders lifted the lad onto their shoulders and carried him, to great fanfare, across the volcano, to the large communal hut of the Fainga Clan. The rest of the village, and the Americans, followed.

Once they were all inside the communal hut, torch lights shone all over the stage where Chip was being given the wings of the Bird Man by the priest, Father Perez. Perez spoke to the gathered assembly in their own language, and there was some commotion. Sinclair wondered what this stir was about.

Suddenly, all the white Americans were being captured by the Orongo warriors. Screaming and kicking, they were carted off into the night.

After the arrests were made, Father Perez sat down beside the Bird Man, Chip Jefferson, on his stage of glory. Around them, naked Orongo women danced and cast lusting glances toward their new leader for the coming year.

"What did you tell them?" Chip asked, knowing the answer, yet wanting to hear it in English. Father Perez did know how to speak English, although he never let Ericsson or Sinclair know this fact. In fact, it was Father Perez who had the most control over the island and its peoples because he was not a priest at all; he was an American scientist, Doctor John Garvey, from Harvard University. He spoke twelve languages, and he was, at one time, the head of the Department of Anthropology.

"I told them I had deciphered their rongo-rongo tablets and that you were the black prince, the answer to all their prayers. They are now confining all the white people inside a prison down in the Maunga Terevaka volcano on the other side of the island. Tomorrow will mark the new year of the Black Bird Man. Each month, you will officially appease Meke-Meke by offering him a white person as a sacrifice. We will also start farming and using the tools of Ericsson to create a new, more vital civilization on Easter Island."

Chip Jefferson, Black Bird Man of Easter Island, stood up, stretched out his feathered arms, and began to laugh. Below him, all the bronzed dancing women and the dark-skinned, warrior males, also began to laugh, until the communal hut was ringing with joy!

PART IV: THE LAST JOURNALS

September 3, 1863 - September 30, 1863

CHAPTER FIFTY-NINE: AMELIA ERICSSON'S JOURNAL

September 3, 1863

We were dragged across the island into a dark tomb. Each of us was given a cell, etched into the side of the mountain, and this was to be our confinement forever, or so it seemed at that moment. We were given writing utensils on the second day, and I am now writing by the light from a torch affixed to the cavern's wall. We lived in complete darkness and intermittent light from the torches. We were able to shout to each other inside our separate cells, and this was the only way we could interact with our doleful reality.

My husband, John, immediately confronted Captain Sinclair about our predicament. He found out that Sinclair had arranged with the priest, Father Perez, to train Chip Jefferson to win the Bird Man contest. However, it seems, the priest had decided to take the newly acquired power under his own control. Thus, we were thrown into prison cells with rats and insects too disgusting to imagine.

My husband incessantly questioned Sinclair about what he had planned for his own control of the island, but Walter refused to confess. John said that if we were ever able to get out of this prison he would beat the information out of Sinclair, but the Captain just laughed and said we were fools.

It was several days before I discovered what our tormentors had planned for us. Actually, we were all given a lecture by one who introduced himself as Professor Garvey, who had been previously portraying himself as the priest, Father Perez. He came into the cave one morning with a contingent of large male natives at his side. He spoke to us all using a megaphone apparatus of some sort that he had procured from our ship. He kept pacing back and forth in front of our cells as he delivered this sermon, looking inside, as if he were expecting us to respond to his brilliant wit.

"You will now be serving the greater good. Your weapons have given us the protection we have been without, and for this we thank you. As has been ordained in our writings, the Black Bird Man has come, and each of you will serve a unique purpose under his rule. I shall not tell you the exact reason for your existence, only our God can do that, but you will know in due time how you will serve us. Thank you again for all you have brought to us. The future of our society will be that much better for it." Almost as quickly as he appeared, he was gone.

Of course, I do not have much contact with reality as it used to be, once the darkness falls, but when they came back to get me, I really had no idea what day it was. The others kept shouting at me concerning these things, especially my husband, but my mind took on a life of its own, and I began to fantasize about life back in England. However, my life in London did not involve human beings. Instead, I kept seeing different places and objects that I remembered from my life there. I could touch the chair in my parents' house where my father would sit of an evening and smoke his pipe. I was enthused with comfort as these objects were touched, and my life inside that prison was not as horrendous as it would have been otherwise.

The rest of this journal will depict what happened to me after the day they came to get me. I have been told by authorities that my record could be used in legal proceedings, so I must tell as much of it as I can recollect with an attention to accuracy. My husband is the scientist, and I am not, so I beg the reader's forgiveness for my lapses into emotion, as it was quite an emotional ordeal.

I was taken to a large hut on the top of the volcano where we had viewed the Bird Man contest days earlier. Six native women came into the room and began to dress me in scanty, yet colorful clothing. They also began to bathe my body in what felt and smelled like coconut oil, and one of the women painted my nails with a dark red polish of some sort. What came next was quite a painful experience, the recreation of which sends a chill throughout my person as I describe it. I was given some kind of alcoholic beverage, and then one woman brought in a bowl of black liquid and what looked to be a sharp seashell of some kind. As the others held me down, she began to drag the sharp end of this shell across the bare contour of my leg. I must have shrieked rather loudly because they began to laugh and pour me more liquor. Soon, I became quite intoxicated, and the pain receded.

When I awoke the next morning I discovered that my legs had been inscribed with a fine, lace pattern beneath a reddened swelling on the sides of the lines. I could barely move my legs, they were so terribly sore. Three men came into my hut to get me. I was taken to another hut nearby where there were seven other women dressed for an occasion of some sort. I didn't know the full extent of this occasion until Professor Garvey came to explain it all.

"You women are chosen to serve at the sacrificial ceremony. This is quite an honor, as the Black Bird Man will be in attendance, and he may perhaps choose one of you to be his concubine. If chosen, a concubine lives in the prince's hut and shares all the food and other pleasures of the chosen one. You will learn to dance, to entertain and to perform ritual duties for the day of the sacrifice."

"What if I choose not to participate?" I asked, still not understanding that I was a virtual slave to this new "prince."

"Choice is not of consequence from your perspective, my dear," said the priest, an obvious smirk on his lips. "To be chosen is the thing that matters!"

I was not allowed contact with any of my fellow travelers, and I spent the rest of my days preparing for the first sacrificial offering. I knew in my subconscious that it would be one of our group who would be selected as scapegoat, perhaps even John, my husband, but the will to live kept me in line. I will continue to keep this journal and perhaps there will be a way out of this before it's too late for us all.

CHAPTER SIXTY: CHARLES MCCORD'S JOURNAL

September 10, 1863

All hell broke loose when we was inside the blasted stone hut at the Rano Cao volcano. I was already feeling trapped inside the confines of their communal monstrosity, when three of them bugbears grabbed me and put some kind of noxious rag over my face. I was straight away woozy, like I had me five pints 'o dark, and then, the next thing I knew, I found myself inside some kind of earthy jail. There were metal bars in front of me, and they wouldn't budge an inch when I tried to pry them, so I shouted out to see if they had the rest of us in there too. I soon learned all of us, except for the colored lad, Chip, were locked inside this cavernous mountain.

It was soon that this wild man came into our prison and began shouting at us about how we was each going to serve the new Bird Man. I knew this was our Chip he was speaking about, and I wondered at the time why the lad would have us arrested, and that's when this crazy Dr. Garvey gave me these writing utensils. I must confess, with all the activity going on, I wasn't keeping any records in my journal. This now gives me a chance to tell what happened and what my fate may be in the coming days.

On the fourth day, this Dr. Garvey came to get me. He was

quite the chipper lad that morning, telling me I was going to serve a special duty for the new Bird Man and that I should be quite proud of my new responsibility. I was taken across the island to another cave, and inside, there was a locked room where three natives stood guard. These natives wore all kinds of bones on their bodies, and they were painted all over with the most outrageous designs and symbols. Some of these symbols were of a rather obscene nature. This Dr. Garvey then told me I was to be in charge of the distribution of all the medicines inside this chamber. "Medicines?" I asked him, not believing my ears. Did he not know that I had my own problems with medicines?

"Yes, Mister McCord. These are the sacramental drugs that are taken during the sacrificial rites. We need someone to watch over these and be certain only the Shamans have access to them at the proper time."

"Just what do these drugs do?" I asked, unable to contain a certain joy that flowered in my heart. This was the joy I had abandoned for several weeks, but it was once more knocking on the door of my brain like an old friend. However, in my case, one must take the "r" from "friend" to describe the true nature of the lurking beast within me.

"In order to perform the sexual and religious fertility rites, we need to have our initiates in a more receptive mood. Their inhibitions must be lowered, and these drugs give the user a most phantasmagoric state of mental bliss. They are concocted from a certain mushroom, which grows inside the craters of the volcanoes on the island. These are given to participants by the Shamans during the ceremony. It will be your duty to keep guard over this storehouse of magical mushrooms."

Yes, it was my new job, and I did it. Where else was I to go? They brought me my food, and I began to experiment with the drugs. At first, I took only a small bit of drug. I saw the compartment where I was begin to expand and to contract as if it could breathe! Colors began to vibrate, and I could feel an inner excitement about everything around me. As I increased my intake, my illuminations became more fantastic. I no longer felt I was a prisoner. I was a Shaman! I saw into the depths of life and extracted a magical meaning! It was a much more fulfilling experience than alcohol had ever given me.

I did not tell my captor about my new religious powers. This secret was my own to enjoy. The mushrooms grew in small containers deep inside my cave. I was the keeper of magic, and I was soon to be an official participant at the fertility rights of the island! I no longer cared who would be chosen as the sacrificial lamb. It was meant to be, that was all I knew, and I was the high priest of the order.

I now wear human and animal bones all over my naked body. I have many designs painted into my skin. My favorite is a likeness of the Black Bird Man himself. His wings cover both of my thighs, and his head is on my navel. In some way, I truly believe, I am infused with his holiness.

CHAPTER SIXTY-ONE: ANNA CAMERON-GREENE'S JOURNAL

September 14, 1863

My fear is not for my own safety but for my baby's life. When we were taken to the dark caves, I told my husband not to worry, but he began shouting at our captors and threatening them. They had to bind him up on our trip over here. When Dana and I envisioned our private paradise, we certainly did not foresee such a disastrous place! The land is barren, as are the minds of the people who live here. Thankfully, they had an old woman who is proficient in child birthing, and she visits me every other day. Her hands are chafed from work in the Orongo village, but she is gentle and seems concerned about my welfare. Even though she speaks no English, we are able to communicate as women through physical gestures and pantomime. Our sex has been able to take care of these matters for thousands, perhaps even millions of years, and I do not doubt I can bring my child safely into this new world, such as it is.

I have listened to the men conversing about our plight, but it concerns me little. I seem to have retreated into a womblike existence, and my identity resides with the growing miracle inside me. My complete obsession is to protect this child. If we are to survive this, it will be my child who will become our legacy. My husband is a sensitive soul. I am afraid all of this may damage him irreparably. I need this child to make it through. My being inside this prison cell lets me sense my young one's presence so much more astutely. In Psalms it is said, "Behold, children are a heritage from the Lord, the fruit of the womb is a reward." My reward is coming, and I must make certain it is a comfortable delivery. Oh God, deliver me from this evil so that I may do what's best for my infant! I will give up everything to save this child—even my own life.

This Professor Garvey is insane. First he speaks about each of us serving this false god, this Bird King, and now he takes my husband away from me and our future child. What kind of monster is this Garvey that he would wrest husbands from wives and leave a mother alone to care for a child?

I have changed so much since I found out I am with child. No longer do I think of myself. My entire consciousness focuses upon this growing human inside me. I am a vehicle for God, and God will punish me if I do not do my best! Those who come between me and my duty will taste the wrath of God!

CHAPTER SIXTY-TWO: DANA GREENE'S JOURNAL

September 25, 1863

It seems rather ironic that we have been captured and imprisoned. We all left America to find a new paradise, and this paradise has become our torment. The real irony is the fact that little Chip, our orderly aboard the Monitor, has become a native god, and I, once the captain, have become a powerless hostage. I am more concerned about my wife, Anna, as she is with child. I keep shouting at these fiends that if she is harmed in any way I will kill them all. They just laugh.

Perhaps I have spent too much time with my nose inside poetry books. I did not believe the world could be this cruel and uncaring. Captain Ericsson believes this shaman, Father Perez, to be behind all of our travails. When Perez made his speech to us in perfect English, pacing in front of our cells inside the cave, Ericsson determined he was on a quest for complete power over the island and its natives.

I see that Ericsson and Sinclair were also trying, in effect, to become Bird Men. They wanted power as much as this priest does, but I suppose they were surprised a bit by this Perez character and his confession that he was, in fact, one Professor Garvey from the United States. He made us realize we had all been fooled by the island and by the natives who live here. Captain Ericsson tells me the powerful in the world have always been this way and that they will continue to give us false illusions in order to control us. War, he says, is the ultimate example of the grand illusion.

One night, when Captain Ericsson was certain Sinclair was asleep, he told me about how he thought Sinclair was going to use Chip in his plot to take over the island, but that Professor Garvey got between him and his ruse. "Sinclair is not to be trusted anymore, Mister Greene," said Ericsson, and his voice was adamant. "However, I believe we will have a chance to take back the initiative. This man Garvey is playing with superstitious fire. I have read the traditions of these natives, especially as they concern warfare, and this Garvey will, undoubtedly, make a slip of some kind."

I told the Captain that he was trying to see too much into the future and that he was the one who had believed Easter Island was our paradise to return to. We have no paradise here. One could even argue that we have something worse than a civil war. We have pagan anarchy! I then told him that his wife, his darling Amelia, had been recruited to serve as a handmaiden for fertility rites. She now has tattoos on her body, and she is forced to dance in a most un-Christian manner in front of wild men! Was this the Platonic Civilization that Ericsson envisioned? I think not!

Captain Ericsson did not speak for several moments, and then he said, "Mister Greene, there will be a moment when this tyrant will make a mistake, and when that moment comes, I want you to be ready to do what I tell you. Do you promise me you'll follow my orders?"

I, too, waited several moments before I answered. Could I trust this man again? I suppose it was not his fault that these events had unfolded. He did have motives to give these people what they have been missing for many years. He wanted to restore their island to natural splendor. He wanted to protect them and show them how to protect themselves from nefarious people like Professor Garvey. "Yes, Captain," I told him that night in our prison, and I meant it.

The next morning, however, I was taken out of my cell by a contingent of guards who answered to the Fainga clan. They dragged me off to the other side of the island, and I did not know where they were taking me because I was blindfolded and my arms were tied behind my back.

When they took off my blindfold, I was inside a cavern with lighted torches sunk into the earth, and Professor Garvey was standing in front of me with Charles McCord beside him. McCord looked so strange in his native outfitting that I'm afraid I laughed out loud. He had many birds tattooed all over his pale, naked body, and he wore a feathered headdress. His eyes were encircled with black, and they were wild and insane in appearance.

"Mister Dana Greene fancies himself as a devotee of meaningful poetry," said Garvey. "Therefore, you shall serve as the Bird Man's poet laureate."

I was quite confused by the resolute tone of his voice.

"Mister McCord, give Mister Greene his first sacrament," said Garvey, and McCord handed me a small, wafer-like object. "Put it under the tongue and let it dissolve. You will be fed one of these repeatedly during the coming days, until the day of the sacrifice. On this day, you will read the rongo-rongo tablets and reflect on their true meaning for our tribe. It is quite an honor, and I am certain you will be up for it."

I took the wafer and it dissolved in my mouth, with quite a bitter taste. In about one-half of an hour I experienced my first hallucination. Colors began to melt from objects as if they had been burned by some hidden torch. It then got much more extravagant. I believed I was in a hyper-reality, infused with sound and hidden messages from gods contained in all objects. It was quite magical. I was given all the books of poetry I wanted from the ship's library, and I was told I would be allowed to read from the rongo-rongo when the time approached.

I have at last mastered a skill at writing in this journal, even though the words have difficulty staying on the page. They often lift off, swirl around my head, and then fasten on the objects around me. I hope someone is able to save me before I cannot make meaning anymore. I do not want to float off into insanity! God help me!

CHAPTER SIXTY-THREE: JOHN ERICSSON'S JOURNAL

September 26, 1863

I should have planned for the contingency that befell our group. It is the responsibility of a true leader to plan for all possibilities, and I did not. This was the thought going through my head when they captured us inside the communal hut in Orongo Village and brought us to the prison caves across the island. They separated us by sex and we were in solitary confinement. I suspected that Captain Sinclair might have been behind the kidnapping, but when I heard his booming voice coming from one of the prison cells, I knew it had to be the priest, Father Perez. When we interviewed him during our first week on the island, I was wary of his story about being a priest stranded on the island. First off, his Spanish accent was not authentic. I have spoken with many Latin peoples, and this man's inflection was most certainly not that of a true South American or Spaniard. However, I also thought he may have been under some amount of emotional turmoil, and this could have had an effect on his speech pattern. I have known this to be the case in my studies of the colonization of countries for which occupation created an undue stress on their culture and speech, resulting in such behaviors as seen in Father Perez.

Now, after having heard this Professor Garvey speak, I recall an article by him I once read when he was at Harvard. I don't recall the title, but I do remember that he was concerned with the concept of controlling cultures through the written word. Each world culture had its own set of scriptures, from which a powerful influence over the masses could be extracted with the proper interpretations and definitions. The fascinating element to Garvey, as I remember, was the possibility of totally controlling those masses by simply gaining their trust and becoming the official shaman or spiritual prophet of the scriptures. Now that I see what he has done on Easter Island, it all seems very clear. Dr. Garvey, with our help, believes he has mastered his anthropological hypothesis! However, as I have told Mister Greene, my only confidant, I have knowledge that can combat Garvey's shamanistic power. James Morrison's Journal, given to me by Moses Young on Pitcairn Island, proved to me that the culture of war amongst these people can trump the culture of the gods. Or, at least, I was hoping Dr. Garvey was not familiar with the practices. This was at the heart of my plan to re-take the island from the grip of this monstrous guru! If he reads my journal, which is quite a possibility, I only hope he is intrigued enough to let me live long enough to see what I have to combat his treachery. Does he not realize that those who become drunk with power are often left open to revolution from within?

I have observed that several of our group have been taken out of our cells here and transported to other parts of the island. It seems only Sinclair, Mrs. Greene and I are left to chat amongst ourselves. Needless to say, I cannot share my thoughts with Captain Sinclair, as he has proved most untrustworthy, and as for Mrs. Greene? I dare say, the emotional state of a pregnant female is not to be toyed with either. What I have to share about my plans would not be conducive to this poor woman's smooth birth. I can only hope, along with my compatriots——wherever they are——that my plan will be able to be put into motion at some point in immediate time.

Several of the sentences from Dr. Garvey's journal article stood out when I first read them, several years ago, and they still stand out as I remember them today: "Human sacrifice is the most powerful mechanism to control pagan cultures. Even the Judeo-Christian culture has not been able to totally eliminate the spiritual power that the idea of martyrdom has over the masses. With this power of sacrifice, one can achieve complete control over one's subjects."

As one of my group's members disappears each day, I am fearful that these words of Garvey's may have some potent prophecy. I certainly hope he has not decided to put his theory into practice, but this is what I fear. And it is this fear that brings me nightmares and my prayers for redemption. Yes, I no longer contest the Will of God. I simply invoke a twist of His Fate for the survival of my fellows.

CHAPTER SIXTY-FOUR: PENELOPE SINCLAIR'S JOURNAL

September 28, 1863

I was not completely surprised when we were captured and taken away. What did everyone expect? These are savages, and their actions would logically be conditioned by how they live. I have no problem with their lives. In fact, this captive state has given me the chance to plan how to pursue Mister Greene. When they gave us the journals back, telling us we would be recording history for future generations, I vowed to create my own new history as well. I am so very tired of Walter and his dreams of power. At first, it was romantic to think of him away on his travels, doing what I longed to do on my own but was afraid to risk. When we landed here, I began to see my dear Walter for what he really is and not what I had concocted in my feminine brain. Walter Sinclair only looks out for his own needs. He has no delicate, intuitive side like Dana Greene.

The day they took Dana away, we thought he might return. After he had been gone a couple of days, we knew they were removing each of us, one at a time, to do their bidding. Anna became deathly quiet, and I was afraid she had contracted some kind of disease, but she finally responded to me once I kept calling to her from my cell. "I'm just taking care of my baby," Anna told me, and I suppose this is what she would say under these conditions, but her voice became rather sullen and monotonous.

First they took Mister McCord, the Irishman, then Mister Greene, and finally, they came for me. It was quite a change to see these natives bowing to a person who would be a slave in other parts of the world. What could this Professor Garvey gain by giving authority to our little darkie, Chip Jefferson? These niggers have sub-human intelligence, and they have no leadership qualities at all. However, I soon saw that I would have my chance to woo Mister Greene, when Dr. Garvey took me to the Bird Man's "spirit room." Who should be in attendance as the commander-in-charge of this important facility but Lieutenant Greene! His dark mustache and beard had grown full, and his handsome chest was quite hairy and alluring above his short, sealskin trousers. "Mister Greene will be learning the sacred contents of the rongo-rongo tablets, and you will assist him in his intuitive translations, as will I." Translations? I wondered what was written on these stone tablets that had to be translated. Thus, I asked the question. "Why must they be translated?"

"There are great prophesies about what the future holds for our clan here on the island. Mister Greene, with the assistance of these sacred wafers," he handed me a small, light- brown button that looked like a mushroom cap. "Take one, my dear," said Garvey, and he smiled. Dana was already smiling over at me, so I popped it into my mouth.

"Don't chew. Put it under your tongue and let it dissolve," said Dana.

It was tart and had an acidic flavor.

"Bring her to the dressing room/' said Garvey, and two native women took me by the elbows and led me to an adjacent room, which was separated from the main spirit room by a hanging animal skin of some kind. Inside, I came face-to-face with Amelia Ericsson. She was quite the sight! She wore next to nothing, and there were laced tattoo marking all over her legs. Her bare-breasted nipples were disconcerting, to say the least, and she had the same quizzical smile that Greene and McCord had on their faces. That's when my first vision began to sweep over me. Suddenly, I believed what we were doing was the most important task in the world, and I was infused with an enthusiasm I never knew existed! The native women bathed me in oils and in flower petals and they lay me out to be tattooed in the same fashion as they had been inscribed for thousands of years. They sang and they danced, and they gave me a sweetly intoxicating beverage to drink. The bone-white carvings on their skeletal necklaces revolved around their necks like spinning dervishes. Their music vibrated my body and entered my soul as a dark, ominous shadow. I was becoming one of them!

It was joyous, and my mind memorized each dance step they took and each word they sang. It was a strange and mysterious enchantment. I had a whole new world and language to learn. I also had Dana Greene all to myself, and I would serve him well as we exorcised the hidden secrets from the sacred rongo-rongo tablets. I did not even care about the Black Bird Man. Somehow, even he was important to this passionate experience. After all, he was just a symbol to the tribe, while we were the true keepers of our collective destiny, were we not?

Dear Walter began to fade from my consciousness like my old existence in England, and my parents became quaint toys from another world, which was now far away and seemed unimportant next to this rush of rhythmic drum beats and the quick surge of blood through my veins, as I learned the magic of pagan re-birth!

CHAPTER SIXTY-FIVE: WALTER SINCLAIR'S JOURNAL

September 29, 1863

Was it that Burns fellow who wrote about "best laid plans of mice and men?" The smashing defeat I was dealt was a blow to my pride, but the beating I received by these natives was the work of this Professor Garvey! Father Perez, indeed! My body is bruised and tattered, and I know my head has a variety of contusions, but I will continue my resistance against this unspeakable treachery! Even when they began to separate us, I realized what their plan required. This Professor Garvey used me as the fool all along, and I cannot abide this. And then, as if he expected our total subservience, he began to prance around us like Abe Lincoln and declare his new Republic of Chaos!

This is why I am left to sit in this cell. I can hear Ericsson consoling the whimpering Greene woman. Our number is down to three. Have they killed the others or perhaps eaten them? I do not doubt the possibilities of this madness at the hands of Garvey. The look in his eyes is completely insane! He has even taken my wife, my own Pen! What kind of debauchery can he be up to? I used to wonder about her faithfulness when I was at sea, but now my fear for her is unbounded. I have seen with my own eyes and experienced with my own body the lascivious nature of this island! It is hell on earth! What is he giving to his Black Bird Man? Are the white women serving his bestial nature? This demonic leader, Professor Garvey, shall not live much longer if I have anything to say about it. My rage must be controlled, so I can respond when the time comes. I cannot write in this infernal diary! This is not my command. I am not writing in a ship's log. I will not let this traitor to his own

236

country read my thoughts and then use them against me!

Go to hell, Mister Garvey, and make quick work of me unless you want to be watching your back for the rest of your days!

CHAPTER SIXTY-SIX: CHIP JEFFERSON'S JOURNAL

September 30, 1863

Professor Garvey explained to me that when I became the Bird Man I would now be able to run the island the way I wanted to. He said the rongo- rongo tablets gave me the authority to be almost a god to these people. However, when he also told me that they would be sacrificing a white person every month to their god, Meke- Meke, I knew I had to pretend to go along with his plan, or, I too would certainly be offered up as a sacrifice. This shaman, this professor, is crazy!

I am only able to write in this journal after my nightly "fertility ritual" with a different native woman each night. These women don't really care, as long as I pay attention to them early in the evening. I was never as scared as when I first saw one of these naked women come into my hut in Orongo village. The first one smelled like she had been dipped into a barrel of flowers. She had crazy tattoos all over her, and she began to dance in front of me, wiggling her parts like a woman I once saw in a Baptist revival meeting in New York who was overcome by the Spirit of the Lord. She shook all over, and when she stopped, she reached out her arms to me, she puckered her lips, and she closed her eyes. I walked into her embrace, and that's when my own body parts took over. We began rolling all over the blankets and the pillows, and she started to moan and kiss me all over. I never knew life could be so full of hot activity! All the church teaching I learned from my Mama and the others just went flying out of my brain, and I hope I can be forgiven for my animal passions. But I needed to make certain these women did not suspect I was up to something. They had to think I was the proper Bird Man, and this nightly fertility ritual was part of my job, and I don't expect that I disappointed any one of them.

Professor Garvey seems to think I would want to be the Black Bird Man that he read about in their tablets. He is like so many of these white men who expect us to want everything they have. My Papa told me about these kinds of men. He said, "Some white men expect us to seek the same power they seek. What they don't understand is all we want is to be seen as equals." Slavery is not a good thing for any human. Professor Garvey keeps these natives slaves to the Bird Man because they can then be allowed to compete in the yearly competition and raid the other villages for prisoners and love slaves. It makes me wonder if mankind had been created so we could persecute each other. What makes us believe in leaders like this Mister Garvey? I know, Captains Ericsson and Sinclair also wanted to have power on this island, but now I am the Bird Man! We are all fighting to have our own way in the world of Easter Island. However, this shaman, this Professor Garvey, does not want to share his power with any other white man. What does he plan to do with me? Will he get rid of me when I no longer can serve his purpose? As the Bird Man Prince, I couldn't even speak to my own subjects. I didn't know their language. But that's when I met Kaimi.

Kaimi was the third woman I met in my hut one night during the fertility ritual. She was very young, only sixteen, and she was really scared. In fact, when she came in she didn't look me in the eyes. She just stood in the corner, looking all beautiful and petite, and then she spoke to me in English! I never heard any of these natives speak any words in English, so this was quite a surprise. She said her name was Kaimi, which meant "the seeker," and she asked me what my name was. I told her my Christian name was Charles Jefferson, but that my slave name had been Reginald Sims. Kaimi told me she had learned English from a passing British merchant ship's crew member, and she was very curious about my slavery, so I told her about living on the Sims' plantation in Virginia and about how we were finally purchased and given freedom. Kaimi said she had a sister who had been captured by the Peruvian slave traders, and she had even received a letter from her sister a year later. She told Kaimi that she could now speak Spanish and that her owners were treating her much better than how the Fainga treated their women. She no longer had to participate in sex orgies or perform in the fertility rights with the Bird Man. Kaimi then wondered if slavery were not better than what she had to live under with the Fainga. However, Kaimi's sister wrote another letter, about six months after that first one, and in it she explained that she had become deathly ill with fever. She had been worked relentlessly in the banana fields until she contracted the disease from which she was then dying. The only medicine she was administered was from the slaves' partera, or midwife. No real doctor would touch her. Kaimi's sister died shortly after, and that's when Kaimi knew that slavery was a much worse condition than life on Easter Island.

I told Kaimi that the shaman, Professor Garvey, was now instituting a practice just as evil as slavery. He was going to sacrificially murder the white people with whom I traveled to Easter Island and steal all their inventions and weapons. He wanted to control everybody, and I told her I was not ready to let him do that. I told her that she was the most beautiful woman I had ever met and that she could perhaps help me save my friends from this evil man who was posing as her tribe's shaman.

That's when Kaimi told me a secret of her own. She told me that the white people were not the only ones who were to be sacrificed. She asked me if Garvey had told about fekitoa, or the "gathering of two men." Of course I knew nothing about this, and she explained that it meant that when my year was up as Bird Man that I would be taken off by natives to be thrown down into the Rano Cao volcano. I would then meet up with Meke-Meke, the other man, in the "other world."

This explained everything. Garvey was going to do away with his Black Bird Man as soon as the year was over. He was going to steal all the inventions of Captain Ericsson and all the weapons of Captain Sinclair. That's when I knew I had to learn Kaimi's language, and I had to learn it really fast! We needed to find a way to stop Professor Garvey from killing the others and establishing his own dictatorship on Easter Island. Unless the natives could understand their Bird Man, we had no chance to foil Garvey's plan.

Kaimi took my shoulders and melted her chocolate eyes into mine. "Yes, my love, I will teach you," she said, and I kissed her with the truest love I have ever felt in my seventeen years of life on this earth. I just hope we can live to see one more year together, that's all.

EPILOGUE: THE WINNERS

December 25, 1863, Easter Island

The ship docked at Hanga Pika was being boarded by the only passengers headed back to the United States. First, John Ericsson and his wife, Amelia, walked slowly up the ramp. They both stood at the gangway and waved at the only other couple near the bottom. Dana Greene and his wife, Anna, who held their new daughter, Cristina Marie, were following the Ericssons and were half-way up the ramp.

The ship, the American merchant *U.S.S. Wachusett*, under Captain Robert W. Schufeldt, had arrived despite the plague of smallpox. All crew members had been inoculated with the vaccine of cow pox, the same vaccination that Captain Ericsson had used to save the remaining natives on Easter Island.

Captain Ericsson walked alone into Captain Schufeldt's cabin and sat down in a chair in front of the commanding officer's desk. Captain Schufeldt sat behind it, smoking a long briar pipe. He was a tall man, distinguished with large mutton chops and a thick, New York accent. He pointed to a stack of papers on his desk. "Thank you for coming, Captain Ericsson. These journals will be collected and used in our inquiry when we arrive back in the States. As we are still in a state of war, you and Lieutenant Greene will be considered my prisoners until we can consider the evidence in this matter."

"I appreciate it, Captain," said Ericsson, and he cleared his throat. "I welcome your understanding of the delicate nature of our plight. The experience of my group needs to be kept secret from the prying eyes of the public. I am happy the government believes this to be the best possible solution to the problem we have at present."

"Yes, President Lincoln has been advised concerning your adventure. Because your monitors are doing much to assist our naval advances against the rebel forces, it has been Mister Lincoln's decision to keep the details of your trip a secret. However, the matter of the deaths of Mister and Missus Walter Sinclair, Charles Jefferson, and Charles McCord will be thoroughly investigated in the official inquiry. That's why these journals will be important."

"Thank you, Captain. I appreciate the importance of these documents. It is rather ironic that our captors allowed us to keep these journals even during our internment. I suppose it could be considered our Babylonian captivity, of sorts. I have been reading the Bible regularly during these last few months, and it occurs to me that I never really appreciated its relevance to mankind's travails until it related to my own experience. I shall continue to read it with utmost scrutiny in the future."

"Captain Ericsson, as it is Christmas, I would like to take this opportunity to allow you to tell me, in your own words, what occurred over these months at this god-forsaken island. It will be completely off the record, mind you, and I shall give you my word as an officer and a gentleman that none of it will ever be revealed."

"We came to Easter Island because we wanted to establish a civilized colony modeled after the Platonic ideals of the Republic. Sadly, what we found here was a land ravaged by wars between the elite, which resulted in the obliteration of most natural resources and the alienation of the population into a cult that followed a pagan god of fertility and practiced contests such as the Bird Man competition. This was an event that occurred each year to determine a god-man who would be given complete rule over the island and its remaining resources. The people who followed this Bird Man were called the Fainga, and they were the elite group that survived following the Moai statue wars between the Hanau Eepe and Hanau Momoko. When we arrived, a man who was posing as a Jesuit priest, Father Perez, tricked us into competing in the Bird Man contest and he used the winner, our own steward, Mister Chip Jefferson, as his ruse to take over the island populace. At that time, there were only over eight hundred natives, as fifteen-hundred of them had been captured by Peruvian slave traders one year previously."

"Yes, we have heard of these slave traders. They bring disease to the natives, and many thousands have been killed off all over the Polynesian islands," Captain Schufeldt interjected.

"Indeed, and it was this disease that saved our lives, Captain, if you will bear with me. Father Perez turned out to be renegade Harvard Anthropologist, Dr. John Garvey, who had written about a theory he had to control native populations through their original scriptures. In this case, the islanders had what are called the rongo-rongo tablets, which contain hieroglyphic symbols that have meaning only to the shamans of the tribes. Garvey came here to see if he could prove his hypothesis, and when we landed, with our inventions and our weapons, he at last had his chance to take total control."

Captain Schufeldt tapped his pipe with the back of his hand and shook burnt tobacco out. "Go on, Captain, this is quite intriguing. What did he do with these tablets to obtain control?"

"After our Chip won the Bird Man contest, Garvey got his natives to arrest all of us, and he told the lad that Chip was the prophetic coming of the so-called Black Bird Man. This was the special person who would come from afar to establish a new era of peace and abundance here on the island. The natives believed him, and our Chip played along with this false shaman, Garvey, until the day the sacrifices began."

"Sacrifices? What were they sacrificing?"

"I'm afraid to say that Garvey had gone over the edge into madness. He was going to sacrifice one of us each month until their god of fertility, Meke-Meke, was appeased. The first sacrificial offering was to take place on November fifteenth. But first, Garvey had to get all his participants into their proper places. Thus, he recruited Mister Charles McCord, my lead draftsman, to become the master-at-arms of his cache of hallucinogens, a type of mushroom that grows in the base of the island volcanoes. He also added Missus Walter Sinclair and my Lieutenant Dana Greene to become officials at these drug- induced fertility rituals that were conducted in what he called the 'spirit room.' I am sad to say that my own wife, Amelia, was also chosen to become a pagan handmaiden at these rituals of debauchery and carnal revelry. Of course, as I was still being held in our prison at the Maunga Terevaka volcano on the other side of the island, I did not know exactly what each of my compatriots was doing. However, I was soon to find out."

"How dreadful! All this seems to prove how mankind will indeed revert to savagery when Nature and God have been forsaken," said Schufeldt, twisting in his seat and leaning forward in anticipation of the next part of Ericsson's story.

"Savagery is a friendly word for what began to take place on this island, Captain. The Captain of our ship, Mister Walter Sinclair, was residing with me in our prison, and I suppose he was becoming increasingly desperate. I did not realize just how desperate until November the fifteenth arrived. We had been confined in our prison cells for over a month, along with Missus Anna Greene, who was then quite heavy with child. Meanwhile, Professor Garvey had continued with his fertility rituals and the so-called 'translations' of the rongo-rongo tablets. Nobody, not even the Bird Man, knew who was to be sacrificed first, but when they came to take Anna away, we all knew."

"Good God, man! How monstrous!"

"Yes, Garvey wisely kept Mister Greene away from the sacrificial hut. The death blow was about to be struck on the poor woman and her child when Dr. Garvey began to vomit profusely. His entire body began to shake, and he fell into a visible swoon upon the floor. Of course, the sacrifice could not continue, and it was the smallpox that had reached its first victim. It seems the Peruvian slave traders must have brought the virus with them when they ravaged the island, and it had not developed until that very night when Professor Garvey was struck down. Luckily, Anna Greene was taken back to her cell, and we were given a reprieve. Lieutenant Greene came back with her to watch after his wife."

"Good! Now what happened?"

"At last, I had a bargaining chip to play. I had brought with us a small amount of cowpox vaccine, first developed by Edward Jenner in England in 1796. I knew if Garvey were given it soon enough, there was a good chance his smallpox would recede, and I told him so when he came to see if I could do anything for him. He had already taken charge of our vessel, the *HMS Caine*, yet he knew nothing about my storehouse of drugs. Thus, I offered to give Garvey the vaccine if he would, in exchange, allow me my freedom to vaccinate others in the populace, to protect them from almost certain death in the coming days."

"Well, he didn't refuse, did he?"

"No, I was given my freedom, and he was given his life. He was soon to regret his decision. I gave him his inoculation, and I also met with the Black Bird Man to give him his. That was when I discovered that Chip Jefferson had convinced the one-hundred tribesmen of the lower village of Hanga Roa, together with King Maurata, their leader, to attack the Orongo Village. It seems a native girl named Kaimi could speak English, and she had become enamored of Mister Jefferson. She was able to persuade the men to make war that following night."

"Bold move, Captain! I could not have done better myself," said Schufeldt.

"Indeed, but that night, when the natives began attacking, many of the warriors of the Fainga clan in Orongo Village were too sick to fight. Professor Garvey saw that his men were being overcome by the healthy men of the King's tribe, and he panicked. He realized that Walter Sinclair still had the keys to the ship's armory, which held the only weapon that could equalize the odds at that moment in the battle. He sent two natives to fetch Sinclair from his cell, and that's when the tides changed. Sinclair opened the locked armory, but he soon picked up a weapon and shot the two natives dead. He then carried the Gatling Machine Gun up to Orongo Village and set it up in the village square."

"The Gatling? What a stroke of luck! That monster can fire over 600 rounds per minute."

"Indeed, but the person firing it became enraged with jealousy when he saw his wife dancing nude for the Black Bird Man, Chip Jefferson, inside the spirit hut. Did I mention that Walter Sinclair was a racist and supporter of the Southern cause? He shot and killed his own wife, Penelope, Mister Charles McCord, and poor Chip Jefferson, and the tribal chaos that ensued was disastrous. When Sinclair finally ran out of ammunition, over one hundred Fainga warriors were dead, and Walter Sinclair was stabbed to death by the remaining men. What Sinclair and Garvey did not know was that the culture of war amongst the Polynesian peoples is not an affair of complete annihilation as it is in the so-called 'civilized' countries such as our own. Instead, the victorious warrior will take on the name of the warrior he kills in battle—strictly a hand-to-hand affair— and his entire tribe will afterward have a feast to honor the dead enemy. What Sinclair did to these natives broke all bounds of civility and justice for these people, and it proved the undoing of Garvey's anthropological experiment. The natives revolted, and the remaining natives became quite enraged when they discovered Garvey's identity and trickery. He was pushed down into the Rano Cao volcano, together with the sacred rongo-rongo tablets. They also blew-up our ship, exploding the armory, and the craft was nothing but cinders the next day. I officiated in the crowning of the new King, and the Bird Man cult was officially banished from the island. You arrived months following, and the rest will come out at our inquiry state-side, I trust."

Captain Schufeldt stood up and vigorously shook John Ericsson's hand. "Thank you, Captain; I am glad you have been honest with me. I am certain things will go well for you at the inquiry. You are a man of reason and compassion."

John left the captain's stateroom and walked amidships to his own cabin. Amelia was standing in the doorway, but she was frowning. "What's the matter, love?" Ericsson asked, taking her softly by her supple shoulders and kissing her cheek.

"This is the first time in months we will be sleeping in a proper bed," she said, wrinkling up her nose.

"Yes? I agree. It will be quite a change," John said.

"John, do you still love me?" she asked, slowly dropping her dress to the floor, exposing her lattice pattern of native tattooing all over her bare legs.

This was the first time Ericsson had seen his wife's legs under a light, and he enjoyed what he saw. The thought of his wife's native intrigue under the stars on Easter Island would be their secret for years to come. "Dance for me, love," said John, and Amelia began to shake.

* * *

At the base of the ship, standing among the remaining population of Easter Island, one hundred and nine citizens in all, were Chip Jefferson and his new wife, Kaimi Jefferson. Chip was dressed in native attire as was his lovely young wife, and their expressions told the story of the pain and tragic adversity that had taken place over the last few months.

As the *U.S.S. Wachusett* pulled out from the bay, Chip and Kaimi turned their backs to it as the sun retreated into the South Pacific. They did not want to watch the ship leave because they had the beginnings of a new family right where they were. Although Chip knew he could never be the Bird Man again, he was happy to start over. Captain Ericsson had agreed to lie about his death so he could stay on Easter Island, and Chip would forever be grateful. Ericsson said that it would be most difficult to explain away Chip's conspiracy with Dr. Garvey, and it was best that he settle with his new love. The land would again begin to flourish, under the careful husbandry of the remaining natives, and no longer would racism and greed rule the day. Chip knew they were a microcosm of what happened in many other lands, all over the world, and the lessons they learned were well worth the experience.

HISTORICAL NOTES

The two main characters used in this novel that were not fictitious were John Ericsson and Samuel Dana Greene. Part III until the end of the novel was a completely alternate history, although much of the research came from many verified sources, including a great debt of gratitude to Professor Jared Diamond, author of the best-selling non-fiction works, Guns, Germs and Steel and Collapse: How Societies Choose to Fail or Succeed.

Later, Ericsson worked with torpedo inventions, in particular the Destroyer torpedo boat, and in the book *Contributions to the Centennial Exhibition* he presents the so- called "sun engines", using solar power as propellant for a "hot air engine". Once again bitter and plagued by economic difficulties, his invention of the solar engine would not have practical applications for another 100 years.

Although none of his inventions created any large industries, he is regarded as one of the most influential mechanical engineers ever to live. After his passing in 1889 his remains were brought from the United States to Stockholm by the *U.S.S. Baltimore* and to the final resting place at Filipstad, in his Varmland.

On December 11, 1884, while at the Navy Yard, Samuel Dana Greene committed suicide by shooting himself with a .38 caliber revolver. The Concord [New Hampshire] *Evening Monitor* reported on December 12 that "He had been observed to act strangely for some time, and had been watched for fear that he might take his own life." His suicide was attributed by some to criticisms of his actions on the *Monitor* after Worden was wounded. Recent articles in the press had brought old rumors to light and it was believed that

Greene had not been able to cope with the resulting publicity. There is also some indication that he was in poor health at the time of his suicide.

Read other fine titles published by EMRE Publishing, LLC by going to the website: emrepublishing.com

Sign-up for the newsletter and download the app for access to multimedia (ePub3) titles.

ABOUT THE AUTHOR

 Jim Musgrave was born in Fall River, Massachusetts (home to Lizzie Borden). He worked for Caltech in Pasadena (home of the "Big Bang Theory") and continues to use his fascination with technology in his "Detective Pat O'Malley Steampunk Mystery" series. Jim was also a professor of English for 24 years, and he runs a publishing business with his wife, Ellen, in San Diego. He has won many awards, including being a finalist in the Bram Stoker Awards and the Heekin Foundation Awards. His mystery, *Forevermore*, won First Place in the Clue Historical Mystery Contest in 2014. This is the first novel in the best-selling Steampunk series starring Detective Patrick James O'Malley set in post-Civil War New York City.

Printed in Germany
by Amazon Distribution
GmbH, Leipzig